THE
TREA
SEEKER

Frankie J. Jones

Bella
BOOKS

2014

Bella Books, Inc.
P.O. Box 10543
Tallahassee, FL 32302

First Bella Books Edition 2014

Editor: Katherine V. Forrest
Cover Designer: Sandy Knowles

ISBN: 978-1-59493-406-3

Acknowledgments

Peggy J. Herring—Thanks for reading the manuscript.

Martha Cabrera—Thanks for everything you do. You make life a treasure every day.

Katherine V. Forrest—Thanks for your patience and editorial skill.

About the Author

Frankie is an award-winning artist and freelance nature photographer. When she isn't working she loves to travel and fish.

For Martha
My greatest treasure.

CHAPTER ONE

As the footsteps grew steadily closer, Rylene Shelton held her breath and wished she could make herself invisible. Despite her anticipation of what was about to occur, she still flinched when the door flew open.

"I thought you weren't going to work late tonight," Kate said in a tone of voice Ry knew only too well. "This is the first weekend I haven't had to work in months. I don't want to spend it sitting at home watching you work." Kate stood staring at her with crossed arms. Her stance and the tight pinch of her mouth left no doubt of her unhappiness.

Ry stared back at Kate, her lover of six years, an emergency room nurse who made no secret of the fact that while she loved her job, she still valued every free moment away from the hospital.

"I don't know why you get so upset about my hours. We both knew the store would require a lot of sacrifice," Ry said. Lately this had been an ongoing argument between them, and she had grown tired of having to defend herself. She loved the shop. Although, in a weak moment, she would admit it was much harder and more time consuming than she had ever imagined.

Previously, Ry had worked as a designer for a firm in San Antonio for five years. Then the firm began having financial problems and Ry was laid off. When she was unable to secure a position with another design firm, Kate began to urge her to follow through on her dream of opening an antique shop.

Kate had been supportive throughout the entire process of locating and opening the shop. They visited several small towns surrounding San Antonio before they decided to move to Jackson City. The location offered everything they wanted. Ry especially liked the area because it was where she had grown up. Her parents and brothers lived a few miles outside of town. Kate was happy there was a hospital that served Jackson City and the surrounding area. They agreed that Kate's salary would have to support them until the business became financially stable. An additional bonus to relocating to Jackson City was its already booming antique trade.

They located a one-hundred-and-twelve-year-old, two-story brick building that was strong on charm and atmosphere. Ry's father, a construction contractor, looked the building over and declared it sound. Another major plus was that they would be able to live in the twenty-one-hundred square feet space upstairs.

Ry's father offered them the "family discount," which meant he would provide his crew to do the work. Ry and Kate would pay for expenses only.

As they had anticipated, Kate had no problems securing a position as an emergency room nurse at the local hospital. Ry's family pitched in and helped them move their belongings from San Antonio to Jackson City.

Ry spent hours cleaning the enormous old building, hand buffing the stunning hundred-year-old oak floor planks and bead board walls until they glowed. She climbed to the top of a ladder so high it made her head swim to shine the beautiful hand-hammered tin ceiling and brass lighting fixtures. She polished windows and antique glass display cases until they sparkled. There were times when she was so tired she could barely move, but the exhaustion magically dimmed as soon as Kate came home from work and Ry was able to share with her what had been accomplished in that day's work.

Ry hit the road looking for merchandise to stock the store. She lost count of the number of miles she traveled going to farm auctions, estate sales, thrift stores, yard sales and business closeouts. The best times were always the ones when Kate wanted to go with her.

Finally, after weeks of hard work, The Antique Nook opened with blazing success. For the first few months, business was so brisk that Ry could barely keep up. She hired a part-time employee, Sally Watkins. Then the economy worsened and sent sales into a downward spiral. Now, the shop was barely making enough to cover expenses.

"Well?"

Ry stifled a groan of frustration. She wouldn't be getting any more work done tonight, if she wanted to avoid an argument. It was clear Kate was working herself up for one. She stopped typing and couldn't help giving one last try. "I still have to log all these items and price them." She waved her hand toward the jumble of boxes and furniture stacked around her.

"Can't you get Sally to help with that later?" Kate asked. "Isn't that what you're paying her for?" She began to examine her nails until suddenly she shoved her hands into the pockets of her gray tailored slacks.

Ry tried to ignore Kate's fidgeting. There was always an air of nervous energy about her. Maybe it came from having to maintain such a hectic pace at the hospital. Early in their relationship, Ry had liked Kate's nervous energy. It made Ry push herself harder to keep up. Now it mostly irritated her. She remained silent while Kate continued her tirade on Sally earning her pay.

She considered confessing to Kate that due to the decline in business Sally only worked a few hours a week now. That in fact, all of the startup money they had put aside for the store was gone, along with most of Ry's personal savings. If business didn't pick up soon she would have to close the store.

The business wasn't the only thing in a downward spiral. Her relationship with Kate had recently started to take an uneasy turn. They argued constantly and seldom did anything together. These days Kate went out with her friends from the hospital.

Ry stared at Kate and finally admitted to herself that while she cared for Kate she wasn't sure if she still loved her.

"I'm bored," Kate said. "I don't want to spend another Saturday night alone while you sit down here working."

"You could go without me." Ry hoped her eagerness for Kate to leave didn't show.

Kate gave her a sour look. "Yeah, well that hasn't proved to be much fun. Always being the odd wheel is starting to get old."

"You could sit in here with me." Ry tried to keep her rising irritation out of her voice as she pulled her hair behind her ears. In an effort to save money wherever she could, she had put off getting a haircut, and now it was much longer than she usually wore it. She had been keeping her hair pulled back into a ponytail but had lost the rubber band somewhere earlier that day and hadn't bothered to look for another one.

"And do what?" Kate asked as she idly reached into a box and picked up a book. "I don't want to sit around and watch you work." She dropped the book and picked up another. "Who did you buy all this stuff from anyway?"

"There was an estate sale off of Highway Two Eleven. I was driving to San Antonio when I saw the sign on the highway."

"You don't normally buy books. Why did you buy these?" She crinkled her nose in distaste. The movement highlighted the sprinkling of freckles across her nose. "I hope you aren't planning on adding a used-books section."

Ry rubbed her forehead. "I only bought them because there are several nice current first editions. A few customers ask about books. Besides, the estate sale guy was practically giving these away. I only paid a dollar a box." At this point, she was willing to try just about anything that would boost sales.

Kate seemed to forget her boredom as flipped through the books. "Well, since you're so good at finding things, maybe we'll get lucky and you'll find a few hundred-dollar bills tucked between the pages."

Ry smiled in spite of Kate's sarcasm. If there was anything that Ry was truly good at, it was finding things. For as long as she could remember she had been able to find things that others lost—keys, glasses, toys, whatever. As a child, she had spent hours daydreaming about finding buried treasure.

For her twelfth birthday, her parents had bought her a metal detector. She dug so many holes in the yard that her mom quickly banned its use to the woods behind their house. For weeks, she came home each afternoon with a canvas bag filled with treasures that ranged from old bottles with corroded lids to pieces of rust-encrusted farm equipment.

As she grew older, she started antiquing. Her childhood dreams of finding buried treasure gave way to dreams of discovering some phenomenal historical object that others had overlooked. Kate on the other hand was a total realist. She thought buried treasure was better suited to children's literature.

Ry often wondered why Kate had ever been attracted to her. In most ways, they were complete opposites. While she was tall and thin, Kate was short and constantly watched her weight. Ry's idea of a fun weekend was camping and fishing. Kate's perfect weekend was a five-star hotel and endless shopping in stores with prices so high they gave Ry vertigo. Ry was most comfortable in jeans and T-shirts, Kate preferred tailored suits.

Whatever sparked the original attraction between them was definitely growing dimmer. Ry shook off the thought and focused her attention on the antique school desk she had bought from the estate sale. "Did you see the desk?" she asked as she pointed out the small Chandler birch desk. "I was expecting to pay at least a hundred for it, but he only wanted twenty-five."

Kate laid the book down and stepped over to the desk. "It's beautiful." She opened the lid and checked the joints and hinges. "Why did he ask so little? What's wrong with it?"

"He didn't have the chair, but there's nothing wrong with the desk." Ry pointed to the top of the piece. "Look, it still has both of the glass inkwells."

Kate closed the lid and shrugged. "I guess he didn't know what he had, but I know you told him." She removed one of the glass inkwells and peered at it before she replaced it. "What's it worth?" She ran her hand across the top.

The unexpected spark of desire that shot through her as she watched Kate's hand move across the desk surprised Ry. She quickly turned her attention to the brass tacks studding the arm of the leather chair she was sitting in. "It's worth a couple of hundred dollars without the chair." The defensive tone in her voice irritated her. "And yes, I told him. I couldn't rip him off. But it didn't matter. Even after I told him what the desk was worth. He said he just wanted to get rid of everything as quickly as possible." She rushed on. "You should have seen the old upright radio he had. I really wanted to buy it, but he refused every offer I made."

"So, are we going out or what?" Kate asked as she suddenly turned back to Ry.

"I guess so. I did promise you we could do something." Ry hit the save button on her keyboard and pushed it away. She would have to get up even earlier in the morning if she was going to get the merchandise on the show floor tomorrow. Luckily, it would be Sunday and the shop didn't open until noon.

In a rare moment of tenderness, Kate brushed a lock of Ry's hair back from her face. "You look tired."

Again, Ry almost gave in and confessed her fears. She worried about how Kate would take the news of the recent setback. She had mentioned in passing that sales were down, but she hadn't told Kate how drastically they had dropped. She knew that Kate would explode if she ever found out that Ry had cashed in her 401K and most of that money was now gone. Rather than confess, she said, "I never dreamed running a business could be so time consuming." She fought her frustration that was on the verge of bubbling over.

"Are you sorry you opened the shop?"

Surprised by the question, Ry tried to read Kate's face. Was Kate sorry she had moved here? "On a bad day I'm sorry, but overall, no. I love finding pieces for the shop and I like living here."

"You know we could move back to San Antonio," Kate said. "I can always find a job at one of the hospitals. You could take your time job hunting until you found something you would enjoy doing."

Again, Ry tried to read Kate's face. Where was she headed with this conversation? As usual, Kate didn't allow much to show. "Are you tired of living here?" Ry asked. "You're the one who's always bored."

Kate shrugged and moved back to one of the boxes of books. "I guess I just miss you. It seems like you're always down here working or gone somewhere."

Ry stood and wrapped her arms around Kate's waist from behind. "I'm sorry. I know I spend too much time working." She rested her forehead on Kate's shoulder. "Give me time for a quick shower and we can go to the Cove. I'm sure Alice and Janet are still there."

Alice and Janet were friends that Kate had met at the hospital. They had been together for twenty-two years and still acted as if they were in a brand-new relationship. Ry envied the easy way they had with each other.

They stood quietly for a moment before Kate turned and put her arms around Ry's neck. "I have a better idea. Why don't I stay down here and help you finish this, and then in the morning we'll have time to go out for breakfast or even a short drive before you open the shop."

"Are you sure?" Ry asked, hoping her relief wasn't showing.

Kate pulled away. "Where do you want me to start?" Without waiting for an answer, she grabbed a box of books and set it on the large wooden worktable near Ry's desk. "I'll separate all the first editions and start researching and pricing them." She took a book from the box and glanced back at Ry playfully. "Of course, I'm going to go through them first just to be certain there are no hidden hundred-dollar bills."

"Feel free to keep anything you find," Ry said. At this point, she would be grateful to find a few ten-dollar bills. "Any of the books that aren't suitable for the store, I'll take to the nursing home next week. I already have a stack of magazines set aside."

Ry picked up an old cardboard cigar box and opened it. This had been her favorite find of the day. The box held eight small woodcarvings of farm animals. The rather crudely worked pieces had captured Ry's attention. She wanted to know more about them and the person who had carved them. At first, the man at the estate sale had seemed hesitant to sell them. His grandfather had carved the pieces. Normally, that would have made Ry stop asking, but when he admitted he hadn't bothered to look at the pieces close enough to know what they were, she persisted until he agreed to sell them. The objects obviously hadn't held much of a sentimental value to him. She picked up the horse and studied the slightly square head. Hairline cracks in the wood suggested it was old. The blade marks were still clearly visible but worn smooth as if the piece had been handled a lot. She chose another item. It was a rabbit or at least the head of one. The body was still locked inside the small block of wood. She wondered why the carver had never finished the piece. Ry realized she was wasting time. She returned the items back to the box and quickly logged them into her inventory spreadsheet. There would be time later to decide whether she wanted to keep the pieces for herself.

When Kate finished going through the books, she tucked her shoulder-length auburn hair behind her ears and began polishing the furniture.

They worked in easy companionship until almost midnight when Ry finally checked the last item off her list. She quickly downloaded her file to an offsite data-storage service and pushed back from her desk. "That's the last of it," she said as she yawned and stretched. "Everything has been logged and researched. All I have to do is finish making the price tags, and I can do that tomorrow."

Kate gave a last swipe across the small side table she had been polishing. "There's still another box behind the desk."

Ry glanced down at the notebook. Everything was crossed off. She used the book when she shopped. She would jot down each item as she negotiated the price. It helped her to remember the amount they had agreed upon and to make sure she didn't leave any purchases behind. Once she was back at the shop, she would check the items off as she entered them into her inventory. "There shouldn't be anything else. It's probably just an empty box."

Kate went behind the desk and bent over. "It's definitely not empty. It has some magazines and an old metal box."

Ry shook her head. "I didn't buy anything like that."

Kate placed the cardboard box on the wooden table where she had worked earlier. "There's a stack of *Old West* magazines, some books and this old beat-up metal file box." She tugged at the rusted latch. It seemed to be stuck.

When Ry saw the cardboard box, she sighed. "How did that get mixed in?" She rubbed her tired neck. "Crap. He probably thinks I stole it from him. I tried to buy the magazines, but he didn't want to sell them. In fact, he wanted to keep everything in that box." She tried to quell her frustration. The trip out to return the box would be another hour or more wasted tomorrow. She didn't have a phone number for him, so she would have to drive back over there as soon as possible to return it. Hopefully, he would still be there. "With my luck, he'll call the cops."

Kate finally succeeded in opening the metal file box. "Well, the good news is, he can't shoot you. At least not until you return this to him." She held up a pistol.

Ry gasped when she saw the revolver. "Please tell me that thing isn't loaded," she said as she carefully took the weapon. "That box was bouncing around in the back of my truck all afternoon." The pistol was obviously old. She checked it and frowned. What sort of fool stored a loaded weapon in a cheap file box? She pressed the cylinder release latch to open the cylinder. It was loaded with two half-moon clips. She removed them. Her father had taught her never to leave a loaded gun lying around the house. Then she examined it closer. It was a beautiful weapon.

"This is a Smith and Wesson M1917," Ry said. "It was manufactured around World War One." She turned it over in her hands. "It has been well taken care of." She studied the hammered silver grips. "These grips look handmade. They must have cost a fortune." She continued to study the revolver. "I used to have a Smith and Wesson forty-five-caliber Model 625. It was my favorite target pistol." She took one of the half-moon clips from inside the box. It held three shells. "I've heard guys at the range talk about these half-moon clips, but this is the first one I've ever seen."

Kate gave a loud uninterested sigh.

Ry took the hint and placed the revolver and clip back into the metal box. She had grown up around a wide assortment of target and hunting weapons. Her father, three brothers and every other male Shelton over the age of eight were avid hunters. Even though she refused to hunt, Ry's father had encouraged her to learn how to shoot and handle a weapon. On her first trip to the range she discovered she enjoyed target shooting and by the time she was fifteen she could hit a target's bulls-eye four out of every five shots as easily as she could tie her sneakers.

She placed the metal container back inside the cardboard box. "I'll return it to him first thing tomorrow morning." She glanced at Kate. After the earlier outburst, Kate had been in a decent mood, so she took a chance. "Would you like to ride out there with me?"

Kate linked her arm through Ry's arm. "I'll ride out with you if you buy me breakfast at the Pancake Hut afterward."

Ry held her breath as she thought about her already burdened credit card. Surely there was enough left on her credit limit to cover a couple of pancake breakfasts. She could wait awhile longer for a haircut. Or maybe she could get her mom to cut it. Her mom had cut her brothers' hair when they were younger.

She realized Kate was still waiting for her to answer. "That would be nice," Ry said as she headed toward the stairs. "Would you mind checking to make sure everything is locked up? I need to shower."

"Sure." Kate turned and headed into the front area of the shop.

Ry rushed through her shower. She wanted to take advantage of Kate's good mood. It had been weeks since they had made love. When she dashed out a few minutes later, Kate was in bed fast asleep.

She envied Kate's ability to fall asleep so quickly. It was already after one in the morning, but Ry knew she would toss and turn for an hour or more before falling asleep. She considered going back downstairs to start pricing the new stock but didn't feel like working. Too exhausted to read, she turned off the lamp and stretched out next to Kate.

Despite the fact that they lived practically in the center of town, the night was quiet. All of the surrounding shops closed between six and nine. The only business still opened at this hour would be Leroy's, a bar nearly a mile away, out on the highway.

Ry lost track of time as she mentally arranged and rearranged the new furniture into displays. She was just beginning to doze when a loud clatter jarred her awake.

Kate groaned and rolled over. "What was that?" she asked.

Ry put an arm around her and snuggled against her back. "It sounded like the raccoons turned over the trash can again."

"Did you put the straps back on the can?"

"Yes. Try to go back to sleep." Ry smiled slightly. Kate's breathing had already settled back into a steady rhythm. I wish I'd follow my own advice, she thought wearily as she stared into the darkness. Damn raccoons. If there was one creature on earth she wouldn't mind shooting, it would be raccoons. They got into everything and destroyed anything they touched. She had to strap the trash can lids down with the vinyl-covered wire used for bicycle locks. She had tried using bungee cords, but they chewed through them. She thought about the pistol downstairs. Its six measly bullets would be useless against the destructive creatures that seemingly numbered into the hundreds.

The unexpected noise of a car engine cranking interrupted her thoughts. It sounded as though it had been at the corner. She listened as it drove away into the night. As she drifted off to sleep, she dreamed of mutant raccoons running rampant through the streets, breaking windows and stealing cars.

CHAPTER TWO

Ry opened her eyes to find Kate sitting in the middle of the bed drinking coffee and messing with her phone. Ry smiled. This was the private Kate who no one other than Ry was ever allowed to see. Not the never a hair out of place perfectly tailored Kate, but the Kate with one side of her hair frizzed out in a wild mess and a ratty sweatshirt that Ry had discarded long ago.

"Good morning," Ry said as she sat up. She glanced at the clock and suppressed a groan when she saw it was after nine. She had overslept. There was no way she would be able to return the cardboard box, follow through on the promised breakfast with Kate, tag the new merchandise and move it onto the sales floor before noon. Her chest felt like a vise was squeezing it making it difficult to breathe. She closed her eyes and pushed everything but the moment at hand out of her thoughts. One thing at a time.

Kate said, "Mom wants us to have dinner with them on Friday night. Want to go?"

"Don't you have to work on Saturday?" Ry liked Kate's family, but the thought of working all day Friday and then driving the seventy miles roundtrip to San Antonio didn't appeal to her. Neither did the idea of the argument that was sure to develop between Kate and her father. They couldn't be in the same room for more than ten minutes without finding something to disagree about.

"Yes, but that's not a problem. I'll be fine." Kate typed something into her phone. "I get off at three on Friday. We can leave as soon as I get home."

Ry bit her tongue. Kate was well aware that the shop didn't close until seven. If Ry went, she would have to ask Sally Watkins to fill in for her. More expenses she couldn't afford. The vise around her chest began to tighten again. She fought it off. "That's fine."

To avoid any further conversation, Ry pulled on her clothes. "While you're getting dressed, I'll go see how much damage the raccoons did." Without waiting for a response, she hurried down the stairs.

After a quick cup of coffee, Ry grabbed Kate's keys from the table by the stairs. Kate didn't like riding in the truck unless she had to. Ry then went to her office to retrieve the box of items she needed to return. She shivered when she stepped outside. The area had been experiencing an unusually early cold front. After she had locked the box and the gun inside the trunk of Kate's car, she decided to take the items for the nursing home as well. She smiled as this one brief ray of sunshine brightened her day. By dropping the box for the nursing home off today, she would save a trip out there next week. After placing the nursing home box in the backseat of the car, she went to see how much of a mess the raccoons had created.

Just as she expected, the trash can had been tipped over. Luckily, the devious critters hadn't managed to get the lid off. She set the can upright and started back into the house. As she rounded the corner leading to the back door, something on the ground caught her eye. A cigarette butt was on the ground below the back window. It lay on the narrow strip of grass that separated the building from the pavement. The paved spot, barely large enough for four cars, had once been used as the store's parking lot.

She glanced toward their vehicles and saw something glittering on the pavement. Even before she walked around her truck, she knew what she was going to find. The driver's side window had been smashed and the door was only partially closed.

"Oh, my gosh, what happened?"

Ry turned to find Kate behind her. She had already showered and was dressed in a pair of cream-colored slacks and a striking multihued lightweight sweater. "Somebody has broken into my truck." Ry held onto the door for strength. Less than two weeks earlier, she had dropped everything but liability on her truck insurance. Kate was going to have a stroke when she found out. She looked at Kate's car. It seemed to be fine. "I don't think your car was bothered."

"Why would someone break into your truck? Did you leave your cell phone or something valuable lying on the seat?"

Of course, it's my fault. She swallowed her anger. "No." She felt her hip pocket. "I have my wallet and my phone."

"I'll call Victor."

Victor Orozco was the Jackson City sheriff. He'd become a good friend of theirs after his wife and two-year-old son had been seriously injured in a hit-and-run accident. She and Kate had been coming from San Antonio and happened upon the accident. Kate was able to stabilize both victims until the ambulance arrived. The doctors told Victor that Kate's actions probably saved both of their lives.

"No. Don't call Victor, yet," Ry said. "Wait until we get back. I don't know how long the report will take, and I have to return that box before it gets any later." She decided she would wait until after Kate had finished her pancakes to tell her about the insurance. Surely, the mega-dose of sugar and carbohydrates would help curb her anger.

Kate shrugged. "Okay." She started toward her car. "You drive."

* * *

The estate sale sign was still posted on the side of the highway. Ry turned onto a county road that if the potholes were any indication, the county had stopped maintaining years ago. She drove slowly; the last thing she needed to do was damage one of the car's tires or knock the wheels out of alignment. She breathed a sigh of relief when she finally spotted the white ranch-style house with the green sedan in the driveway. "I was worried he wouldn't still be here." Ry eased the car into the short driveway behind the green sedan.

"It's a creepy looking place," Kate said and shuddered. "It looks like something out of one of those slasher movies."

Ry popped the trunk latch. She hadn't noticed yesterday how poorly maintained the house and yard were. "It's just old and run-down. I don't think anyone has lived here for quite a while." Her phone rang. She took it from her pocket and glanced at the screen. It was a vendor she knew from San Antonio. Ry decided to call her back later. She laid the phone on the console before she opened the car door and stepped out. "You can wait here if you want. I'll only be a minute."

Kate nodded. Then in a rare moment of playfulness she added, "Yell if anything gets after you." She waved Ry's phone at her. "I'll call nine-one-one."

"My s-hero," Ry replied drily.

"Hey, I always leave the butch stuff up to you," Kate replied quickly.

Ry walked to the back of the car and raised the trunk. She started to take both the metal file box containing the gun and the cardboard box, but they were so heavy she decided it would be better to make two trips. She grabbed the metal box and closed the trunk.

The smells of autumn filled the air. Fallen leaves and dead grass crunched under her shoes as she made her way across the yard. The large, dark, empty windows stared out of the forsaken house. She couldn't stop the slight shiver that crawled up her back as she realized how quiet it was. Sounds from the main road didn't carry this far back. Signs of neglect showed everywhere. Three sides of the isolated house were hemmed in by expansive tree-lined fields dotted with dead, shredded cornstalks, and despite the abundance of trees and brush around, there were no bird sounds. Not even the buzzing of an annoying cicada. She glanced looking for the endless grasshoppers that had been plaguing the area for weeks. Nothing moved.

Ry couldn't help but flinch when the weathered planks squealed in protest as she stepped onto the porch. She tried to shake off the eerie feeling. This is all Kate's fault, she told herself. Why did she have to make that dang slasher movie reference?

Ry's unease increased when she knocked on the door and it slowly swung open with a teeth-aching squeal. No matter how hard she fought against the memories, every gruesome movie she had ever seen or heard about came back to her. Not caring whether he was home or not she turned sharply to leave and ran squarely into Kate. Ry couldn't stop the yelp of fright.

"You scared the crap out of me," she snapped, embarrassed that she had given way to such juvenile fears.

"I felt guilty about sending you in alone. I thought I'd help out by bringing the box of stuff up here for you." Kate was staring at the door. "Why is the door open?"

"I don't know. It opened when I knocked." With Kate nearby, Ry found a new sense of confidence. She stepped back up to the door and knocked loudly on the doorframe. "Hello." Inside she could see the large, floral print couch was still there. He had tried to give it to her after she had declined buying it, but it was too modern to be of any use to her.

"Maybe he's still asleep," Kate offered, as she leaned inside the doorway and shouted. "Hello! Is anyone here?"

Ry studied the car in the driveway. She hadn't paid much attention to it the day before, but she was certain it was the same one. "It's a new car," she began. "I don't think it's something someone would just leave sitting out here."

"It's a rental."

She looked at Kate in surprise. "How do you know that?"

"There's an Avis sticker on the back window." Kate shoved the door fully open.

"Hey, we probably shouldn't…" Her protests were cut short as Kate bolted into the house, dropping the box of books and magazines just inside the doorway.

Ry started to follow but froze when she saw what had propelled Kate into action. A man covered in blood lay on the floor. From the pools of blood and his ashen color, Ry didn't need a medical degree to know he was dead. Her stomach started to churn. She quickly backed out of the room. Her head spun as she struggled to breathe. She sat down on the porch and leaned her head against the cool metal of the file box. She was still sitting there when Kate came out talking on her cell phone.

Kate hung up and sat next to Ry. "Are you okay?" she asked, as she put an arm around her.

Not trusting her voice, Ry simply grunted.

"I called nine-one-one," Kate said. "The sheriff and an ambulance are on the way."

"He looked like it was too late for an ambulance," Ry said as she tried to push the images away.

"A medical examiner still has to come out."

"What happened to him?" Ry asked.

"He was shot, twice. I think. There's so much blood, it's hard to tell without moving him." She stopped. "I'm sorry. I know it's hard if you're not used to it."

Who could ever get used to that? "Do you think someone robbed him?" The house had been filled with furniture and household items. He had probably taken in quite a bit of cash yesterday. She had given him a little over three hundred dollars herself.

"I don't know. All I know is he hasn't been dead long. The blood was still fairly fresh."

Ry's head began to spin again as she recalled the river of blood. Just as she leaned her head down, a loud crack split the air. The bullet made a shattering thud as it dug into the wooden post and filled the air with splinters. Instantly, the side of Ry's face was on fire as the tiny slivers of wood dug into her flesh. Before her brain had time to register why, Ry had Kate by the arm, dragging her into the house. She heard Kate screaming something about her phone as she tried to pull away. Ry tightened her grip. It had been a few years since she'd heard the sound, but that was definitely a gunshot. Another shot shattered the front window as they dove inside. They hit the floor hard.

Ry slammed the door shut with her foot as two more shots exploded in rapid succession. She rolled away from the door, knowing it wouldn't do much toward stopping a bullet. Still hugging the floor, she crawled beneath the window that had been shot out. She had to move shards of glass out of her way as she crawled.

Kate followed. "I dropped my phone." She was clearly angry. "Why didn't you let me pick it up?"

"Because, we both would probably be dead now," Ry's voice came out in choppy spurts. She knew this wasn't a safe location for them, but needed to see what was going on. She couldn't remember if the outer house covering was wood or aluminum siding. Not that it mattered much, since neither would offer much protection from a high-powered rifle.

Ry sat up slowly. To her left, beams of sunlight streamed through the bullet holes in the door. "What have we stumbled into?"

Kate started to sit up just as another shot smashed through the window to their right, showering glass around them.

Ry threw herself over Kate. When a second shot didn't follow, she sat up and motioned for Kate to move. "Get behind that couch." Without waiting to see if Kate moved, Ry carefully peeked through the window. She saw a blur of blue as someone disappeared behind a tree.

"Watch that glass," Kate warned.

Ry turned back to her. "I told you to get behind the couch." She instantly regretted the sharpness of her voice. "It's a miracle he hasn't hit one of us already."

"You're bleeding." Kate reached to touch Ry's face.

"It's nothing but splinters from the post." Ry gently moved Kate's hand away.

Another bullet smashed through the wall on the other side of the door. "He's not sure where we are. He's hoping for a lucky shot," Ry said. "We need to move." She knew their best bet was getting back to the car and getting the hell away from there. To do so, they would have to cross the open yard. Suddenly she remembered the sunken den. She had nearly tripped on the stairs yesterday when she was looking around the house. She grabbed Kate's hand. "Follow me, but stay as close to the floor as you can."

Afraid the shooter would continue to pump random shots into the front of the house, Ry made her way to the middle of the room where the couch sat. From there she could see the doorway to the den. They would have to cover about twelve feet of open space before they reached the sunken den. She'd noticed yesterday that the sunken area of the room was actually below ground level. The dried water stains along the wall indicated how impractical the design had been, but right now Ry could have kissed the architect. She pointed toward the den. "We've got to get in there as quickly as possible." She looked at Kate. "We're going to belly crawl as fast as we can."

Kate nodded. Her brown eyes looked large against her ashen face.

"Are you ready?"

Again, Kate nodded.

Ry clung to the metal file box as she began to crawl.

Another single shot entered the house and struck the floor beside the couch. The noise brought them both to their feet. Ry threw herself over the edge into the two-and-a-half-foot deep hole. She almost cried with joy when she saw the behemoth old sleeper sofa that sat against the front wall of the room.

"Help me," she said as she bent low and made her way to the sofa.

"What are we doing?" Kate asked.

"Turn the sofa over so it's sitting on its arms." She started tugging on the piece. "This thing is old and it weighs a ton." She grunted as she tugged. Cowering behind the sofa didn't give her any real sense of safety, but at least it would help protect them from the flying debris and hopefully any stray ricochets.

It took them three more tries before they finally managed to tip the beast forward.

"Get underneath there," Ry said, pointing to the cave-like opening the overturned sofa created.

Kate opened her mouth but whatever she had intended to say was interrupted by an explosive sound that caused the floor beneath them to vibrate. They both scrambled into the cubbyhole beneath the sofa.

Ry held Kate closely as the walls of the living room disintegrated beneath the hammering of the rapid fire. The shooter had obviously grown tired of peppering the house with a single shot or two. He was now literally tearing the house apart with an automatic weapon of some sort. After what seemed like an eternity, the noise stopped. The silence that filled the room caused Ry's ears to ache. They continued to cling to each other.

When the silence held, Ry prayed that he had run out of ammo. She started to move away from Kate, but another round of destruction stopped her. This time the madness was directed at the wall mere inches above where they huddled. As long as he was outside all he could do was fire into the house at ground level. The only thing they had to fear was a ricochet, which was still very much a danger considering the number of bullets flying around the room.

Ry didn't know much about assault weapons—her family had never owned any, only rifles or an occasional shotgun to hunt and pistols for target practice—but judging by the length of time he was able to maintain a constant onslaught, she guessed the shooter was using something with at least a one-hundred-round drum.

As the room continued to disintegrate around them, they flattened themselves against the floor. Ry kept her body between Kate and the wall, praying she was right in remembering that the sunken area was completely below ground level. She watched with a strange sense of detachment as pieces of glass, aluminum from the miniblinds and tattered fragments of cloth from the curtains danced in the air. Shards of wood flew across the room. The wooden spindles that ran alongside the steps leading down into the room exploded into a shower of splinters, some of which embedded themselves into the opposite wall from where she and Kate lay. She was vaguely aware of Kate's screams or maybe they were her own. At this point, she could no longer be sure of anything. She tried to whisper words of comfort into Kate's ear, but she felt certain that nothing she said could penetrate the deafening roar around them. She realized that he wasn't going to stop until they were dead. "Stop screaming," she shouted in Kate's ear. "He won't stop unless he thinks we're dead." Her words must have reached Kate because she stopped. Ry tried to determine how much time had passed since Kate's nine-one-one call.

Silence.

Ry held Kate closer and silently counted the seconds.

"The sheriff should be here any moment," Kate said. "If you'd let me grab my phone, I could have called again. Why don't you ever carry your phone? If you'd paid attention to what you were doing yesterday, we wouldn't be in this mess." Kate seemed on the verge of hysteria. Her body was trembling, her teeth clattering together. "This is entirely your fault."

Ry ignored the accusations and held her tighter. She didn't want to scare Kate more by reminding her that the county sheriff's office was responsible for the safety of the entire county. There was no way to know how long it would be before they arrived. She kept counting. Would the shooter reload and continue firing? How many drums did he have? She remembered the double-sided drums as being rather large. They certainly weren't something he could slip into his pocket. If he ran out of ammo would he leave, or would he come after them? She counted to fifty-three before the third round of destruction started pouring into the house. Everywhere she looked, there was damage. Nothing had managed to escape the havoc created by the hail of gunfire.

A thunderous crash at the front of the house startled Ry. When she flinched, her elbow struck something solid and sharp. She glanced back and saw the metal file box. It took some maneuvering, but she finally managed to get it pulled from behind her.

"What are you doing?" Kate demanded.

Ry opened the box and removed the revolver. Her hands trembled as she grabbed the clips she had unloaded from it the previous night. "He's not going to stop until he kills us," she said. Her voice sounded flat, even to her own ears. What was she planning on doing with six bullets? She prayed the bullets weren't as old as the revolver. The last thing she needed was for this thing to explode in her hand when she squeezed the trigger.

"The sheriff will be here any minute," Kate insisted.

Another burst of bullets ripped through the interior walls sending out a billowing cloud of drywall dust. From the sound of the destruction, it seemed he was now simply sweeping the weapon's aim back and forth across the front of the house.

"Are you willing to bet our lives on that?" Ry asked, recovering her voice. "I'm sure he figures we called the police. There's bound to be other people living nearby, they'll hear the shots." She pressed the cylinder release latch, inserted the two clips and carefully closed the cylinder. She wondered if he still had ammunition for the rifle. Or maybe he had other weapons. If he simply intended to drive away, why hadn't he done so already? A shiver ran down her back. He didn't intend to leave anyone alive here. "He's going to get tired of standing out there and eventually he's going to come in after us."

"Ry, please." Kate must have seen something in her face, because she stopped in midsentence.

This time when the pause in gunfire occurred, Ry was ready. She rolled from beneath the sofa and poked her head above the edge. The destruction that greeted her was beyond comprehension. She stood slowly as she took in the damage. Enormous holes had been blown through the outer wall. The siding, framing timbers and Sheetrock looked as if some maniacal beast had chewed them up and spat them out. A large section of the interior wall between the den and living room no longer existed. Her legs nearly buckled when she realized that had the den not been partially below ground level, she and Kate wouldn't have had a chance of escaping. Mindful of the debris, she moved closer to the battered wall and peered over. The shooter stood less than fifteen feet away. He was loading a bolt-action rifle. She didn't recognize the make or model but she knew enough about guns to know that the rifle he was holding was not the weapon that had created all this damage. It took her a moment to notice the discarded assault rifle lying on the ground several feet behind him. Next to it were three double round drums.

Even as her brain fought to make reason of all this, Ry couldn't help but notice that in his white shirt and black dress pants he looked more like a man heading off to church than a mad gunman.

Sun glinted off one of the bullets he was feeding into the rifle and snapped her out of her reverie. She aimed the pistol at him. "Drop the rifle," she yelled.

He jumped back at the sound of her voice. Several shells fell from his hand.

She saw his eyes settle on the pistol. Startling him had given Ry an odd sense of satisfaction. It quickly disappeared when he failed to drop the rifle. "I said drop the rifle."

Time slowed for Ry as the rifle started to swing upward and at the same moment, his right hand worked the bolt to inject a shell. Without conscious thought, she widened her stance, took a deep breath, pulled back the hammer and squeezed the trigger. Her first shot struck the inner side of his left shirt pocket, shots two and three quickly followed and were exactly one inch on either side of the first. She watched the red stain spread across his white shirt. His body seemed to deflate. He fell to his knees. The rifle slipped to the ground as if the impact of his falling had jarred it from his grip. Then slowly he fell forward and landed facedown in the yard.

CHAPTER THREE

Ry didn't know how much time passed before Kate's voice cut through the fog that had engulfed her.

"I should go out there and see if there's anything I can do for him," Kate said. Her voice sounded hollow.

"There's no need," Ry said. She knew where her shots had gone and she knew the damage they had caused. "He's beyond help."

Kate made a small choking sound. "Dear God, you killed him."

Ry started to turn to comfort Kate, but a sense of unease still nagged at her. She scanned the yard again, double-checking any area that looked large enough to hide another person.

"Did you have to kill him?" Kate's voice was starting to sound panicky. "I'm sure he would have left had he known you were armed."

Ry glanced at her in disbelief. Had she lost her mind? "Kate, look around you. Does it look like he was just trying to scare us off?" Her throat was parched. She licked her dry lips. "Besides, I told him to drop the rifle. He saw I was armed."

Kate began to bounce her fists against her thighs.

Ry recognized the gesture as something Kate did when she was highly stressed. The almost paralyzing sense that she had missed something kept her gaze glued to the yard. What was she not seeing? She continued to the scan the area.

"You didn't have to kill him?" Kate asked again. "You're a good shot. You could have shot him in the leg or something?"

Ry shook her head. "Kate, I did what was necessary. Look around you. He wouldn't have stopped until he killed us both." Her eyes continued to search the area. She didn't bother to mention that had the floor not been below ground level, it would be the two of them lying there bleeding out. The sofa could not have protected them from direct fire. But then, Kate lived in the medical world where they saved lives, not took them. Still not seeing anything that caused alarm, she turned to her thoughts back to the nine-one-one call. How long had it been? Thoughts of the sheriff made her realize what was about to occur.

"I'm going to go get your phone from the porch where you dropped it." Ry had left her own phone in Kate's car. She gave the yard one last scrutiny before starting toward the living room. The den stairs were splintered and too dangerous to step on. She climbed out of the sunken den and carefully made her way toward the porch. She was shocked to find that the large crash they had heard earlier had been the small porch collapsing. The bullets had eaten through the two thin support posts.

Amazingly enough, Kate's phone was undamaged. Ry picked it up and dusted it off, while still holding the pistol in her other hand.

"Will you please throw that thing away," Kate said and nodded toward the pistol. "Who are you calling?" she asked as she took the phone from Ry.

Suppressing a spark of anger at having the phone snatched from her hand, Ry took a deep breath before replying. "I was going to call my dad. I'm going to need a lawyer."

"It was self-defense," Kate said, her eyes wide.

"Yes, but there's two dead bodies here and we're going to have to explain them."

Kate began to dial. "In that case, let's call my dad. Your dad's lawyer probably knows more about business law than criminal. As a former state senator, I'm sure my dad knows a few criminal lawyers." She stepped back into the house as she placed the phone to her ear. Kate's willingness to get her father involved so quickly frightened Ry more than the thought of having to face hours of police questioning. Kate had one hard-and-fast rule and that was never to ask her father for anything.

Ry looked at the pistol she was still holding. She considered laying it down, but somehow she felt safer holding it. She followed Kate back into the living room. In the six years that she and Kate had been together, Ry had never known the former Republican State Senator Edwin Prescott Elliott and his daughter to agree on a single thing. Both were hardheaded and set in their stubborn ways.

Mindful of the splintered wood and glass shards, Ry resumed her study of the yard. As she listened to Kate quietly talking on the phone, she fought against the cold knot of panic that was trying to form deep within her. She was sickened by what had happened, but she knew without a doubt that he would have killed them both. *He created the situation that led to his death by shooting at us*, she told herself. *It's not as if I shot him without warning. He clearly saw the pistol.* Why had he taken the risk of shooting at them?

Kate returned to stand by her. "He said not to answer any questions until we get to the station and have a lawyer present. He's sending his lawyer to the Bexar County Sheriff's Office. We're outside the city limits, so that's where they'll take us."

"Won't not answering their questions make us look like we're hiding something?" Ry asked.

Kate shrugged.

Neither of them spoke again until nearly ten minutes later when a county sheriff's car finally arrived. There was no room in the short driveway for his car. He drove his car up into the yard.

Ry could see the look of surprise turn to shock on the young officer's face when he spotted the dead man in the yard and then eyed the damaged house.

"What do we do?" Kate asked, her voice trembling.

"We probably should go out," Ry said. She shook her head after giving it some thought. "Maybe we should wait until he tells us to come out." Ry continued to study the young officer. He looked as though he should still be in high school. She watched as he picked up the radio mike and spoke into it.

"How do we explain all this?" Kate waved her arms at the destruction around them.

"We tell the truth." The pistol felt heavy in her hand. She had never fired a weapon at a living thing until today. She turned her attention back to the cop as he continued to sit in the car.

"Why isn't he getting out?" Kate asked.

"I think he called for backup. From the looks of him, he probably hasn't been at this long," Ry said. Suddenly exhausted, she staggered slightly. How had things gotten so horribly out of hand? Maybe she was dreaming. Hoping to wake herself from this terrible dream, she rubbed her free hand over her face harshly and winced. She had forgotten about her face full of splinters. The burning pain in her cheek ruled out the possibility of all this being a dream.

"I guess we'll just stay here. He's bound to tell us to come out eventually." Ry turned to study the living room. It looked much worse than she had first noticed. The large double front window was now nothing more than thousands of glittering shards scattered across the floor. The fragmented remains of the front door dangled at an odd angle from the twisted top hinge. Tiny particles of the cotton stuffing and floral fabric on the old couch still drifted aimlessly through the air.

"Why is this happening?" Kate asked in a burst of tears.

Ry reached out a hand to console her, but her offer of comfort was rebuked as Kate stepped away. Ry tried to ignore the stab of pain the rejection caused. "I don't know," she said, "but he was definitely trying to kill us. Maybe we were just in the wrong place at the wrong time." She didn't wait for Kate to respond. "It doesn't make sense. He knew we didn't see him kill this guy. Why would he take such a chance in coming after us?"

"Maybe he planned on robbing us and he just assumed you weren't armed."

"That was a pretty stupid assumption on his part. It's Texas." Ry shook her head. "Besides, he didn't give up even after he saw I had the pistol. He was after something."

Kate waved her hands, clearly annoyed. "Oh, come on. He had no way of knowing we would be here this morning."

"That's true." Ry stared out of what had once been the window. Her brain was overly stimulated. She couldn't concentrate. She closed her eyes. What was she was missing? There was something there just out of her reach. Her thoughts flashed around like a school of minnows in a pond. Frustrated with trying to corral them she turned back to Kate. "You said the guy in here hadn't been dead long." She pointed toward the dead body. They both avoided looking directly at the man lying in a pool of drying blood. "So, maybe I'm wrong. It could have been bad timing for us and we just happened to arrive as he was being killed." She drummed her fingers against her leg and searched for a logical answer. "Maybe the guy out there had been intending to get away in the rental car." Even as she said it, Ry wasn't buying the idea. Where had he been when they arrived? Where had he gotten the assault rifle and the three one-hundred-round drums? He could have easily carried both weapons at once, but the fully loaded drums would have made it more difficult. He had to have a car nearby.

"Or he might have seen my car and wanted it instead of the rental," Kate said. "Don't they put those tracking devices on rental cars?"

Ry shrugged, but she had stopped listening. She had noticed what was left of the cardboard box containing the books and magazines. They had been directly in front of the window and had taken a lot of the abuse. Now, they were little more than confetti. She expressed her thoughts to Kate. "I think this all has something to do with either that box or something I bought yesterday."

"Why does everything have to be so over the top with you?" Kate demanded. "As usual, you're reading too much into this," she said as wrapped her arms tightly around herself. "This isn't one of your fantasy treasure mysteries. None of this has anything to do with us. We were simply in the wrong place at the wrong time."

Ry stared at the destruction around them. The front of the house looked as though it had been fed through a gigantic shredder. She and Kate were covered in dust and small pieces of debris. One knee of Kate's slacks was ripped. She glanced down at her own jeans and absently brushed them off as she recalled the cigarette butt beneath the shop window. "Someone was by the shop window last night. I found a cigarette butt outside beneath the window."

Kate grew pale. Ry caught her arm as she swayed.

"Are you telling me that someone was watching us last night?" Kate asked, as she pulled away.

Ry shrugged. "I don't know that we were being watched, but someone dropped that cigarette butt. I'm betting it was that same person who broke into my truck."

"I don't think it was anything that sinister," Kate said as she began to hammer at her thighs again. "Who knows how long that cigarette butt's been there? As for the truck, it was probably kids screwing around. Saturday night in a small town with nothing much to do and they end up doing crap like that."

Ry shook her head. "We've lived there two years and never had any problems. So why now?" She thought about the raccoon knocking over the garbage can. Shortly after hearing the can fall, she had heard the sound of a car motor cranking. She decided not to mention the car. She had spouted enough wild accusations already. "What if it wasn't kids and the raccoons scared him off?" she said instead.

Kate looked at her as if she was skeptical of Ry's sanity. "I seriously doubt a raccoon is going to scare a cold-blooded killer."

"No. I don't mean the raccoon itself. What if he heard the racket of the can being tipped over and didn't realize what caused it? Maybe he thought it was someone taking their garbage out and he was afraid of being seen."

Her speculations ended as a second county sheriff's car rolled into the yard, immediately followed by a third one.

"I don't think you should start spewing your silly ideas to them," Kate said as she stared at the cars.

Ry's heart pounded as the officers climbed out of their cars with their weapons drawn. "Don't make any sudden moves," she whispered to Kate. "I'll go out first. You stay close behind me."

She felt sure they were clearly visible to the officers, but to be certain she slowly stepped closer to the gaping doorway. "We're in the house," she yelled out of the mangled door. "I'm going to toss the gun out the door first." She wasn't about to throw a loaded gun, so she quickly unloaded the pistol and dropped the clips on the floor.

"Keep your hands where we can see them," the first cop yelled as they all aimed their weapons toward the front door. "Toss your weapons and come out one at a time."

"Stay here until they tell you to come out," Ry told Kate, "and whatever you do, don't make any sudden movements."

"I'm so scared. I'm not sure I can even move," Kate admitted.

Ry tried to give a reassuring smile, but it wasn't easy. "It'll be fine." She tossed the gun through the open door and stepped out with her hands high in the air. "That's the only weapon we have," she yelled.

"Keep walking this way," the young cop shouted.

When Ry reached him, he motioned for her to stop. His eyes darted wildly from her face to the house. "You badly hurt?" he asked.

Without thinking, Ry touched her cheek, causing it to start stinging again. "No. Not bad."

He nodded and cleared his throat.

She could see his Adam's apple bob as he struggled to swallow.

"Who else is in the house?" he asked, in a voice shrill with excitement.

"Kate Elliott. We drove out here together. There's also a dead man inside. I don't know his name, but I think this guy," she nodded toward the man she had killed, "shot him."

The young cop's eyes bugged at the mention of a second body. "Who shot him?" he asked, nodding to the body in the yard.

"I did." She remembered the warning that Mr. Elliott had given them about waiting for a lawyer, but any fool could see this was self-defense.

The young cop licked his lips nervously before he finally waved her on back to the second cop. This guy was older and seemed to be watching the rookie.

"Walk on over here to me," the older officer said and motioned to Ry.

The young cop waited until Ry had been patted down and was in handcuffs before he yelled for Kate to come out.

Ry watched with her heart in her throat as Kate slowly made her way across the yard. It was obvious that the young guy was new to the job. He was clearly nervous. The back of his shirt was stained with sweat. His hands shook. He gripped the pistol so tightly his knuckles were white. She took some consolation in the fact that his index finger was still along the side of the weapon and not on the trigger.

The third officer searched and handcuffed Kate. She and Kate were placed in separate cars before the three cops split into two teams. The one who had handcuffed Kate went to examine the man in the yard and the older man and the rookie carefully made their way into the house. A few seconds later, an ambulance bounced across the lawn followed by more squad cars. After several minutes of hectic activity, the car in which Kate was being held left.

Ry tried to get Kate's attention as the car drove away, but Kate kept her head turned away from her. Kate's refusal to look at her worried her more than the older officer and the Emergency Medical Technician who were approaching the car where she waited.

The officer opened the back car door and motioned for Ry to step out. As he helped her out of the car, Ry noticed that his badge indicated he was a deputy sheriff. His nametag read Ward.

"This is June," he said and motioned toward a woman Ry judged to be in her late thirties. "She needs to look at your cheek."

"Thanks, but it's not bad."

June turned Ry's face slightly before speaking. "Sorry, but those splinters need to come out. With these older houses you never know what might have been used in the wood and paint." She turned to the deputy. "Richard, let's move over to the ambulance."

Ry and the officer quietly followed her.

"Have a seat there on the bumper," June said and pointed to the ambulance bumper. "The sun is bright enough for me to see by." She reached into the back of the vehicle and removed a large case.

Ry tried to sit down but the handcuffs made it difficult.

"Richard, can you remove those cuffs or at least switch them to the front?" June asked. "She's having trouble trying to sit down."

He eyed Ry for a moment.

"Come on, Richard," June said as she winked at Ry. "If she starts to run, you can always shoot her."

He reached for his keys and nodded. "That's true." He glared at Ry. "You're not planning on trying to run, are you?"

Without thinking, Ry glanced at the body in the yard. "I've never been much of a runner."

Richard followed her glance before slowly nodding. "I guess not," he said as he unlocked the cuffs and refastened them with her arms to the front.

June slipped on a pair of dark-rimmed glasses that were hanging on a cord around her neck. "This may sting a little," June said as she started cleaning the wounds on Ry's face.

Ry bit her tongue against the fiery burn that the antiseptic created. It hurt but was bearable. But when June began to remove the splinters, she couldn't stop the tears of pain. Embarrassed by the tears she squeezed her eyes shut trying to stop them.

"Richard," June said. "Do you remember back two or three years ago when I had to extract that double load of buckshot from Miller Jensen's backside?"

"Good Lord, why did you bring that up? I've tried to block that memory," Richard said with a slight chuckle.

June patted Ry's shoulder. "Miller was about, what, seventy-three or seventy-four then?"

"About that, I reckon," Richard agreed.

"Well," June continued, "Miller was dating Ms. Emily Trousdale. She was a spry sixty-eight or so then. According to

Miller, he had gone over to her house on this particular day to pop the question. What Miller didn't know at the time was that Ms. Emily had another suitor, J. Reilly Cones, who was about the same age as Miller.

"It seems that earlier that day when Miller was going to pop the question, J. Reilly had decided to go dove hunting and he just happened to be near Ms. Emily's place. J. Reilly gets tired of hunting and since she's so close by, he decides to drop in on Ms. Emily and surprise her. And to make a long story short, he gets to her house and when she doesn't answer his knock he gets worried about her and breaks in. He gets through the front door just in time to see Miller's bare butt disappear out the back door and there sits Ms. Emily on the couch trying to hide the gifts God gave her with the sofa doilies."

Ry smiled when she heard Richard's deep chuckle.

"Being a gentleman, J. Reilly instantly assumes Miller has taken leave of his senses and accosted Ms. Emily. So, he tears out after Miller. About halfway across the backyard J. Reilly starts to run out of steam so he stops and cuts loose with his old shotgun that was loaded with birdshot."

"It must have taken you an hour to pick all those pellets out of Miller's rear end," Richard said.

"I can honestly say, I know Miller Jensen's butt better than I do my own," June said. "And all the time I was working, Ms. Emily kept crying 'Don't you hurt my Miller,'" June said. "Then when Richard tried to take J. Reilly in for questioning she started yelling at him, 'Don't hurt my J. Reilly.'"

"So, which one did she end up marrying?" Ry asked and laughed.

"Neither. She ran off a few weeks later with Cyrus Vancil. He was only sixty-five and still had his driver's license." June patted Ry's shoulder. "That's the last splinter. None was very deep, but you need to watch for infection. I don't think you'll have any problems, but keep an eye on it anyway. If you see anything unusual, make an appointment with your doctor." She stopped suddenly.

Ry stopped smiling. Tears again burned her eyes when she remembered where she was. She swallowed. "Thanks for taking care of this," she said as she pointed toward her cheek. "And, thanks for making up that story to distract me."

June rolled her eyes. "I wish I had made it up. To this day, I can't look at a roadmap without seeing Miller Jensen's butt."

CHAPTER FOUR

When Ry arrived at the police station she was relieved to discover that Alice Sinclair, the attorney Mr. Elliott had acquired for her, was there waiting. Alice had demanded that she be given time to talk to her client. She informed Ry that Kate was fine and was being represented by a different attorney. Ry tried not to read anything into that fact. She didn't have long to ponder the where or why of the matter before Alice made her go through the entire events of the day. She told Alice everything that had happened, including the cigarette butt and her broken truck window. She was surprised when Alice waved the additional information off with "there's no need to muddy the water." She told Ry to stick to what had happened at the house that morning. Ry was to tell the police why she was there but not to expound on anything that had happened at the shop the previous night. Then she made Ry go through the events again. The second time around Ry did as she had been instructed, even though she didn't much like the thought of doing so. After hearing the second run-through, Alice nodded and told her to stick with the theory that they were simply in the wrong place at the wrong time. Ry reluctantly agreed. She couldn't help but wonder if Alice had heard or read Kate's statement because it certainly sounded like Kate's theory.

Ry had anticipated the police questioning would be difficult, but it proved to be little more than retelling her story repeatedly. She lost track of how many times she told her story. And, of course, there was a long delay between each telling. Ry had finally been released pending further investigation. No charges had been filed against her. Alice had assured her that everything would be fine. It was an obvious case of self-defense. The police were simply going through the necessary motions to ensure they hadn't missed anything. Ry asked about Kate, but again Alice put her off.

It was dark when Ry finally stepped out of the police station. Alice was standing beneath a streetlight waiting for her. "Here are the keys to Kate's car." She handed Ry the keys. "The car is in the lot across the street."

"How did the car get here?" Ry asked as she looked around for Kate.

"I believe Mr. Elliott had it picked up and left here for you."

"Where's Kate?"

Alice glanced away. "It seems she was cleared and released earlier in the day. I believe she left with her parents. They probably drove her home."

Ry tried not to make too much out of the fact that Kate hadn't been waiting for her. She couldn't imagine driving off and leaving Kate here alone. Ry focused her attention on the keys. "You have my address," she said. "You can send the bill there or I…"

Alice cut her off. "Mr. Elliott has taken care of everything."

Ry shook her head. "I'd rather you bill me direct." She had no idea how she would pay her, but she'd find a way.

Alice shrugged. "I can't do anything about that. You'll have to take it up with him." She stuck out her hand. "I'll call as soon as I hear something. Until then don't talk to anyone about the case, especially the press," she warned as she shook Ry's hand.

Ry had no trouble finding the car. She called Kate's cell. When she got no answer, she tried the shop and sighed when the call went directly to voice mail. She tried sending Kate a text, but still nothing.

* * *

The clock on the car dashboard indicated it was after nine when Ry parked Kate's car in the lot behind the shop. The streets of Jackson City were deserted. The only light came from the dim glow of the pseudo-eighteenth century street-lamps.

More tired than she had ever felt in her life, Ry pulled her exhausted body out of the vehicle and staggered. She grabbed the car door to steady herself before she started toward the back door of the shop. She walked past her truck and remembered she still hadn't notified the local police of the vandalism. The mere thought of having to answer more questions was more than she could handle. It didn't really seem worthwhile, since they would probably never know who broke the window.

Kate was almost certainly right. It had probably been a couple of kids with too much time on their hands messing around. Her time and energy would be better spent by installing a better security light back here or putting a lock on the gate.

She glanced toward the upstairs windows. The house was dark. Kate must already be in bed. Her stomach growled loudly to remind her she hadn't eaten all day. She considered grabbing an apple from the kitchen, but she was too tired.

Ry fumbled with the keys on Kate's keychain. She knew one of them belonged to the back door of the shop. It was hard to see in the dim light emitted from the lights of the side street.

When she finally found the right key and tried to insert it, the door swung inward. Her heart nearly stopped. This was the second time today that she had stumbled upon an unlocked door. She froze, terrified of what she would find if she made a move. This couldn't be happening. Maybe she had forgotten to lock the door before they left, or Kate had failed to lock up when she went to bed. Her heart pounded so hard she could barely hear and her hands began to tingle. She reached inside the door and flipped on the overhead light.

Her workroom looked as though a tornado had gone through it. The furniture appeared to have been hacked to pieces with an ax. Books ripped apart lay scattered around the room; their pages carpeted the floor. The artwork she had so carefully framed and hung lay smashed and torn in piles of shattered glass and splintered frames. Her laptop had been snapped at the hinges and the screen shattered. A jumbled mass of plastic that she vaguely recognized as the printer was in the corner.

Ry's throat ached. She hadn't realized she had been screaming Kate's name. Heedless of the dangers of the broken glass and twisted metal scattered about the floor, she raced into the showroom. There she found an even worse mess. She almost fell as the room spun around her. There was no time to give in to the shock. She had to find Kate. Without bothering to stop, she ran to the stairs that led to their living space. Even the stairway hadn't been immune to the devastation. Several of the steps and risers had deep gashes hacked into them and parts of the banister had been completely broken away. The stairwell glittered from the jewel-like shards of glass from the numerous vases and glassware that had been shattered against the stairs. Ry fell twice. Ignoring the pain in her hands and knees, she kept going. Her fear grew to an almost unbearable degree when the brutal damage continued into their living quarters. Her own personal safety never entered her mind as she raced through each of the rooms screaming for Kate. Terrified beyond reason she ran, lost her balance and slammed backward onto the splintered mess that had once been the doorframe to their bedroom.

The room had not been spared. Clothes yanked from the closet and dresser drawers had been ripped to shreds. The bedding slashed and flung into scattered mounds on the floor. A layer of debris from the disemboweled mattress had settled over everything.

Her throat burned as if she had swallowed a hot coal, but she couldn't stop screaming Kate's name. She lost track of the number of times she checked each room before she raced back to the stairwell. The heel of her shoe caught on a gouge in one of the stair steps. She tried to grab the banister to break her fall, but the weakened wood gave way. Time seemed to stop as she tumbled and crashed hard to the bottom. Her left wrist bent at an odd angle sending a white-hot bolt of pain shooting through her arm. When she finally stopped tumbling, it took her a moment to gather herself enough to stand. Her wrist throbbed, but she could still move it so nothing was broken. A thin trickle of blood oozed down her arm.

She slowly assessed the damage around her. Nothing within the room had been spared. Everything from merchandise to display cases had been smashed. She hobbled through the mess and continued to call for Kate, by now her throat emitted little more than a harsh whisper. Finally satisfied that Kate's body was not among the ruins, she dropped to the floor.

As she stared at the mangled wreckage, her empty stomach rebelled. Dry heaves racked her body. She fought them back and forced long breaths of air deep into her lungs. As she struggled to breathe, a dark, murderous rage filled her. Who would do this and why? She had done nothing to cause this sort of anger.

She eased herself to her feet, ignoring the pain in her left wrist. With slow determined steps, she made her way back to Kate's car to retrieve her cell phone. The screen swam before her eyes as she scrolled through the list of numbers. When she finally located the one for Kate's parents, she dialed and waited. She tried to think of words to lessen the devastation she had walked through. When Kate's mother answered, all she could do was ask for Kate.

"Who is this?" Mrs. Elliott asked.

"It's Ry." She realized her voice was little more than a hoarse whisper.

"My gosh, Ry. What's wrong with your voice, honey?"

"Please, is Kate there?"

Mrs. Elliott hesitated before replying. "Well, yes, she is. We thought that given everything that had happened, maybe it would be best if she spent a few days here."

"Can I speak to her, please?" Ry was confused. Why would Kate be staying with her parents?

"Please. Tell her it's important," she added when Mrs. Elliott continued to hesitate.

"Um...well...she's asleep. The doctor gave her a sedative. You know, she was terribly upset over all this."

"I really need to talk to her."

"Why don't you call back in the morning? Or better yet, come on over and spend the..." There was a loudly hissed "*no*" and Mrs. Elliott stopped sharply.

Ry recognized Kate's voice. Kate didn't want her there, and she didn't want to come home.

"Uh...what I meant was maybe you should go over to your parents." Mrs. Elliott cleared her throat nervously. "I'm sure Kate will go home tomorrow."

Exhausted beyond reason Ry didn't bother to hide her anger. Why should she care if Kate didn't want to come home? If she preferred being with her parents, fine. She could stay there. "Tell her to not bother. There's nothing left to come home to." She hung up.

Ry slipped the phone into the pocket of her jeans and started back toward the shop. She still needed to call her own parents. It would only be a matter of time before the news made its way to them and she wanted it to come from her. She glanced at her watch and was shocked to see it was after ten. Everything in her ached, but there was still so much to do. She needed to call Victor to report the vandalism. She stopped. Vandalism seemed too minor a word to describe what she had just seen.

She flinched when her phone rang. When she saw Kate's name on the display she turned the phone off and returned it to her pocket. She looked around the room and thought to hell with it. This could wait a few more hours. She was going home. She started upstairs to pack a bag, until she remembered: there was nothing left to pack.

Ry shivered as a she stepped outside into the cool air. With the truck's side window missing, she was in for a cold ride. She remembered a jacket she had seen in the trunk of Kate's car that morning. When she opened the trunk, the first thing she saw was an *Old West* magazine. It took her a moment to remember that she hadn't taken the cardboard box inside the estate sale house that morning. Kate had. Kate must have mistakenly taken the box from the backseat—the box intended for the nursing home. Ry tugged on the jacket. It was too tight through the shoulders and too short, but it stopped the wind. She grabbed the box from the trunk and placed it inside her truck. Maybe there would be something in the box that could explain why her store had been wrecked.

She tossed Kate's keys beneath the front seat and locked the car doors. There was a spare set of keys in the kitchen somewhere. Kate could dig them out. Without a backward glance, she got into her truck.

CHAPTER FIVE

Ry parked her truck in front of her parents' two-story log and stone house. She had grown up in this house and had nothing but happy memories of her childhood. Her parents had purchased two hundred and sixty-five acres of land the year they were married. Decades of poor farming habits by the previous owners had worn out the land. Nothing grew there except scrub oak, mesquite and cactus. The property's one redeeming value, other than its low price tag, was a large pond that had never been known to go dry. Despite its seemingly poor soil, her parents had had dreams of turning it into something much better. Her father had started building their dream house. It took him six years to complete the work. During that time, her parents lived in a small mobile home on the property. James, her oldest brother, had been born two years into the building. Eighteen months later Lewis came along, followed less than two years later by Daniel. By the time her father finished the house, the mobile home was practically bursting at the seams with the Shelton brood. Ry had been born six months after they moved into the new house. Over the years, the house had become an integral part of all their lives.

She sat staring at the darkened house. It must be around eleven o'clock. Because her parents were such early risers, they were always in bed by ten. She hated to wake them, but she didn't dare take the chance of using her key and being mistaken for a burglar. She had been shot at enough today to last her several lifetimes.

Ry got out of the truck and grabbed the cardboard box. The closer she got to the door the more exhausted she felt. She knew she should have called Victor to report the break-in, but she couldn't deal with it.

The porch light popped on as soon as she stepped onto the porch. Her father's massive frame dressed in a T-shirt and jeans filled the doorway. He pushed opened the screen door and stepped aside as her mom scooted past him. "Rylene, is that you?" No one but her mom called her Rylene. Her mother was fussing with the belt of an old flannel robe that she refused to throw away. She had been given several new robes, but she obviously preferred this one.

"I'm sorry it's so late." Ry stumbled.

Her father caught her and took the box.

"Honey, are you sick?" she asked as she took Ry by the arm. The love and tenderness of her mother's voice was nearly her undoing.

Ry fought the tears. She knew if she started crying she wouldn't stop. "No. I'm just tired."

As soon as they were inside, her mom turned on a lamp while her father placed the box on the floor.

Her mother gasped when she saw Ry's face. She started to say something when she noticed the blood on Ry's shirt. "Dear God, Seth, she's bleeding." Her mother eased her down onto a chair.

"Mom, it's just a scratch." She tried to turn her arm.

"Seth, get the first-aid kit out of the kitchen."

He left without comment.

Ry tried to stand up. "I don't want to get blood on your chair."

Her mom was a tall, and what some would describe as, a raw-boned, woman with an incredibly tender nature. But she could take on the disposition of a grizzly bear if riled. She gently pushed her back down. "It's just a chair, Rylene. Now stop squirming so I can see. You never could sit still."

Her father returned with the first-aid kit. He and Ry waited patiently while her mother worked.

"It's not deep," her mom said. "You don't need stitches, but it could get infected." She washed the wound with something that felt like liquid fire. Ry tried not to squirm, but her mom was making it difficult.

Her mom finally stepped back. "That's all I can do. We'll have to watch and make sure it doesn't get infected. Now I want you to stretch out over here and rest." She helped Ry to the couch.

Ry's father said, "Doreen, maybe you could make us a pot of coffee."

Ry smiled. Her father could face the apocalypse head-on as long as he had a pot of coffee.

"I think you're right." She rushed off to the kitchen with the first-aid kit.

Ry closed her eyes and let her body sink into the couch. Her bones ached and her muscles felt like jelly.

"Here, drink this, but don't tell your mother I gave it to you."

She opened her eyes to find her dad standing beside her with a shot glass of whiskey. She took the glass and downed the contents.

"I've never been able to convince your mom that a shot of good whiskey has medicinal value."

The fiery liquid seared her throat. Her empty stomach lurched when the alcohol hit it. "Dad, can you lock that box up in your safe?" she asked as she pointed toward the cardboard box. She watched his gaze travel over the box's contents.

She sensed his curiosity but no longer had the strength to explain. "It's a long story, and frankly, I'm not sure it's anything more than my imagination."

He picked up the box and empty glass and left the room.

Ry leaned her head back and again closed her eyes. Her wrist was still tender. She rubbed it as she tried to think of how she could even begin to explain everything that had happened in the past twenty-four hours.

"Sit up. Try to eat some of this."

Ry opened her eyes to find a tray in front of her containing a steaming bowl of chicken soup and pot of coffee with three cups. Her father was sitting in the chair across from her.

"Mom, you didn't have to do that."

"I know I didn't have to, but you look half-starved," her mom said. "When was the last time you ate?"

"I don't even remember," Ry admitted. She ate a couple of spoonfuls. "I don't even know where to start."

"You just jump in anywhere and we'll catch up," her father said as he poured coffee into each of the three cups. He handed one to his wife, slid one closer to Ry and took one for himself.

Slowly the events of the past several hours began to pour out of her. Her mom or dad would occasionally stop her and ask for clarification, but mostly they listened. As she spoke, Ry watched the myriad of emotions cross her parents' faces: the clenching of the muscle in her father's jaw, the shock on her mother's face, the slight widening of her father's eyes and heard her mom's gasp of horror when she related how she had shot a man. By the time she finished describing the destruction she found at the shop, they looked as exhausted as she felt. She waited as her parents sat in stunned silence for several seconds.

Her mom finally asked, "Where's Kate?"

"She went home with her parents after she left the police station," Ry said.

Her father gave a slight grunt then he stood and set his cup on the tray. He placed a large hand on Ry's shoulder. "It's late and you're exhausted. You go on up to bed and we'll work this out in the morning." He helped her up and hugged her tightly. "I don't want you to worry about anything. You'll be safe here."

When he stepped back, she dried her eyes. "Thanks, Dad. I'm sorry I had to drop this all on you."

He shook his head. "A load is always easier to carry on two sets of shoulders."

Her mom hugged her. "You should have called us sooner," she scolded, as she stepped back and examined Ry's face. "There's some antibacterial ointment in the hall bathroom if you need it. Your room has fresh sheets." She kissed Ry's forehead. "You let me know if you need anything."

Ry kissed her parents goodnight and went upstairs. She was so tired she didn't even bother to turn the bedding down. She simply kicked off her boots and stretched out across the bed, certain she would be asleep before her head hit the pillow.

Despite her exhaustion, sleep was slow in coming. When she finally did sleep, she dreamed of glass raining from the sky. She tried to escape it and found herself running through a maze screaming Kate's name. In the distance, she heard Kate calling for her. Ry fought the heaviness in her feet and legs. She had to find Kate. Each time Ry reached the location where she thought Kate's voice had been coming from, she encountered a man in a blue shirt.

Something about him scared her. She ran harder to escape him. It was useless. He kept closing her in tighter and tighter until she had nowhere left to run. Terrified, she watched him raise a rifle and point it at her. She tried to run but her feet seemed to be bound to something. Unable to run, she could only watch as his finger closed around the trigger and squeezed. The barrel grew to a monstrous size, allowing her to see the bullet spinning through it. She couldn't take her eyes off the bullet, even as it continued to blaze through the air, directly toward her. It grew so near she could smell its metallic scent. She waited and silently lamented every wasted moment of her life. She regretted never telling her family how much they meant to her. She felt guilty for the financial mess she was leaving behind that her family would have to straighten out. She was ashamed that she had taken another human's life. But most of all, she was sorry for all the times she had put her relationship with Kate second.

As if conjured by the thought, Kate suddenly materialized directly in front of her. Ry smiled and reached out her hand. As she did, she realized the bullet was still moving toward her. Only now, the bullet was going to hit Kate. Ry screamed for

Kate to move, but Kate seemed frozen in place. Ry threw her body forward. She saw the bullet spinning wildly toward her. Just before it smashed into her body, she screamed.

Ry sat upright in bed. Her heart pounded. Her sweat-drenched clothing was making her cold. Someone had placed a blanket over her during the night. Her tossing and thrashing had left it entangled around her feet. She wiggled it free and pulled it beneath her chin. The movement caused her wrist to start hurting again. She gently massaged it.

As the fog of sleep slowly faded, she heard distant voices. Her room was directly above the kitchen. The air-conditioning duct in the floor beside her bed had always allowed her to overhear most conversations held at the kitchen table. She closed her eyes and listened. She had grown up with these sounds, the deeper voices of her father and brother, Daniel, along with the lighter sounds of her mom and Daniel's wife Elise. The voices today were softer and lower in volume. She realized they were trying not to wake her.

All of her brothers lived within ten miles of their childhood home. Each of them had bought land and built their own homes just as their father had.

As she continued to listen to the low comforting sounds, her stomach growled loudly. She knew that despite the fact that her mom had probably put enough food on the table for a small army, her brother could eat through it quickly. If she didn't get down there soon there would be nothing left.

She showered. The hot water felt good on her wrist. Afterward, she dug through her closet in hopes there would be something there she could still wear. All that was left was the formal she had worn to her senior prom, her school jacket and an assortment of old hunting jackets that belonged to her dad. She could imagine her mom trying to get rid of them only to have him hide them up here. She finally managed to find an old sweatshirt and pants tucked away in a dresser drawer. They were old and faded but they still fit reasonably well. More importantly, they were clean and warm.

As she dressed, she glanced around the room. It had been nearly a decade since she had been in here but her shooting trophies still filled the top shelf of the bookcase and the better items of her "treasure finds" from her metal detecting years still sat in the case that her father had helped her build. She winced as she remembered the number of times she smacked her thumb and fingers with the hammer during the process of building the case. That had been when she decided she wanted to work with him during the summer as the boys did.

A large corkboard displayed a wide array of photos. She went over to them. The first photo caused a twinge of sadness. Linda Sue Adams, her first love and the cause of her first broken heart. Linda Sue, Ry, Jana Scott and Lucy Bennington had become best friends in kindergarten. The four of them had been inseparable. Things had been great until sometime during the tenth grade when Ry realized her feelings for Linda Sue weren't the same as her feelings for her other two friends. For six months, Ry struggled to find a way to tell Linda Sue how she felt. She finally gathered her courage and decided to make her intentions known on Christmas Eve. Before Ry found the opportunity to speak to Linda Sue alone, Linda Sue had proudly shown them the ring that Roger Collins had given her. He'd made the ring from a nickel that he had hollowed out in shop class.

The grandfather clock in the entryway struck nine and ended her trip down memory lane. Ry quickly made her bed and headed downstairs.

CHAPTER SIX

Ry stopped at the bottom of the stairs and let the sounds of the house settle over her. The low murmur of voices drifted to her from the kitchen. Even though she was unable to make out what they were saying, simply hearing their voices was comforting. Her brother Daniel's deep voice seemed more serious than normal. He was the family jokester. She would never admit to loving one brother more than the other two, but Daniel held a special place in her heart. Age wise, Ry and her three older brothers weren't far apart. James, the oldest, was only four years and seven months older. Now that they were grown the years separating them seemed miniscule, but it had been different growing up. James and Lewis had always referred to her and Daniel as the babies of the family. She and Daniel had always thought of James and Lewis as being no fun, James in particular. All he did was go to school and follow their father around. Lewis at least had girlfriends that she and Daniel could torment with their practical jokes.

As they grew older, she had left the practical jokes behind. Daniel hadn't. He could still turn the household upside down with some prank or other. She sometimes found it hard to believe he was married with two children.

She crossed the living room and started down the hallway toward the kitchen. She smiled when she saw Daniel and Elise sitting with her parents at the ten-foot-long rough-hewn log table that had once belonged to her dad's grandparents. Worn smooth from several decades of use, it sat before two oversized windows that filled the room with morning sunlight and provided a view of rolling native grasses. Her parents had been working with a state land conservationist during the last few years and the land had made a remarkable comeback. Even the natural underground springs were coming back.

When Ry walked into the kitchen, silence fell. She studied their faces. Would they judge her for what she had done? She needed everyone at this table to remain as they had throughout her lifetime. As she scanned their faces, all she found was love and concern.

Her mom broke the awkward silence. "I was just about ready to go wake you before Daniel ate everything," her mom said. She poured coffee into a cup and placed it at Ry's usual spot at the table.

"Hey, some of us have already put in half a day's work," Daniel chimed in. "We need the extra nourishment." He scooted his chair back and stood. "Glad you're safe, little sister," he whispered as he hugged her.

Ry made her way around the table hugging her family, relieved that at least here nothing had changed. "What are you guys doing here on a Monday morning? Don't you have jobs anymore?" She teased as she caught the biscuit Daniel tossed at her.

"Stop horsing around with the food," her father said as he poured himself more coffee. "You're going to break something."

"Don't worry, Dad. It wasn't one of Elise's biscuits, so we're safe," Daniel teased.

"That's why I let you wear the apron at home," Elise said and smiled at him sweetly. Elise was only five-foot-one, but her sharp wit kept Daniel on his toes.

Ry laughed. It was true that Elise made awful biscuits and overall Daniel probably was the better cook. He certainly would never admit to it, though.

"You're going to wound my manly pride," he said, puffing out his chest.

"Careful or your 'manly pride' is going to pop the buttons right off that shirt," Elise countered.

"She's right, Daniel," Ry said. "A man your age needs to start cutting back on the calories."

"What do you mean my age?" Daniel protested. "I'm still a young and mighty stud."

"Daniel, be careful of boasting," his mother warned. "Even the largest stud can be brought down by a tiny termite."

Ry laughed as Daniel struggled not to roll his eyes at his mother.

"A guy has no chance around here," he said as he patted his slight paunch.

Her father ignored them all. "Ry, I called Victor Orozco last night and told him about the break-in." He sipped his coffee. "He was pretty upset that you hadn't called him, until I explained everything that happened yesterday. He wants you in his office this morning."

Ry nodded. "I'm sorry. I should have called him last night."

"Don't worry about it. You were exhausted," her father said as he stood. "Victor wanted to see your truck also, so Lewis drove it in early this morning."

"My truck?" she asked.

"Yeah. I guess Victor is looking for fingerprints or some other clue as to who broke into it. I doubt he'll find anything now."

Ry sighed. One more thing she had screwed up. "Dad, I'm sorry. I should have called him before I came out. It never occurred to me there might be any evidence on the truck."

"Don't worry. Odds are whoever broke into the truck wore gloves anyway." He set his cup down. "Daniel and I are going over to see if there's anything we can do to secure the building."

"I'll go with you. Give me time to grab my jacket." Ry started to stand.

Her Dad put out a hand. "Eat your breakfast," he said. "You have plenty of time. Your mom is driving in later." He turned to Daniel. "Ready?" He left without waiting for an answer.

Daniel slid his chair back and turned to his wife. "Are you riding with Mom?"

Elise nodded as he gave her a quick kiss and rushed after his father.

Ry followed their voices through the living room. Just as they reached the entrance door, they were delayed by the arrival of her other two sisters-in-law, Michelle and Annie.

As she listened to their voices, Ry ate as her mom and Elise loaded the breakfast dishes into the dishwasher. Ry liked her sisters-in-law. They were all funny, intelligent women. Of the four siblings, only Ry's spouse had failed to blend into this loud and fun-loving family.

Each year, the entire Shelton clan spent the first week in April camping along the Guadalupe River on property owned by Ry's paternal grandfather. Over the decades, the family had built a multitude of cabins, a boat dock, a fishing pier, even a shooting range. There was a central location where all the meals were cooked and the family ate together under an arbor constructed from an enormous cypress tree that had run aground on the riverbank during a flood.

The cabins contained fireplaces to ward off the occasional cool morning. Even during the summer, they never seemed to be too hot due to the large oak and cypress trees that shaded the area and the ever-present cool breeze from the water. There was electricity, but her grandfather insisted there could be no televisions, video games or electronic devices that distracted anyone's attention from nature. He wanted his offspring to have a taste of what he referred to as "the good life." This was meant to be one week out of each year when everyone's troubles were temporarily set aside and all thoughts focused on being with family, fishing, swimming, boating and enjoying the beauty of the natural world. Well, that was her grandfather's dream, at least. What it had turned into was a weeklong competition of who caught the biggest fish, swam the farthest and fastest or outshot the others at the range. The competition never stopped.

Kate had agreed to go on the camping trip the first year they were together. It had gone badly from the beginning. She didn't like the constant competition and left midweek. Afterward, she always found some excuse never to return.

Michelle and Annie burst into the kitchen carrying several shopping bags. They dropped the bags and hugged her tightly. The two women couldn't be more physically different. Michelle was tall, thin and leggy. Annie was short and constantly struggling to control her weight. The battle was even tougher now that she was five months pregnant with her fourth child. She and Lewis already had three girls, and had chosen to wait until this baby was born to discover its gender. They both said it didn't matter as long as the child was healthy. But, Ry suspected they would both be ecstatic should it be a boy.

"What is all this?" Ry asked and pointed to the bags. Her mom and Elise joined them at the table.

Annie grabbed a bag and handed it to her. "We thought you might need these."

Ry looked inside the bag and tears sprang to her eyes. The bag contained clothes and shoes.

"I hope the sneakers fit," Annie said. "We weren't sure what size you wore."

Touched by their kindness, Ry removed the shirts from the bag and kept her head down to hide the tears.

"Now, don't do that," Michelle said and patted her knee. "If you get Annie started crying it'll be an hour before we can get her to stop."

"Don't pick on my raging hormones," Annie said as she sniffled. "Besides, I'll bet her eyes are watering from that god-awful green shirt you picked out," Annie teased.

"Hey, earth tones are in now," Michelle defended, as she flipped her long, blond hair over her shoulder. "Ry, look at that shirt. Don't you love it?"

Ry located the rather dull green shirt in question and held it up. She doubted she would have ever chosen the shirt for herself, but it was far better than the stretched-out sweats she was wearing. "I love it." She smiled.

"There! I told you," Michelle shouted with glee.

Annie waved her off. "What does she know? She still wears that bright orange knitted hat and scarf."

"Wait a minute," Ry protested. "Granny Shelton gave those to me." A mental image of the tangled remains of the scarf lying in the wreckage of the bedroom floor hit her. For a moment, she lost her breath.

"Oh, God, Ry, I'm sorry." Annie ran and put an arm around Ry's shoulder. "I'm such a dunce."

Ry shook her head as she struggled to regain her composure. "It's fine." She waved toward the bags. "I can't thank you two enough. How much do I owe you? I can stop by the ATM."

Michelle gave a dismissing wave. "Your dad gave us his credit card."

Ry looked at the mound of bags. "Now I know why Elise wasn't with you two." They all laughed. Elise was a shopaholic.

"I can't help it if I excel at shopping," Elise said defensively. "It's my one true talent."

"We knew you wouldn't have time to go shopping," Annie said. "Hopefully, these things can tide you over at least until the insurance company settles with you."

"Rylene, go get dressed," her mom said. "I'm sorry we don't have time to wash the new clothes, but I promised your dad I'd get you to town before eleven."

Ry gathered the bags and hurried upstairs. As she unpacked what was practically an entire new wardrobe, her eyes blurred with tears several times. Michelle and Annie had thought of everything right down to a toothbrush.

* * *

As soon as they were on the highway, the women began to discuss Annie's pregnancy. They laughed and joked about her late night cravings. Then they spent several minutes discussing what would be the best gender-neutral paint colors for the nursery.

Ry tried to join their banter and get into the swing of the moment, but nothing felt right. Kate wasn't here. She hadn't tried to call again after Ry had ignored her call the previous night.

Everything felt off-kilter. Even the clothes she wore, except for her boots, were foreign to her. Someone else had chosen them. She started to tremble when she realized practically everything she had was gone.

"Are you okay?"

She turned to find her mom watching her. Ry shook her head. "What am I going to do?" She rubbed her face, ignoring the pain that flared in her cheek.

Her mom took her hand. "It's going to be fine. I'm sure Seth already has a plan."

"Mom, I can't keep depending on you and Dad to bail me out of every jam I get into." She turned to look out the window. "Why do I keep screwing up?"

Her mom made a hissing dismissal sound. "How have you screwed up? This wasn't your fault."

"Mom, I've always been a screwup. I changed my major three times before I settled on design. It took me almost a year to finally get a job, and they fired me after six months."

"After you lost that job in Dallas, you eventually got a much better design job that brought you back to San Antonio," her mom reminded her.

The sisters-in-law had gone silent.

"A job I couldn't keep."

Her mom's voice suddenly changed and grew sterner. "Rylene Shelton, I won't have you sitting here feeling sorry for yourself. Yes, what happened is horrible. I can't begin to imagine what you went through yesterday. I know how much you value life of any kind." She took Ry's hand and her voice grew gentler, "Honey, you and Kate are safe. That's all that matters. I'm sorry about your store, but it's only wood and glass. It can be fixed." Her voice broke slightly. "When I think of what could have happened to you and Kate…"

"Mom, Kate's mad at me." She wondered how to explain. It seemed silly when she thought about it. "I got my feelings hurt when she went home to her parents. Then she wouldn't talk to me and I told her not to bother coming home." She saw Michelle and Annie exchange glances. Elise had suddenly become engrossed in the passing landscape.

Ry knew they were listening. They were probably thinking here we go again with Ry and her rocky relationships. Her fourth in thirteen years.

"So call her and apologize," her mother said. "You two should sit down and talk. Almost anything is possible with a little give and take." She didn't allow Ry time to deny the possibility. "Your father and brothers are at your store right now. They're already looking the damage over to see what needs to be done to get the shop open and running again."

Ry cut in, her voice sharper than she intended. "Mom, you don't understand. There's nothing left. Someone took an ax and destroyed everything."

Doreen Jeter Shelton seldom ever lost her temper. When she did, everyone scattered for safety. Now, a small spark of that temper flared. "No, Rylene, he did not destroy everything. Whoever this horrid person is only destroyed material items." She grabbed Ry's hands. "You still have everything that truly matters." She looked Ry in the eyes. "You still have your health and your family. Nothing else matters in the end and don't you ever forget that."

The conversation ended abruptly when Michelle parked in front of The Antique Nook. The women sat staring at the yellow crime scene tape stretched across the door for a long moment before Doreen took charge.

"Let's go see what can be done," she said. She gave Ry's knee a quick, affectionate slap.

"Don't they have to process the crime scene?" Annie asked, as they climbed out of the vehicle. "They won't let us go in, will they? I mean, don't they keep the crime scene tape up for days or weeks?" Annie's habit of stringing questions together had been annoying when she and Lewis were first married, but over the years, it had become endearing.

Ry stared through the front display window. The interior damage was clearly visible even from the curb. "I guess the investigation will be handled by the city. If so, I doubt their budget will allow for little more than a cursory once-over." Ry knew her family was there for moral support and she was grateful she wouldn't have to face the ordeal alone.

"Ry."

She turned to find Ben Harrington, the owner of the bakery from across the street. She wasn't surprised he would be the first to appear. The man never missed anything. She couldn't help thinking it was too bad Ben didn't live above the bakery, because nothing got past him. He would have seen whoever had broken in and called Victor.

"I'm so sorry about what happened to your shop. Nancy and I were so relieved to hear neither you nor Kate was home when this happened." He glanced at the women with her. "Where's Kate? Is she okay?"

Doreen quickly intervened. "Kate had to attend to some other things."

"I can't believe this sort of thing happened in Jackson City," Ben said. "We moved here from the city because we thought it would be better for our kids." He continued shaking his head. "I just can't believe it."

Carlos and Lupe Sanchez joined them. They owned the hardware store a few doors down. Shortly afterward, Lacy Wayne, the owner of the small gift and stationery store across the street, came over. The crowd steadily grew as various business owners and townspeople stopped by to offer their help whenever she was ready to reopen.

Ry lost count of the number of times she fielded inquiries about Kate.

When the crowd's focus changed from reassuring themselves that Kate and Ry were safe, to speculation on why and how something like this had happened, Doreen took charge and gently urged the women toward the side entrance and away from the mass of well-wishers. After they were free of the crowd, Michelle turned to Ry. "I'm sorry. I should have parked around back."

"No, it's good they were able to see that's Rylene is safe," Doreen said. "This is a small town and in some ways this horrible thing happened to everyone here. They needed to talk about what happened." She squeezed Ry's hand. "You're not in this alone."

When they reached the corner, the sound of saws and other power tools met them. "What are they doing?" Ry asked. She looked to her mom for an answer.

"I don't know. Seth just said he and the boys were coming over to see what could be done."

As they drew closer, Ry's step faltered when she remembered the scene that had unfolded before her last night. Who could have done this? Trying to imagine the degree of anger needed to inflict such destruction made her stomach cramp. The first thing she noticed was that the old weatherworn wood fence was gone. James and her father were off to one side where they had established a work area by tossing an old door over a set of sawhorses. Daniel and Lewis were manually digging postholes.

Daniel spied them first. "Hey, reinforcements," he called. "Who wants to take over here?" He held up the posthole digger and grinned. "This is so much fun. You guys will love it."

"You've got to do a lot better than that, Tom Sawyer," Elise said and waved him off.

Seth met the group of women. "Have you seen Victor yet?" he asked Ry.

"No. We just got here," she replied. "What are you guys doing?"

"We can't touch anything inside until the insurance company gets over here and does whatever it is they do," Seth said. "Victor told us the fence back here wasn't involved so we could start by replacing it. We'll set it with metal posts in concrete this time and use better lumber."

"Dad, I don't know when I'll be able to pay. At this point, I'm not even sure I'm going to reopen the store." Ry was as surprised by her statement as her mom seemed to be.

"Nonsense," Doreen insisted. "You love the store. You can't let some vandal scare you off."

Her dad stunned them both by adding, "Maybe she's right, Doreen." He looked at Ry. "If you don't want to reopen, don't. What we're doing now won't amount to much, but it might help you get a better price for the place." He put an arm around Doreen. "Ry, you go on over to the sheriff's office and talk to

Victor and then call your insurance company. We'll be here when you're done."

As he started to turn away he lowered his voice slightly. "By the way, Kate came by a few minutes ago."

Ry stopped sharply. "She's here?"

"No," he said. "After seeing the shop she was understandably upset." His eyebrows rose slightly when he added, "She wasn't too happy when she discovered you'd locked her keys inside the car."

Ry cringed. "I shouldn't have done that. I guess I was a little pissed off at her. Plus, I didn't know what else to do with them. Did you get the door open for her?"

He rubbed his hand across his chin. "No. She opened it herself."

"So she found the spare keys," Ry said, relieved.

"Nope, she was so mad she knocked out the side window with a rock." He shook his head. "I think it's safe to assume you two are about to see a big jump in your insurance premiums."

They stood silently for a moment before Ry spoke. "I'll see you guys after I talk to Victor." She hesitated. "Dad, did you tell Victor about the box I gave you?"

"No." He was watching her closely "I didn't think it was my place to do so."

She nodded and left.

On the way to the police station several other shop owners, customers and townspeople stopped Ry. Their words of comfort and confusion over how something like this could have happened made Ry realize her mother was right. This catastrophe affected the entire town. When she finally had a free moment, she called her insurance agent, Wilma Brown, who was located just across town.

"I heard about what happened," Wilma said as soon as she heard Ry's voice. "Are you and Kate all right?"

"We're fine. We were gone when it happened." She didn't want to get too deeply into talking about Kate. "What do I need to do to get things started on your end?" she asked to divert any more questions.

"How bad is the damage?"

Ry swallowed. "The contents, both personal and business, are completely destroyed." She heard the gasp through the phone but continued, "There's also a lot of damage to the building, doors, stairs and window frames." She stopped and took a deep breath. "It's a mess, Wilma."

"Ry, don't you worry. I'm going to do everything I can for you. Is the building currently habitable?"

"No. I'm staying at my parents."

"So you and Kate are staying at your parents. I've looked over your policy. Do you want to stay on there? If not, *Loss of Use* is included in your policy."

"I think we're fine for now. Can I let you know in a couple of days?"

"Of course you can. Now, let's get the ball rolling. I'll need a copy of the police report, of course. I also need a copy of your current inventory." She stopped and cleared her throat. "By that I mean what it would have been as of yesterday. Do you have that?"

"Yes, I keep it stored on an off-site computer data storage service. I can email a copy to you."

"That would be great."

"I'm on my way to see Sheriff Orozco now."

"Good, he can fax a copy of the police report to me and I'll get a claims adjuster over there. If you and Kate change your minds and decide you don't want to stay with your parents let me know and I'll make the necessary arrangements."

Ry used her iPhone to retrieve the inventory report from the off-site storage location and email it to Wilma. She checked her messages again. There was still only the one call from Kate from the previous night. Kate had left a voice mail, but Ry wasn't ready to listen to it. She knew how mad Kate would have been at being ignored.

When Ry finally made her way into the police station, she could tell that Victor wasn't happy with her either.

"I'm glad you could finally make it in," he said as he waved her into his office.

"I'm sorry. I just couldn't handle any more."

He got up, poured two cups of coffee from a pot behind his desk and put one in front of her. "I heard you had a rather busy day." His dark eyes probed hers as he waited for her to respond.

"I guess you heard what happened in Bexar County?" she said as she picked up the cup.

"Deputy Sheriff Ward called me asking about you."

"What did you tell him?"

"The truth." Victor sipped his coffee.

Ry sat patiently and waited as he dabbed a napkin to his immense handlebar mustache. On most men she would have thought the mustache silly, but somehow it fit him.

When Victor had finished grooming his mustache, he continued. "I told him you were quiet, that I'd never had a complaint from any of your customers or the locals and that Jackson City was fortunate to have you and Kate as citizens." He sat down suddenly and picked up a pen. "So, tell me what happened. The longer we wait around, the less chance we'll have of catching whoever did this."

Ry stared into her coffee. She didn't know where to start.

Victor seemed to sense her dilemma. "When do you think this started?"

"I could be wrong," she said, lifting her gaze from the coffee cup.

He grinned slightly. "Hey, we all have to be wrong occasionally."

Some of the tension eased from Ry's shoulders. "I think it started when I stopped by the estate sale." Slowly she filled him in on every detail of what had transpired from the time she stopped at the estate sale until she had found the shop destroyed. The only thing she omitted was the fact that the wrong cardboard box had been damaged during the shooting.

Afterward, he sat staring at her for a long moment before he began asking her random questions about individual events. He questioned her at length about the items she had purchased from the sale and then switched abruptly to questions about the cigarette butt she had found beneath the window and her broken truck window. He asked about the man at the estate sale.

Had she ever seen him around? Did he tell her anything about himself? On and on he went. Then he asked about the man she shot. Without warning, he surprised her with, "What exactly was in the box that you picked up by mistake?"

She blinked. "Um, I didn't look in it too closely, but I remember some *Old West* magazines, a few books and the metal file box that held the gun." As she told him, she realized that she hadn't really looked in the box. Kate had been the one who poked around in it. "Kate may remember something else. She looked in it closer than I did."

"Let's go back to the guy you shot," he said without pausing. "You said you'd never seen him before."

"That's right."

"And you're sure there was only one shooter? He was by himself."

She started to answer but hesitated when in her mind's eye she again saw the flash of blue. "I'm not absolutely sure. After the first couple of shots were fired, I looked out. I thought I saw a blue shirt." She shook her head. "I'm probably mistaken. The guy I..." she swallowed. "...shot was wearing a white shirt."

"Could you identify the guy if you saw him again?"

"No. Honestly, I'm not even sure it was a man. All I really saw was a blue blur."

He nodded. "Do you remember anything else?"

She closed her eyes and tried to concentrate. She could see the two weapons clearly, but something wasn't right. She struggled to figure it out, but whatever it was stayed just out of her reach. Finally, she gave up and told him what she did remember. "The first couple of shots sounded different. They didn't have that same loud..." she searched for the word she needed to describe the sound.

He waited quietly.

"Punch," she said at last. "The first shots seemed to make less of an impact than the bullets from the bolt-action rifle and it certainly wasn't the assault weapon he used." She tried to remember every detail. "I guess he could have been using different size loads in the rifle."

He leaned back in his chair. "I followed up with Ward this morning and they found shell casings from a thirty-thirty Winchester."

She shook her head. "No. He was firing a bolt-action rifle." She had a clear image of him working the bolt as he was turning toward her. "My brother James has a similar rifle. I think it's a Remington."

He nodded approvingly. "They found a Remington Model 798 and an AR-15 assault rifle near the body of the man you shot." He looked down at the papers in front of him. "The guy in the house was shot with a thirty-eight."

She leaned forward. "So that clears me. The pistol from the file box was a forty-five."

He made a dismissive gesture with his hand. "It just means there are some missing weapons. They didn't find the thirty-eight or the Winchester." He eyed her again. "It seems the first officer on the scene was a rookie. He failed to check your car." Victor hesitated slightly. "You didn't remove anything from the car between then and this morning did you?"

Ry felt her blood pressure spike. "I did," she admitted. "I took a jacket out of the trunk last night."

"Nothing else was removed?" he persisted.

"After I took the jacket out, I locked the keys in the car and left." She flattened the tail of her shirt against her thigh. She could feel his eyes boring into her. "So you think there was someone else involved." As she said the words, a chill crept down her spine.

"It seems like there might have been. I recommend you and Kate stay extra vigilant until we can find out more about what's going on." He laid the pencil down. "Are you going to be staying with your parents until your place is repaired?"

She sighed. She hadn't given it much thought. "I don't know. I mean I guess so. I can't live at the shop." She leaned back in the chair. "When can I start cleaning up?"

He sipped his coffee before answering. "First, let me tell you that we didn't find much in the way of evidence. As you can imagine, trying to fingerprint the store was a nightmare. So many people have gone in and out of there that trying to get

DNA evidence would have been useless. Even if the perpetrator had left prints behind and we finally caught him, he could simply say he had been there shopping at some point." He scanned the papers in front of him.

"We did find an ax in the rubble. We discovered it belonged to the furniture shop behind you. They'd been using it to bust up packing crates and left it out by accident." Again, he sipped his coffee before continuing. "I'm sure it was the ax used to wreck your place. There were several fresh nicks in the blade and a couple of smudged prints on the handle, but nothing useful. We encountered the same problem with the back door knob. I'm guessing whoever did it was wearing gloves. We found the cigarette butt." He stopped and frowned. "By the way, did you cut yourself while you were in the shop?"

"Yes." Her shirtsleeve hid the bandage. "I cut the back of my arm when I fell against the bedroom doorframe."

He sighed. "That's too bad. I thought we might have gotten lucky with the blood and had some DNA we could use if we ever catch this guy."

"What about the cigarette butt? Can't you get DNA from it?"

"It wouldn't do any good. It was found outside the building. I was hoping for something that would put him inside." He stood suddenly. "Come on. I'll take you back out front. Deputy Ross will help you fill out all the forms." He walked out of his office with her. "You can remove the crime scene tape, but I'd recommend you don't remove anything or clean up any until after the claims adjuster comes."

She gave him Wilma Brown's information and asked him to fax over a copy of the police report.

He walked her to a small room that contained a table and two chairs. "Ross will be over in a minute." He shook her hand. "If you think of anything else, let me know. If we come up with something, I'll call you."

It was almost two hours later when Ry finally left the police station.

CHAPTER SEVEN

By the time Ry returned to the shop, Daniel and Lewis had finished installing the posts and were busy building the six-foot-wide fence panels that would eventually be erected between the posts. James and her father were building a gate. The women were nowhere to be seen.

Ry stopped to talk to Daniel and Lewis. "Where's Mom?" she asked.

Lewis set the drill he had been using down and arched his back. At six-foot-four, he was the tallest of her brothers. His lanky frame made him look even taller. "They went home."

"Yeah," Daniel said. "I think the mess in there really freaked Mom out."

"Dang, Daniel, it freaked us all out," Lewis said. He turned to Ry. "I don't know how you kept it together. Man, if I came home to find something like that…" He let the sentence trail off and shook his head. "I don't know if you're just crazy brave or plain crazy. I can't believe you actually went inside."

"I thought Kate was home," Ry admitted. "Otherwise, I'm not sure I could have gone in."

"Oh." Lewis nodded.

"Are you going to try to reopen?" Daniel asked.

"I don't know." She looked around to make sure her father wasn't within earshot. "To be honest, I'm not sure how much longer I could have kept the store open. Business has been so bad recently."

"That seems to be a problem everywhere," Lewis said. "Our job ratio is down twenty-seven percent from where it was this time last year. Thankfully, that big job earlier this year for Henderson International has helped keep our earnings up."

Daniel looked at Ry and smiled. Not only was Lewis the tallest of her brothers he was also the smartest when it came to crunching numbers. When he was younger, they had teased him to no end about being an egghead. Now they begged him to prepare their income tax returns.

If he saw their exchange, Lewis ignored it and continued. "If you like, I might be able to help you reevaluate your business plan. I couldn't help but notice whenever Annie and I came over that the antique stores here all carry very similar stock. Maybe together we could come up with an idea that's a little different for you, something that would give you an edge over the other shops."

"Thanks, Lewis. I appreciate that. I'll certainly keep it in mind." She stepped back. "I guess I'd better go tell Dad what Victor said. Are you guys going to be at Mom and Dad's for dinner tonight?"

They both nodded.

Ry went over to where her dad and James were working on the gate. "That thing looks massive. Will I be able to swing it open?" she teased.

James grinned at her. "When did you become such a ninety-seven pound weakling?" He was her oldest brother and the most methodical. When he wasn't working at the construction company, he designed and built beautiful chairs.

"When we're finished you'll be able to open the gate remotely," her father explained. "That's more secure than a padlock."

Ry suspected her father was going to go overboard on the security measures. She started to say so but stopped and tried to put herself in his shoes. It couldn't be easy for anyone who cared about her to look at the destruction inside and not be worried. In truth, part of the reason she was not sure if she was going to reopen the store was because she didn't know if she'd ever feel safe in the building again. Rather than tease or scoff, she simply thanked him. "Victor said I can start cleaning up as soon as the claims adjuster comes out."

"It'll probably take them a couple of days to get someone out here," James said.

"Your mother and the girls went back out to the house. She said for you to come on home whenever you're finished." Her dad nodded toward her truck. "Victor's deputy came over earlier and checked the truck. He even checked the interior, but didn't find anything that was helpful."

"How much longer are you all going to work?" she asked.

Her dad pointed to the gate. "I want to get this finished and maybe a couple of more fence panels. We won't hang anything until tomorrow to give the posts plenty of time to set." He patted her shoulder. "You go on home and tell your mom we won't be long."

Ry went to her truck. As she started driving out of town, she saw the hospital and considered calling Kate. She knew it was nothing more than sheer stubborn pride that was keeping her from dialing the number. But Kate had left her at the police station yesterday. Then she'd told her mom to lie about her being there. Ry had lashed out and told her not to come home because she was hurt by Kate's action. A chill ran down her spine. Kate had only tried to call her once. It wasn't like her to give in so easily. This is just a spat, she told herself. It certainly wasn't something worth breaking up over. Surely Kate didn't think Ry meant that she should never come home. She grabbed her cell phone and dialed Kate's number. All of her worries subsided when Kate answered on the second ring.

"I'm sorry," Ry said. "I was an ass. Forgive me?"

Kate hesitated a moment. "It was my fault. I should have talked to you last night." She paused. "Listen, we need to talk. Can you meet me somewhere?"

There was something different in Kate's tone. A sick feeling began to build in Ry's stomach. "This is beginning to sound a little ominous," she said and gave a weak laugh.

"I'd rather not discuss it on the phone."

"Okay, but at least give me a hint as to what we have to talk about." Ry rolled her eyes at the stupidity of the statement. Of course, they had things to talk about. Who wouldn't after what they had gone through over the last twenty-four hours?

"Things have changed," Kate's voice broke. "I think it's best if we—"

Ry cut her off. "Kate, are you breaking up with me?"

"God, Ry, don't act so surprised," Kate snapped.

Ry's heart felt as if it were trying to push itself out of her throat. "I don't understand what you're saying."

"I told you I don't want to do this on the phone."

"Why? Do you think it's going to hurt less if you're staring me in the face?" Barely able to breathe, much less drive, Ry pulled her truck into a convenience store parking area and stopped.

"Of course it has to be your way," Kate spat. "Fine, have it your way. Yes, I'm breaking up with you."

"Why?"

Kate gave a bitter laugh. "How can someone as smart as you are be so dense? The very fact that you're so surprised by this should tell you something. Ry, you have not noticed anything since you opened that store."

"I thought you wanted the store as much as I did."

"Maybe I did at first, but then it started to consume our lives. I got tired of sitting at home alone. Damn it, Ry. Anybody would have gotten tired of being alone. You can't blame me for what happened."

Ry held her breath. Surely Kate didn't mean what it sounded like she was saying. She tried to tell herself that Kate was blaming her for yesterday, but something told her it was much worse. She replayed the conversation in her head, hoping it would come out differently.

"Say something!" Kate hissed.

Ry tried to form a word—any word, but nothing came.

Kate's voice filled the silence. "You practically shoved me into her arms. We didn't mean for it to happen. You can't blame either of us."

Ry squeezed the steering wheel with her free hand. Kate couldn't have made it any plainer than that. It was over. There was nothing left except to try to walk away with her dignity. She took a deep breath and slowly exhaled. "Fine," she replied in a voice so eerily calm it frightened her. "I don't blame *either* of you. Have a good life, Kate. I'm sorry I made the past six years so hard for you." She hung up before she started screaming for the name of the low-down dirty, lower than worm shit, piece of crap that Kate had left her for.

Ry mentally replayed the conversation. How had things gone so badly so quickly? As she thought back to their lives over the past few months, she realized she had been dense. She should have noticed that Kate was coming home later and later. When had she had stopped asking why? She tried to think who it could be. There had been an emergency room nurse Kate talked about a lot. Ry tried to recall her name. It was something cutesy like Bambi. "Hell, no more than I listened, it could have been Lotus Blossom." Why hadn't she paid more attention? She slapped the steering wheel in frustration and cried out in pain as her already injured wrist struck the hard surface.

The cool breeze of earlier was turning cold. Even the weather was messed up. It shouldn't be this cool yet. She shivered as a gust of wind came through the gaping hole where the side window should have been. She continued to sit, even after the cold wind had seeped all the way to her bones. Her body trembled, but she refused to move. She intended to stay until the cold froze the pain coursing through her body and made her numb. She visualized her body turning into a solid block of ice. She waited. Surely the ice block would fracture under the force of her pain and burst into a million pieces. She waited.

"Hey, Ry. What're you doing?"

Startled, Ry jumped away from the window, her knee striking the steering column. "Blast you, Daniel Shelton. Why did you sneak up on me like that?"

His eyebrows climbed halfway up his forehead. "I didn't sneak up. Heck, I called out to you twice." He leaned closer. "Are you all right?"

She rubbed her knee. "No. I'm not. You made me practically dislocate my kneecap."

"You are such a drama queen."

"Leave me alone before I get out and kick your butt."

"You couldn't whip me even if I were on my death bed with both my arms tied behind me," he teased with an old childhood taunt.

Ry couldn't help but chuckle. "You're crazy."

"Hey, I'm not the one sitting in the cold, staring into space," he reminded her.

"I wasn't staring into space," she said. "I was trying to decide where I was going to take the truck to get the window fixed." Lying to him produced a twinge of guilt. It was better than telling him the truth and having to see the pity in his eyes that was sure to appear.

"I have an appointment in San Antonio tomorrow. How's about I swing by Pick-n-Pull and see if I can find you a window glass there. You and I can install it. If we do the work ourselves, it'll be a lot cheaper than taking it to a body shop."

Tears burned the back of her eyes at his kindness. She started digging into her pocket for cash.

"No, don't give me any money now. I don't know how much it will cost. We can settle up after I get it." He removed his jacket and handed it to her. "Here. Put this on before you catch a cold. You're such a weenie when you get sick."

She took the jacket and gratefully wiggled into it. "I love you," she said, surprising them both.

"I love you too, sis." He gave her arm a swift swat before turning away. "I'll see you back at the house. Dad's going to have a conniption if I don't hurry back with his coffee." He tucked his hands into his pockets and ran off.

CHAPTER EIGHT

The grandfather clock in the entryway struck midnight. Ry sat on her old desk chair and stared at the cluttered mess on her bed. After her parents turned in for the night, she had retrieved the box from her father's safe. He hadn't changed the combination in the twenty-odd years he had owned the safe. She'd spent the last three hours going through each magazine and book and had found absolutely nothing. Not even an old shopping list.

"One more thing you were wrong about," she muttered as she stacked the items back into the cardboard box. She had been so sure that something from the estate sale had led to the events of the last couple of days. Maybe he had found the item he was after in the shop and the damage was intended to hide whatever was missing. She shook her head. That didn't make sense. If he simply wanted to prevent anyone from knowing what he'd taken, he could have torched the building. That would have made more sense. How long had his rampage taken? He must have made a colossal amount of noise. Granted, the shops around her closed at six on Sundays, but he had still taken a big chance. The occasional car drove through town after hours, and the city police did random patrols through the business area until midnight.

She absently tapped her fingers against her knee. She was missing something. The utter devastation seemed more personal. A chill ran down her back at her next thought. He hadn't found what he was looking for. There had been nothing unusual in or about the furniture, no secret papers or lost treasure maps. She or Kate would have found whatever it was when they cleaned and polished the items.

Kate.

She tried to set aside any thoughts of Kate. Why should she cry and grieve over someone who was no longer interested in her? Kate had made her decision. One small, rough patch and she threw away a six-year relationship. "I don't need the grief."

She went to shower. Afterward, she crawled into bed with a pad and pencil. Over the next two hours, she made two lists. The first list indicated everything she needed to have taken care of in order to reopen the shop. The second one listed what she would need to do in order to sell the shop. She tossed the pad on the side table. She wouldn't be able to make any plans until she received the claims adjuster's report and settled with Kate. They owned the building together. If Kate didn't want to keep the building, Ry knew she couldn't afford to buy Kate's share.

Tired but too wired to sleep, Ry turned off the light and stretched out in the bed. The whirlwind of thoughts kept swirling about. Selling the building made the most sense. She wondered if she could ever feel safe living there again. The size of the building was both a blessing and a curse. A smaller place would have less overhead and maintenance, but it would also limit the size of her showroom.

She sighed and turned over. Beneath all the agonizing about the store, she couldn't stop thinking about Kate. Would Kate ever want to live there again? Was this new relationship serious or a ploy to get her attention? She shook her head. Kate didn't play games.

The more practical side of Ry told her they should sell the building. Then she could find a nine-to-five job, one that provided a steady income. The high probability of running into Kate everywhere she went made living in Jackson City less than desirable, but she certainly wasn't eager to move back to San Antonio. The crowds no longer appealed to her.

At some point, she finally drifted off to sleep, but there was to be no rest for her. She spent a restless night trying to find her way out of a maze of tunnels. No matter which one she took it brought her back around to where she had started. She woke several times only to resume the same dream as soon as she dozed.

The clock beside her bed read 3:22 when she finally surrendered and got up.

When she reached the kitchen, she was surprised to find her mom sitting at the table with a cup of coffee.

"Mom, what are you doing up?"

"I couldn't sleep." Her mom pointed to the counter. "There's coffee if you want some."

Ry poured herself a cup and joined her at the table.

"What brought you down so early?" her mom asked. "You're dressed already. Are you going somewhere?"

Ry sipped her coffee as she tried to organize her thoughts. When she finally set her cup down, she said, "Kate's met someone else."

A look of incredible sadness crossed her mom's face. "Sweetie, I'm sorry." She took Ry's hand and hesitated a moment before asking, "Is it just a fling or something more serious?"

"I don't know." She kept her eyes on her coffee. She didn't want to see the pity in her mom's eyes.

"So, you don't think you two can work through this?"

Ry responded without thought. "I'm not sure I want to." Surprised by the statement, she looked up and said, "On some level I love Kate, but things haven't been right with us for a long time. The shop took too much of my time. I think she came to regret moving here." She cleared her throat. "I think I used the shop as an excuse to get closer to home. I hated living in the city."

As Ry spoke, events began to make more sense. It hadn't been hard for her to consume herself with work and ignore Kate, because some part of her had already started withdrawing. Early in their relationship, she had suspected that their real attraction to each other was the sex. Once that declined, there was nothing else left for them to build on.

Her mom squeezed her arm. "Be kind to each other and you'll find your way."

Ry nodded. "So why are you up so early?'

Her mom smiled sadly before replying. "I suppose I'm a little depressed. Today would have been your Granny Jeter's birthday."

"That's right. With everything that's been going on, I'd completely forgotten." Ry thought about her high-spirited great-grandmother Granny Jeter. "She was something else."

"I don't know what my little brothers and I would have done if she hadn't taken us in when Mama and Daddy were killed in that car accident." She shook her head in wonder. "Do you realize that she was fifty-seven when she took us in?"

"Your Grandfather Jeter was already dead when your parents were killed, wasn't he?" Ry asked.

"Oh, yes. Grandpa died in an accident in 1937. Daddy was only ten then and my Aunt Jasmine was seven. Granny raised them alone and then twenty-seven years later she had three more little ones on her doorstep. I was ten, Donny was eight and Hank was five." She put her hand to her face. "She was only a couple of years younger than I am now." She looked at Ry with awe in her eyes. "I can't imagine trying to raise three little ones at this stage of my life."

Ry shook her head. She wouldn't want to try it even at her age. "Mom, that would be like you taking James and Michelle's kids. They are almost identical in age as you and your brothers were."

"God forbid." She covered her mouth quickly. "I didn't mean that in a bad way. You know I love all of my grandkids."

"Did you know that Granny Jeter was the first person I came out to?" Ry said. She'd spent a lot of time with her granny on weekends and during the summer before she'd started working with her father. She loved the cabin and the little cubbyhole beside the kitchen that had been her room. She had told her

Granny everything. Whenever there had been problems that Ry couldn't handle on her own, she had gone to Granny Jeter for answers.

"I'm not surprised," her mom said. "She never judged. I can't remember hearing her say a single bad thing about anyone."

"Except for Willard Pritchard."

Her mom shuddered. "Oh, he was a horrible old man."

"Why didn't she like him?"

"It happened so long ago, I'm not sure I even remember." She sipped her coffee before she continued. "You weren't born when your father moved Granny's cabin over by the pond."

"You mean it wasn't always there?"

"No. No. She and Grandpa had a little piece of property over by where Carlson's Dairy is now. Carlson started the dairy the year after your father and I were married. You can imagine how bad the stench was in the summer and poor Granny's cabin was downwind from the place."

Ry crinkled her nose.

"I was seven months pregnant with James. Seth and I were living in that little mobile home. The stench had gotten so horrible that your father and I invited her to come and live with us." Her mom chuckled. "Granny politely informed us that she wasn't ready to live with anyone. She was around seventy then. I kept begging her. I even used my pregnancy as an excuse." She patted Ry's arm. "The pregnancy scare wasn't really a lie. I was secretly terrified." She waved her hand. "Anyway, I guess Granny got tired of us bugging her and told us the only way she would move would be if God picked up her cabin and sat it down by our pond. She really liked that pond." Her mom started laughing. "Well, Granny hadn't learned that there was at least one other person on this earth as stubborn as her."

"Dad." Ry smiled.

"Exactly. Your dad knew how much I wanted her nearby and as always, he found a solution. He went to Granny and told her he wasn't God, but if she'd let him, he would find a way to get her cabin moved over by the pond."

"So, he moved Granny's cabin," Ry said.

"Yes. He got his dad and his brothers Allen and Zack to help him and somehow they put that little cabin on a trailer. The four of them moved it across the county and put it down there by the pond. She lived there another twenty-five years."

"And that's when she moved in here," Ry said. "I remember that. I was in college."

"Yes, she lived here until she died at one hundred and three years of age."

"That's quite an accomplishment," Ry said, awed by her great-grandmother's fortitude. "I wish I had half her spunk."

Her mom tilted her head slightly to stare at Ry. "You know you were named for her. You may not see it now, but there's a lot of her in you." She patted Ry's arm again. "Spunk is not something you have ever lacked. In fact, your spunk has contributed to the origins of many of these gray hairs." She waved her hand over the top of her head.

"You don't have gray hair."

"God bless you Rylene, but you really do need to have your eyes checked." She laughed.

"What is all the jabbering and giggling going on down here?" Ry's father said as he ambled into the kitchen smiling.

"We were just reminiscing about Granny Jeter," her mom said. "Did we wake you?"

"Now there was a woman," he said, shrugging away the question. "I remember when she turned a hundred. I asked her what she wanted for her birthday and do you know what she told me?" He turned to Ry.

"What?"

"She told me she wanted me to plow up a patch of ground back there behind the house so she could plant herself a garden. She didn't like those puny grocery store vegetables."

"Did you do it?"

"I sure did and she grew some of the best tasting tomatoes I've ever eaten." He stopped by Doreen's chair and kissed her on the top of her head. "Why don't you plant a garden? Maybe you could grow some of those great tomatoes."

"That's why the good Lord created market days," her mom responded. "Sit down and I'll get your coffee."

"No, keep your seat. I'll get it." He made his way to the coffeepot. "Ry, do you remember any of the carpentry I taught you?"

She looked up, surprised. "I think so. Why?"

"Granny Jeter's cabin needs some work. Nothing major, mind you. A few loose shingles and the front porch rails need some work. You know. It's a few little things, but if I keep putting them off it won't be long before they become major issues." He poured his coffee. "Looks like it's going to be a few days before the claims adjuster gets around to checking out your place, so I thought you might not mind fixing up the cabin. It shouldn't take you more than a day or two at the most." He sipped his coffee.

"No, I don't mind at all. I always loved going there to visit Granny Jeter."

"Good," her dad said as he sat down across from her. "As soon as it gets light we can toss whatever you might need onto my work truck and you can take it. All the tools you need are already in the truck."

Her mom stood. "You'll need some food," she said and went to the pantry.

"Mom, I'll only be there a couple of days, so don't over pack," Ry said. She knew her mom's version of a snack for the road was enough food to feed a family of four.

"While you're out there, keep your eyes open," her father said. "I received a call from Nat Zucker last week. You know he owns that stretch of land that's southeast of ours."

Ry nodded.

"Poachers have gotten so bad out his way he had to call the Fish and Game Department. They promised to investigate, but you know how busy they are with only two game wardens for the entire county. If you see anyone you don't know messing around out there give me call."

Ry fought the slight nervous twinge that tightened her stomach. The last thing she wanted was another encounter with an idiot toting a gun. "Do you think they're dangerous?"

"No. I wouldn't have suggested you go out there otherwise. You know how Nat gets. He finds a couple of deer carcasses and he overreacts. Those deer may have died of old age. You never know with Nat." He sipped his coffee before continuing, "When I was out that way I looked around, didn't see anything out of the ordinary." He eyed her for a moment. "You can take one of the hunting rifles with you if it makes you feel better."

She waved off the offer. "No, thanks. I'm not sure I ever want to touch another weapon."

"Ry, you can't punish yourself for what happened. You had to defend yourself and Kate."

"Dad, on an intellectual level, I know all of that is true." She looked at him and lowered her voice. "I intended to place those shots exactly where they struck. I could have just as easily wounded him, but at the time, it never occurred to me to do so. Why didn't it? Why was my first instinct to kill him?"

Her father stared into her eyes for a long moment. She could see the conflicting emotions in his gaze.

He cleared his throat. "Instinct maybe. I don't know," he replied. "Thank God you reacted exactly as you did. I certainly don't ever want to be in the position where I have to tell her that her little girl is gone." He stood suddenly. "I need to get going. I have to drive over and pick up James. Then, we're going to go finish up that fence for you. Okay if I drive your truck? I don't like to leave your mom without her car."

"Sure. If you don't mind nature's air-conditioning. The keys are on the entryway table." Ry hopped up and gave him a tight hug. "Thank you, Dad."

He kissed her forehead. "You be careful when you climb up on that ladder to fix the roof. You never were overly nimble."

Ry slapped his arm gently. "Are you trying to say I'm a klutz?"

"Well, you know there's a reason we didn't name you Grace." He winked and left.

CHAPTER NINE

Ry parked her father's Ford F-250 beneath a towering cypress tree. Then she slowly made a circuit around the oak plank cabin. It was exactly what her father had described. There were a handful of missing shingles, a few nails needed to be reset and the front porch banister needed tightening. She sat in one of the four rockers on the front porch. It faced the pond that was less than sixty yards away. As she rocked and watched a couple of mallards swimming around the pond, she began to suspect her father had sent her here more for her mental well-being than that of the cabin. A hummingbird swooped across the porch in front of her. It hovered near her for a moment before zipping away with its iridescent wings sparkling in the sunlight. The bird reminded her of an afternoon she had spent helping her great-grandmother weed her flower garden. There had been a wide variety of flowers, but one particular plant put the hummingbirds into a feeding frenzy. She tried but failed to remember what her granny had called it. The hummingbird returned and hovered near the edge of the porch. His actions made Ry remember the glass feeders that her granny had kept out. She went inside and dug around until she located a feeder in a kitchen cabinet.

Since some member of the family was always using the cabin, it was always fairly well stocked. She put a pot of water on to boil and soon the feeder was filled with the sugary water the hummingbirds so dearly loved. She hung the feeder on the front porch and within minutes five hummingbirds battled for the sweet liquid.

Ry watched their aerial acrobatics for a long while. She marveled at the brilliant flashes of reds and greens as the hummers darted to and from the feeder. After watching them for several minutes, she began unloading the back of the truck.

The cabin was essentially a square box divided into four rooms. Rather than use the bedroom, she put her suitcase in the same tiny niche behind the kitchen chimney that she had slept in as a child. The space was barely big enough for a twin-size bed and tiny side table. As a child, she had pretended the small cubby was her treasure cave. She had hidden her multitude of treasures beneath the bed.

It didn't surprise her to discover that her mother had packed two large ice chests. One filled with a gallon jar of lemonade along with half a dozen frozen dinners her mom was famous for making. The other chest contained nonperishable goodies that included a large can of coffee. Ry transferred the lemonade and the perishable items to the refrigerator and left the rest stored in the ice chest.

Back at the truck, she saw another smaller ice chest. In it she found several beers in ice. "Thanks, Dad," she said and smiled. Next to the ice chest containing the beer was a fishing pole and tackle box. She put the ice chest in the cool shade of the tree and unloaded a large toolbox. It only took a few minutes to reset the nails and tighten the porch rail. Replacing the handful of shingles took less than an hour.

By midafternoon, she was sitting beneath a cypress tree with a fishing pole in one hand and a cold beer in the other. Her mom had packed an entire link of German sausage and Ry had chopped part of it up into small pieces to use as fish bait. The mallards kept their distance, but continued their diligent foraging. From somewhere in the distance came the erratic drumming of a woodpecker. Ry's body absorbed the serenity of the world around her. When she reeled her line in and found the hook cleaned, she laid it aside and began idly tossing the bits of sausage into the water.

For the first time in longer than she could remember, she felt at peace. Several decisions still needed to be made and she'd make them when the time came. She didn't know how everything would work out, but if it was meant to be then she would find a way.

When the sun finally slipped beneath the horizon, she locked her father's tools in the truck and went inside the cabin. She didn't bother with lights but went straight to bed. She was asleep before her head hit the pillow.

Someone called her name. Her body, heavy with sleep, was slow in responding. When her name was called again, she made herself sit up. It sounded like her mother. She turned to get out of bed but something was in her way. She tried again. Something had been moved against her bed. On the verge of screaming at her brothers for pulling one of their juvenile pranks, she suddenly remembered she wasn't at home but rather at the cabin. She turned over and swung her legs off the bed. Moonlight poured through the kitchen windows allowing her to see clearly the woman standing by the doorway. Ry stared in disbelief and surprisingly enough wasn't frightened. "Granny Jeter, is that you?"

"Ry, there's a storm coming. It's a bad storm, honey."

Ry looked beyond the shadowy image of her great-grandmother. The moonlight was bright. There didn't seem to be any clouds obscuring it. "Granny Jeter, I must be dreaming. You're dead." She wanted to run to her, but her feet wouldn't move. "We miss you so much."

"I'm never far away. Ry, you have to be strong. When they come for you, you stay strong and fight them."

Scared, Ry looked around her. "Who's coming? Why are they coming for me?"

"Who doesn't matter. What matters is that you keep fighting and don't give in."

"I promise," Ry said.

"Your life is changing and it'll never be the same. When the weak come to you for help, don't withhold it out of fright. You have a lot to do. Don't be afraid. I'll always be near. And, Ry, remember, it's not a sign of weakness to forgive."

A god-awful racket brought Ry to her feet. Morning sunlight from the kitchen windows blinded her. Frightened by her great-grandmother's ominous words still ringing in her ears, she held up a hand to block the light. She wasn't sure what she was expecting to find. When she saw nothing the least bit scary she breathed a loud sigh of relief and gave a nervous chuckle. It had been a dream. Yet, it had seemed so real. A strange nervousness hit her stomach. Was Granny Jeter trying to warn her of something? She had heard of such things happening to people. Her thoughts were interrupted when the racket began again. It was nothing more than a blue jay shrieking an alarm.

Ry sat back down on the edge of the bed. The bird had probably seen a hawk or maybe a snake. It was his job to alert the other birds. She put on her clothes and boots. Her watch indicated it was after nine. She couldn't remember how long it had been since she had slept so well. After starting a pot of coffee, she brushed her teeth and washed her face in the bathroom sink. She needed to call Wilma Brown and follow up on when the claims adjuster would be out to look over the shop. As soon as the coffee was ready, she poured a cup and retrieved her cell phone from the kitchen table. The day was too beautiful to stay inside the cabin. She decided to have her coffee on the porch. She dialed Wilma's number as she walked.

As she stepped out onto the front porch, the squawking blue jay flew directly at her. Ry instinctively jumped back. As she moved, a strong gust of wind kicked up. She clearly heard the creaking of the massive cypress tree limbs. The hummingbird feeder swung wildly in the blast of air. The liquid inside the feeder caught the sunlight creating a brilliant rainbow. As she watched, the myriad of colors suddenly exploded, sending a multitude of glass shards into the air. The sugar water from the feeder seemed to hang in midair for a second before splattering across the porch.

Confused, Ry tried to comprehend what had happened to the feeder. Then she heard the unmistakable sound of a gunshot. The sound recognition had barely been processed when something hard hit the right side of her forehead. As her knees folded, she felt the phone and coffee cup slip from her hands. She fell face forward onto the porch. Something warm ran down her face. At first, Ry thought it was the spilled coffee, but then she saw the stream of blood oozing across the porch plank. She had been shot. So this was how it would happen. This was the way she would die. Granny Jeter had attempted to warn her. Ry tried to move, but her body no longer obeyed. Nothing on it seemed to work.

Oddly enough, she felt no pain. All she felt was a sense of sadness. No one would come looking for her for at least another day or two. Her father would blame himself for sending her out here. Her mom would grieve. Blackness began to close over her.

Voices filled her head. "*A parent shouldn't bury a child. Fight. Don't give in.*"

Light, blinding light moved toward her.

More whispers.

"*Fight, Ry, don't give in.*"

She fought against the heaviness that was settling over her.

The light dimmed but continued to hover nearby.

"Ry, tell your mother the earring she lost fell behind the baseboard at the back of her dresser. It's a little gold heart with a sapphire in the center."

Was that Granny Jeter's voice? Ry wanted desperately to open her eyes, but they were too heavy.

Couldn't Granny Jeter see she was dying? Why was she talking about earrings? Faces began floating before her. They all seemed to want something from her. She squeezed her eyes tighter.

Even with her eyes tightly closed, the faces of strangers continued to float before her. She fought to push them away. The pleading face of a young woman caught her attention. As soon as she made eye contact, the young woman seemed to jump forward and stand right next to her.

"Don't be afraid. They won't be with you long," her Granny Jeter's voice cut through the clamoring voices around her. "Listen to her. She needs your help."

The young woman leaned down and whispered. "Tell my mother that my diary is hidden in my closet behind a fake panel. Please tell her. She needs to know."

Ry tried to ask the woman's name, but before she could form the words another face was there talking to her. This time an older man, his voice so heavily accented she could barely understand him. "Tell my grandson the one he loves is in Tulsa. My grandson has lost his way. He needs to find his way back to her. It was meant to be."

The light closed in again. It seemed so peaceful, so welcoming she moved toward it. Ry could see silhouettes of people in front of the light. Some were beckoning her to come closer, but there was a much louder group waving her away.

A voice shouted near her ear. "Come on, stay with me. Open your eyes and talk to me. What's your name? Come on, you're making me do all the work. Fight."

Ry ran away from the light. "I'm fighting. I won't let you down, Granny Jeter, I promise."

A sharp spasm of pain shot through Ry's body. The faces and voices disappeared. The pressure in her head was nearly unbearable. She screamed in pain and desperately searched for the peaceful light, but it had abandoned her as well. She called out for her great-grandmother, her parents, Kate, anyone who could stop the pain. The voice that finally cut through the pain was unknown to her, but she clung to it desperately. Somehow, she knew that if she lost that voice, she would die. "Talk to me," she begged. "Don't leave me."

A warm hand caressed her cheek. "I'm right here. I'm not going anywhere and neither are you."

* * *

Water dripped on Ry's face. She tried to reach up and touch her face, but the darkness kept dragging her back.

"Mom, come on. Let the doctors work."

Daniel's voice. Ry tried to call out to him. *Where was the other voice?* She needed to hear the other voice.

"Mr. and Mrs. Shelton, please. You have to leave."

Darkness.

"…get you if…"

Darkness.

"…changes…"

Kate. Was Kate here?

Darkness.

"*Fight, Ry.*"

Darkness.

Ry lost track of the number of times the voices and the darkness pulled her back and forth. She was so exhausted. She again looked around for the comforting light, but it continued to elude her.

Was she doomed for all eternity to hear the voices of her loved ones without being able to speak to them? Maybe this was Hell. After all, she had killed a man. She had gone to Sunday school and the Bible definitely frowned on killing. But, there was that eye for an eye thing. Did that include self-defense? Except for a few minor slips, she had tried to lead a good life. She shouldn't have been so mean to Lenny Morton in the fourth grade. She had superglued the wheels of his skateboard after he put a dead frog in Linda Sue's gym shoes. And she had stolen a couple of copies from Lewis's hidden stash of girly magazines when she was fifteen. Before she could ponder further on whether she was in Hell or not, the menacing darkness gave way to a less threatening void.

Ry pulled herself from the void by following the voices. They were nearby, whispering. One voice seemed familiar, but not the other. She tried to concentrate.

"I'm sure I put my keys in my bag after I got out of the car." That was Kate's voice.

"You probably dropped them," replied the unknown voice.

A hand clasped Ry's hand. Instantly her body grew hot as an image flashed through the blackness. She saw keys in a dark, almost tunnel-like area. She recognized the keys by the small penknife with Kate's initials. Where were they? She studied everything around the keys and finally identified what she was seeing.

"I don't know what I'm going to do if I don't find them," Kate said.

"Keys un...er car seat. In air con..it...on...ent," she tried to tell Kate, but something in her mouth prevented her from speaking. She wanted to yank it away, but her arm wouldn't move.

The voices stopped.

Ry felt herself slipping back into the darkness.

"Ry, can you hear me?"

Someone was gently touching her face. It sounded like Kate. Ry imagined she could even smell the slightly citrusy scent of Kate's favorite body wash. Maybe it really was Kate. She again tried to tell Kate where her keys were and again her words sounded garbled.

"Ry, if you can hear me squeeze my hand."

She struggled to make her hands move. Nothing happened. It seemed as if her body was frozen into position.

From somewhere far away she heard her Granny Jeter say, "Come on, Ry. Be strong. You are now the Seeker. Many people will depend on you."

Ry focused all her attention on making her hand move. At first, all she could do was twitch one finger.

"Yes, Ry. Come on, honey." Kate pleaded. "Squeeze my hand and then you can sleep."

Ry funneled all of her energy into her hand. Finally, her muscles cooperated enough for Ry to close her hand around Kate's fingers. The effort left her feeling exhausted. There wasn't much energy left to squeeze.

It seemed like it was enough, because Kate was laughing happily.

Ry felt drops of water hitting her face. It must be raining, she thought as she drifted off to sleep.

* * *

The next time Ry opened her eyes filtered sunlight bathed the room. Her parents stood beside her bed.

Horrified by the stricken looks on their faces, she tried to reach out to them but couldn't seem to find the strength. Her father looked as if he had aged ten years. Something was terribly wrong. Why did they look so scared? She struggled to clear her head. Ry had known why they were upset, but she couldn't remember now. She tried to speak, but there was still something in her mouth. She reached up to remove it. A hand gently stopped her.

"You have to leave the tube in."

Ry blinked in confusion. Kate was leaning over her. When had Kate gotten to the cabin? Was this still a dream? She had a vague memory of dreaming about Granny Jeter. Maybe this was still part of that dream. If she could just get this thing out of her mouth, she could ask. She tried to grab it again.

"Ry, that's a breathing tube. It's there to help you. Please don't bother it." Kate turned and disappeared.

Ry's eyes kept trying to close, but her parents were talking to her. She struggled to understand what they were saying. When had they gotten to the cabin? Or was she still at the house? She tried to sort things out. Something had happened. What was it? She tried to think, but her head felt as if someone had stuffed it with cotton. If only she could sleep for a while longer. She was so tired. Her eyes closed.

A man's voice jarred her awake. His voice irritated her. It was too loud, and he sounded like he was speaking jibber-jabber. She tried to ignore him, but he wouldn't go away. Couldn't he see she was trying to sleep?

He called out again.

Ry opened her eyes and saw a man in a white coat. He was leaning over her and appeared to be talking to her. What had he said? She could see his lips moving and hear the sound of his voice, but he was talking too fast, nothing made sense. She told herself to focus on his lips. Slowly his words came through.

"Ms. Shelton, I'm Dr. Price. If you can hear me clearly, I want you to blink once. If my voice is not clear, please blink twice." He watched her intently.

She mustered her energy and blinked once.

"Wonderful," he said and rewarded her effort with a huge smile. "Now I'd like for you to follow this light with your eyes only. Don't move your head. Just follow the light with your eyes."

Ry tried to follow the light, but it kept bouncing around. It made her dizzy.

He squeezed her arm. "Don't worry if you can't do it right away. It'll get a little easier each time." He kept talking, but Ry couldn't fight it any longer and closed her eyes.

CHAPTER TEN

Ry opened her eyes. Her throat ached. She tried to swallow, but her mouth was too dry. The room was dark except for a dim light to her left. She turned her head slightly and the room spun wildly. Terrified, she grabbed the side rails of the bed to keep from flying off. The room seemed to be nothing more than blurs of various shades of black. She couldn't focus.

A hand closed around her arm. "It's okay. Breathe slowly."

The familiar voice made her feel safer. She closed her eyes and took several slow breaths. When the bed stopped spinning, she cautiously opened her eyes. The room remained stable. Her heart skipped a beat when she saw Kate staring down at her. Somewhere to her right a series of rapid beeps and pings were clanging loudly. She turned to see what had caused the commotion and set the room to spinning again.

"Breathe slowly," Kate said again in a low soothing voice. "Try not to move your head." Kate went around the bed and did something to stop the machine's pinging. Then she went back to stand beside Ry.

"What's happened?" Ry didn't recognize her own voice. It was little more than a raspy whisper.

"Do you know who I am?" Kate asked.

Ry frowned. "Yes, Kate, I know who you are."

"Can you hold up two fingers?" Kate asked.

"What's wrong with you?" Ry was so tired she could barely hold her eyes open. Her head was pounding and Kate wanted to play games. Why was she here anyway? Maybe the new girlfriend worked long hours, too. She seriously considered showing Kate a couple of choice fingers, but was too tired to flip her off. Instead, she lifted two fingers on her right hand.

"Can you move your arm and leg on the left side?"

Ry began to get scared as she realized that this wasn't Kate, her former girlfriend, talking. This was Kate the nurse. She wiggled her toes on both feet and then moved both her left arm and leg being careful not to move her head. "You're frightening me."

"Don't be afraid. You're doing wonderful." She touched Ry's arm. "Do you remember what happened to you?" Kate stared down at her intently.

Ry tried to think, but everything was such a jumble. "Granny Jeter was at the cabin, only it was dream," she whispered. "She said there was a storm coming."

The blips on the machine became quicker.

Kate put a finger to Ry's lips. "It's okay. Don't get upset." She removed her finger from Ry's lips. "You may have a few memory gaps for a while. That's completely normal." Her hand brushed Ry's cheek. "My God, Ry, you have no idea how lucky you were. I swear you must have a full squadron of guardian angels watching over you."

Ry's throat ached. "I'm thirsty." She was having trouble keeping her eyes open. She couldn't concentrate.

"Here are some ice chips. That's all you can have for a while. The moisture will help your throat feel better." She spoon-fed Ry the ice.

Ry held the ice chips in her mouth. They quickly melted. She swallowed and opened her mouth for more. She felt as though she could guzzle a gallon of water and still be thirsty.

When she had managed a couple of more swallows, she pointed to her throat. "What's wrong?"

"When you arrived at the emergency room you were having trouble breathing. We had to intubate you. You were still having trouble after surgery. They weren't able to remove it until yesterday."

Ry's head was pounding. "Surgery?" She couldn't remember ever being so exhausted. She struggled to remember. Sleep began to overtake her, but she fought it off. "Why are you here? Shouldn't you be with your new girlfriend? Where are Mom and Dad?" She didn't dare move her head again to search for her parents.

Kate seemed to ignore her outburst and gave her more ice chips. "Your parents are fine. I finally convinced them to leave and get some sleep. They hadn't left the hospital since you got here four days ago. They were exhausted."

Ry felt even more confused. "Four days?" she asked after she had swallowed. "Have I been sleeping that long? What day is it?"

Kate gave her more ice. "It's Sunday and it's around three in the morning."

"Sunday," Ry repeated. "So the shooting at the estate sale house, that happened a week ago?"

"You probably won't be able to remember anything that's happened since you were hurt. Can you remember anything?"

Ry forgot and shook her head to answer. When her head moved not only did the bed spin, but her stomach gave a powerful heave.

Kate held a pan beneath Ry's chin until the dry heaves passed.

The excruciating pain in her head brought tears to Ry's eyes. Something was horribly wrong. Panic began shutting down her body. The roar in her ears blocked out Kate's voice. Her breath came in short, ragged gasps. The slightest movement of her head brought another wave of pain. She tried to fight the fear and the pain, but the whirling room and dry heaves weren't helping. And to make matters worse there was a tugging pain in her groin.

Kate's hand caressed her arm as she leaned over the bed. Ry focused her attention on watching the movement of Kate's lips. Slowly the roar in her head subsided, allowing the comforting sound of Kate's voice. Ry tried to comprehend what she was saying, but the words couldn't penetrate the pain. Ry closed her eyes and held fast to the sound of Kate's voice. She didn't want Kate here. Kate loved someone else. Yet, she felt certain that Kate's voice was the only thing that kept her from slipping into a terrifying void. A tiny voice of fear told her she must have a brain tumor or had been stricken with some horrible debilitating disease. That would explain why her parents looked so devastated when she saw them earlier. That was why Kate was here being so kind to her. She was dying. When she finally managed to regain enough control to talk, she grabbed Kate's arm.

"What's that?" she asked. She tried to reach down between her legs.

Kate smiled. "You have a catheter. Try not to disturb it."

"What's wrong with me?" she asked, not bothering to try to hide her panic. "Am I dying?"

"No, Ry, you're not dying. You've been hurt. If you promise to calm down, I'll tell you everything I can." She glanced toward the door. "If you keep this up the night nurse is going to come and kick me out." She leaned close to Ry. "The thing you need to remember is that you're going to be fine. All of your tests look promising. I know what a fighter you are. You'll be up and around in no time." She took Ry's hand. "Will you promise to try to remain calm?"

Ry took a slow breath. "Yes."

"Good. Now relax and keep your head still." She patted Ry's arm. "You were out by your family's pond and someone shot you."

Ry froze. Had she heard Kate correctly? "I was shot?" The machine began beeping rapidly again as she frantically patted her chest and torso. "Where? Where was I shot? How bad is it?"

"Ry." Kate's voice took on a more authoritarian tone. "You promised. You're going to be fine." Kate held Ry's arms until she began to settle down; only then did she reset the machine. "You have to stay calm. The doctor will explain everything to you tomorrow morning."

"You tell me," Ry whispered. Even as she asked, she wasn't certain she wanted to know.

"Do you remember being at the cabin?" Kate asked.

"Yes." Ry was careful not to move her head. She concentrated on recalling what had happened at the cabin. "I did some repairs to the roof and porch." She closed her eyes. "I tried to fish, but I got tired and just fed the fish instead." Her throat hurt. She tried to swallow.

"Try some more of these," Kate held out a spoon with ice chips.

Ry eyed it cautiously. "Will they make me sick again?"

"Maybe, but you need to try anyway."

Ry held the ice chips in her mouth until they melted and slowly swallowed.

"What else do you remember?" Kate persisted.

"I sat outside until it was dark. Then I went inside the cabin. I was tired and went to bed." She thought of the dream about Granny Jeter. Maybe now wasn't the time to bring it up. "When I woke, it was morning. I…" She struggled to remember. "I made coffee. There was a blue jay. He was upset about something." She closed her eyes. "I think I was trying to call someone." A wave of exhaustion rolled over her. She opened her eyes. "I'm sorry."

"You're doing great," Kate said, encouraging her. "Do you remember who you called?"

Ry couldn't think. "No, I don't remember calling anyone."

"You made a call but were shot before you could say anything." Kate hesitated. "Do you remember anything else? Did you see who shot you?"

"No. I don't remember anything else."

Kate gave her more ice. "You called Wilma Brown. She answered in time to hear the shot. When she couldn't get you to respond, she called Victor Orozco. Victor in turn called your dad and discovered you were out at the cabin." Kate pulled a chair closer to the bed and sat down. "Sorry, I guess I'm more tired than I thought."

Ry had noticed the dark circles beneath Kate's eyes. She didn't want to feel any sympathy or concern for her, but couldn't stop herself. "How long have you been here?" She kept her head still.

"Just a few hours," Kate began. "I got here around seven I guess." She quickly changed the subject. "Anyway, while everyone was calling around looking for you, a game warden found you."

"Game warden," Ry said. She vaguely remembered the conversation she'd had with her father the morning she left for the cabin. "That's right. Dad mentioned that Nat Zucker was having problems with poachers." Confused, she hesitated. "A poacher shot me?"

"That's what they think happened, but at this time they're not really sure who shot you. The game warden had been on her way to check the cove over to the east of the pond and that's when she heard the shot."

Ry tried to remember, but there was nothing.

"Long story short," Kate continued, "the game warden brought you to Jackson City Memorial. After we got you stabilized, you were taken by chopper to San Antonio."

"San Antonio." She forgot the rest of what she had intended to say. She struggled to remember, but it had slipped away from her. The invasive sense of weakness in her body frightened her. She tried to fight against the feeling of heaviness settling over her.

"Ry, I need to ask you something before you sleep. Can you hear me?"

Ry fought to open her eyes. "I can hear."

"How did you know where my keys were?"

"What keys?" Ry asked.

"Earlier you were awake for just a moment and you told me my keys were beneath my car seat in the air conditioning vent. How did you know they were there?"

"I saw them," Ry whispered. "Can I sleep now?"

"How did you see them?" Kate persisted.

"I saw…I saw them in my…my…"

"It's okay," Kate whispered. "You need to sleep. Don't worry. You won't be alone. Until you're stable someone will always be here with you."

"You didn't stay." Ry was so tired she wasn't sure if she had said the words or simply imagined them. Either way, she couldn't help but feel safer with Kate nearby. Ry gave in to the velvety softness that closed around her. As sleep overtook her, she felt warm, soft lips against hers. She experienced a small jab of panic. There must be brain damage and she was hallucinating. Kate wouldn't kiss her. Kate was in love with someone else. Ry tried to open her eyes to see if Kate was still standing beside the bed, but stopped. What if Kate wasn't there? Maybe she had imagined the entire thing. The same way she had imagined seeing Granny Jeter in the dream.

"I was not a dream, young lady."

Ry clearly heard Granny's voice.

"Granny Jeter, I'm scared," she confessed. "Why is everyone shooting at me?"

"Don't be scared, Ry. You have a long life ahead of you. Remember, you have to help all those people."

"Promise me everything will be all right," Ry persisted.

"I promise you everything will be fine."

Filled with a new sense of security, Ry stopped fighting and floated into the warm depths of sleep. Granny Jeter had never once broken a promise to her.

CHAPTER ELEVEN

Ry opened her eyes. The cardiac monitor next to her bed was still pumping and hissing. She supposed it was tracking her vital signs. The pain in her head had decreased significantly and it no longer felt as if it were stuffed with cotton. She found she could swallow more easily. Her throat no longer felt parched. She gently began to move her limbs. Everything seemed to work, but she still felt exhausted and weak.

"Seth, she's awake." Her mother materialized by the bedside. "How do you feel?"

Ry moved her head slowly to look at her mom. A small stab of pain pricked the right side of her head. The pain set off a slight tilting of the room, but nothing like before. "Hi, Mom. I actually feel a lot better."

Her dad appeared at the foot of the bed. He was dressed in a khaki work shirt with a Shelton and Sons logo. The shirt was wrinkled and he needed to shave. Her mom's blouse and slacks looked as if she had been wearing them for a while as well.

"You gave us a real scare," her dad said.

It startled her to see how tired and worried they looked. For the first time in her life, the realization that her parents were getting older struck her. To her they had both always been so strong and active that their aging never occurred to her. "I'm sorry I worried you guys. I guess Daniel was right. He always said my head was harder than a rock." She tried to smile.

"This is one time I wish it had been a little harder," her dad said as he squeezed her foot.

The shadows on the drawn window shades suggested it was late afternoon. "What day is it?" she asked, afraid she had lost even more time.

"Sunday afternoon," her father said.

"So, it was earlier this morning when I talked to Kate?" She stopped. "At least, I think I talked to Kate this morning."

"Yes. You did. The doctors have kept you heavily sedated," her mother said. "They all say you're doing remarkably well."

A nurse appeared. "I'm afraid you folks will have to leave now," she said as she began checking the monitor next to the bed.

"But she just woke up," her mother protested.

"The doctor is on his way in. He'll need a few minutes with her. You'll be able to visit after he leaves," she assured them.

"We'll be right outside," her father said as he took his wife's arm.

The nurse began asking Ry the same questions as Kate had earlier. Ry knew it was easier to repeat everything than it was to try to argue. She held up fingers when told to do so, she moved her limbs as directed and she counted from one to twenty and then back to one. She was relieved when the nurse finally left.

The dull ache in her head was growing. Ry closed her eyes and wished she were home in her own bed where she could sleep in peace. She was on the verge of sleep again when she heard the door. She opened her eyes and saw a man in a white coat.

"I heard that you had decided to wake up," he said and smiled. "I doubt if you remember me. I'm Dr. Price. I'm the neurosurgeon who's been poking around in your head." He held out his hand as he approached the bed. His too perfect tan suggested he spent a lot of time in a tanning salon.

Ry took his hand and instantly her head seemed to explode with color that immediately gave way to a scene of a German shepherd sitting by a tree. There was a swing next to the tree. It was one of those western types with the fake wagon wheels on either side of it. As she looked closer, she saw a rope. The dog was tied to the tree and appeared to be malnourished. She couldn't see a food or water bowl anywhere nearby. The scene faded as quickly as it came.

The doctor seemingly hadn't noticed any change in her. He had released her hand and was looking at her chart. "Everything looks remarkably good." He put the chart down and examined the bandage on her forehead. "Have you experienced any dizziness since you woke?"

"There's a little dizziness when I turn my head, but it's minimal."

"Have you had any visual or auditory hallucinations?"

"No." She decided not to mention what she had experienced when she shook his hand.

"How's the pain level? On a scale from one to ten, if one were a hangnail and ten being unable to lift your head."

"I have a dull headache. I guess one or two would be right."

He glanced at the monitor. "Your blood pressure and heart rate are fine."

Ry was trying to understand what had just happened with the sudden vision of the dog. "What exactly is going on with me, Doc?" she asked.

He stepped back and stared down at her. "How much have you been told so far?"

"I know I was shot and I'm in San Antonio."

He nodded. "You were struck by a bullet fragment approximately three millimeters wide and less than half that in length. Three millimeters is slightly less than an eighth of an inch," he explained. The fragment entered here." He placed a finger on the right side of his forehead slightly below his hairline. "It lodged in the right frontal lobe. You were fortunate that the fragment was small. There was very little brain swelling. We were able to remove the fragment without having to make a larger opening in your skull."

The monitor began bleeping wildly. He reached over and lowered the volume.

"I'm sorry. I know this all sounds frightening and it can be. But, as I said, you are doing amazingly well."

"How did I survive a bullet to the brain?"

He laid the chart down. "You're fortunate that only a small fragment of the bullet struck you. It didn't penetrate the frontal lobe very deeply. The police think the bullet hit a tree limb before it passed through a glass jar and hit you."

Ry remembered the hummingbird feeder exploding just before she heard the shot. "That's right. It was a hummingbird feeder." She closed her eyes and let the memories roll over her. "There was a sharp gust of wind just before I heard the shot," she said. "The cypress tree limbs were whipping and the feeder was whirling about." She opened her eyes. She didn't want to recall the impact of the bullet.

He was staring at her. "That gust of wind seems to have saved your life," he replied. "The cypress limb deflected the bullet just enough that it missed any vital areas. And when the bullet passed through the hummingbird feeder it was slowed down so it didn't penetrate deeply." He shook his head in amazement. "It's truly a miracle you're alive."

Too many thoughts were running through her mind. She needed time alone to sort them out and make sense of them. "When can I go home?"

"You've only been awake for a few minutes and you're already anxious to leave us." He smiled. "You haven't even experienced our wonderful hospital cuisine yet. I'm sorry, but at this point I can't give you a definitive date as to when you can go home." He picked up the chart again and flipped through it as he spoke. "Immediately after surgery you had some superficial swelling, which was to be expected. It has since gone down." He motioned toward her face. "You have some bruising, but that will go away soon. There's no indication of infection. Your speech and auditory functions appear normal. There are no signs of paralysis in any of your extremities." He closed the chart. "We're going to get you up and moving around shortly. If all continues to go well, the only physical reminder you'll have of this will be a small scar on your forehead." He fiddled with the monitor again. "Do you have any questions?"

"Will I still be able to do everything the way I did before?" she asked.

He rubbed his chin. "Ms. Shelton…"

"Please call me, Ry."

He nodded. "Ry, you've had some damage to the right frontal lobe of your brain. This area of the brain is responsible for cognitive thought processes." He stopped and held up his hand. "Please understand, I'm giving you a purely clinical evaluation of what could and I stress *could*, occur. This doesn't means that any of these changes will happen to you. It simply means we will be watching for these things over the next few weeks. Do you understand that?"

She fought to remain in control. The thought of not being back to normal for weeks made her nauseous. She kept her voice as calm as she could. "Yes. Please go on."

He nodded and continued, "Damage to this area *could* lead to changes in a person's socialization skills, a decrease in attention span, increased risk taking or changes to a person's sexual habits."

"So I might stop being a lesbian." She couldn't hide her smile.

He stared at her for a long second and cleared his throat. "Well, I'm not sure about that."

Before he could say anything more, the door opened and a tall and very handsome woman dressed in a uniform walked in.

As Ry glanced over at her the monitor next to the bed began its annoying wild beep.

"Officer, if you could wait outside. I'll only be another moment," Dr. Price said.

"Sorry." The woman disappeared as quickly as she had appeared.

He cleared his throat again. "If the sudden elevation in heart rate and blood pressure are any indicator, it appears your concerns about changing your sexual orientation won't be an issue," he said as he held out his hand.

When she took it, she was again overwhelmed by an array of colors before she once more saw the dog. "Do you own a German shepherd?" she asked without thinking.

He stopped short and stared at her. "I do." The sense of tension seemed to fill the room. "Why do you ask?"

Ry told herself to be quiet, but couldn't keep from asking, "Do you know someone who has one of those big western swings with the wagon wheels on the ends?"

His eyes narrowed slightly as he glanced from her to the machine. "Actually, I believe I do," he said.

"I think you should look there for your dog."

He frowned. "How would you know where my dog is?"

"I don't know. I just have a feeling."

"Has someone mentioned my dog to you?"

"No. It's just a feeling." She wished she could take back the entire conversation.

He stared at her for a long moment. "Rest as much as you can. I'll stop by to see you soon." He left her alone.

Ry cursed herself for saying anything. Now she'd probably end up in the psych ward. She flinched when she heard a voice whisper in her ear, "Ry, you must follow your path."

She closed her eyes. "Granny Jeter, you never lied to me. I sure hope you know what you're doing."

"Is this still a bad time?"

Ry opened her eyes to find the woman who had stepped in earlier smiling down at her. She was wearing a Parks and Wildlife uniform. There was a roguish twinkle in her sky-blue eyes. Ry couldn't help but smile back. "No, I'm just having a conversation with the voices in my head."

The woman tilted her head slightly as she idly turned her uniform hat in her hands. "Someone once told me that talking to yourself is often times the only way to ensure an intelligent conversation." She stepped closer and held out her hand. "I'm Nicole Matthews."

Ry held her breath as she shook her hand. She nearly giggled with relief when nothing happened.

"I understand you saved my life," Ry said.

Nicole blew out a loud breath and ran a hand over her short black hair. "I'm glad I could help, but I sure hope I never have to do that again. In all honesty, I was scared to death. I've never seen so much blood." She stopped and shifted her feet.

"Well, Officer Matthews. Thank you saving my life."

"Always happy to rescue a pretty lady," she said and smiled. "You can call me Nicole."

Ry cringed when the blasted cardiac monitor started bleeping like a wild being. "Sorry about the noise," she said. "That thing is apparently broken."

Nicole smiled at her. "I understand completely." She shuffled her feet. "I had to come into the city to testify in court so I thought I'd stop by to see how you were doing."

"The doctor seems happy with my progress," Ry said as she tried not to stare at the way Nicole's uniform seemed to fit perfectly in all the right spots.

"That's good." She spun her hat a couple of times before adding, "You probably don't remember me but we met about a year ago."

Ry study Nicole's face. She was certain she would have remembered her. "Where did we meet?"

"It was a fundraiser. Some group was trying to raise money to fence in that old cemetery out west of town."

Ry frowned and tried to remember. Suddenly it came to her. "I remember the event. It was for the Old Pioneer Cemetery. My mom was on the committee."

Nicole nodded. "I noticed you and wanted to talk to you that night but then I saw you were with someone." She continued to spin her hat. "So, I backed off."

"I was, then."

"Then?" Nicole's attention sharpened.

"She moved out." She stopped. "Not moved out exactly. There wasn't really anything left to move out of."

"I heard about your shop. It was a nice place."

"You've been to the shop?" Ry began to worry about her memory. How could she have possibly seen this woman twice and not remember her. Who could forget those eyes?

"I stopped by once, but you weren't there. Some other woman was working that day, short woman with a long braid."

"That's Sally."

Nicole nodded before suddenly saying. "The doctor told me I could only stay a minute. I was wondering. Would you mind if I stopped by to see you again? I mean, if I get a chance. I never know what my hours are going to be."

"I'd like that," Ry said. She liked this bold woman. Perhaps that was what made her feel a bit more daring than she normally was. "Maybe you should give me your number in case I'm released before you get back this way."

They stared at each other for a long moment before Nicole reached into her pocket and removed a card and a pen. She wrote on the back. "You can reach me through dispatch at the number on the front." She handed the card to Ry. "Or you can reach me directly on my cell number."

"I think I prefer the direct approach," Ry said. Her eyes never left Nicole.

Nicole smiled that devilish smile again. "Somehow, I just thought you might."

"Don't forget to send me your bill for saving my life," Ry teased.

Without warning, Nicole leaned down and gently kissed her lips. "There. Consider it paid in full."

Before Ry could catch her breath or respond, the door to the room burst open. A nurse came flying in with Ry's parents right behind her. It took her a moment to realize the monitor sounded as though it had gone into cardiac arrest.

"Are you okay?" the nurse asked as she began fussing over Ry. She slapped a blood pressure cuff on Ry's arm, took a stethoscope from her pocket and began checking Ry's heart.

"We were just talking and it started going crazy," Ry said. She could feel her face blazing.

"Your pulse is a little high," the nurse said.

"It's that thing," Ry said. "It nearly scared me to death."

The nurse turned to the monitor. "I'll get it replaced."

Nicole gave Ry a wink. "I'll see you soon."

"Thanks again for saving my life," Ry said.

Nicole waved goodbye and left.

After another check of the monitor, the nurse left. As soon as she was gone, Ry's parents approached the bed.

"What happened?" her father asked.

Ry deeply regretted the fright she had given them. "It's the monitor. I think it's broken. It goes crazy every once in a while."

Her mom was watching her closely.

"I'm fine," Ry assured them. She wished her mom wouldn't keep watching her. It felt like she was a kid again. She had never been able to hide anything from her mother. "Any leads on who shot me?" she asked to deflect her mom's scrutiny.

"Victor thinks it was the poacher Nat Zucker's been complaining about," her father said.

She touched the bandage on her forehead. She didn't say anything, but it didn't make sense. Maybe her thoughts were still muddled, but she had been standing on the porch. How could anyone have possibly mistaken her for a deer? She decided not to voice her opinion. Her parents had worried enough already.

Her mom began giving her a complete rundown of messages from her siblings and their families. Ry tried to concentrate, but it was useless. All she could think about was Nicole and that bold kiss. Ry's eyes grew too heavy to keep open. She tried to fight the heaviness, but it was useless. She finally gave up.

CHAPTER TWELVE

It was almost dark when she woke. Her dad was sitting in the large chair beside the bed.

"I'm sorry I fell asleep while mom was talking," she said.

Her dad got up and went over to stand by the bed. "She understands you need to rest."

"Where is she now?"

"She's in the waiting room. The boys and Kate are out there. Your mom is talking to them. The hospital only allows two people to be in your room at a time," he explained. "Your mother can be even stricter." He smiled. "She won't allow anyone but me in while you're sleeping. She nearly tackled a nurse earlier."

"I feel bad they drove all this way," Ry began. She wondered why Kate was still here.

"No. No. I don't want you to worry about anything. They knew they probably wouldn't be able to see you today. It helps your mom to have them here."

Ry reached up, put her hand over the back of her father's hand and squeezed. She knew he wouldn't freely admit that he found comfort in having his sons nearby. "I love you, Dad."

"I love you too, Buttercup."

She grinned. "You haven't called me that since I was a kid."

"It drove you crazy when I called you Buttercup," he said and smiled. "You'd tell me Buttercup was a cow's name and you weren't a cow."

He turned his hand and clasped her hand. Ry's head filled with color and suddenly she was seeing herself as a child.

"You haven't lost me, Dad. I've just grown up." She didn't know where the vision or statement had come from. Both had simply popped into her head.

He stared at her startled for a moment before tears sprung to his eyes. He wiped his face roughly. "Victor is waiting outside to talk to you," he said. "He's been here practically every night since they brought you in. I promised I'd tell him as soon as you were awake and up to talking. Do you feel like talking to him?"

"I think I'm up to it," she agreed. "Why is Victor here?" she asked as an afterthought. "The shooting didn't happen in town."

"He's working with the county sheriff. He seems to think the mess that happened over there at that house, the destruction of your shop and now this are all tied together somehow. I'll go get him."

Victor came in with her parents. They had seemingly forgotten the two-person at a time rule, but Ry held her tongue.

"I'm glad to hear you're doing better." He gave her a slight nod and began to smooth his massive handlebar mustache. He was wearing the heavier weight dark blue uniform that the personnel in the sheriff's department wore during cooler weather. "I'm sorry I have to bother you," he said.

"It's no bother," Ry assured him. "I'm afraid I can't help you any. I don't remember seeing anyone."

"I was hoping if you felt up to it, you could tell me what you do remember. Sometimes people see or hear things they don't think will make a difference, but it oftentimes does."

Ry repeated the same story she told Kate.

Victor nodded. "So you were hit while you were standing on the porch holding a cup of coffee and a cell phone?" Victor asked to clarify.

"Yes. I was calling Wilma Brown to see if she'd been able to schedule an appointment with a claims adjuster." Ry struggled to piece the events of the morning back together. "I remember a gust of wind hit me just as the hummingbird feeder exploded. I heard the shot and then…" She stopped when she heard her mom choke back a sob.

Victor turned his hat in his hands. "I'm sorry to upset you, Doreen. I probably should have talked to Ry alone. I certainly don't want to cause you folks anymore grief or suffering."

Her mom shook her head. "No, you go ahead. I'm fine." She pasted on a smile that was clearly forced.

They all remained silent for a long moment before her dad cleared his throat. "Doreen, I could sure use some coffee. Why don't we run down and grab a cup while Victor's here with Ry?"

Her mom clearly didn't want to leave, but she could take a hint. "Would you like a cup, Victor?" she asked as graciously as possible.

He smiled. "No, ma'am, I'm already three cups over my daily caffeine allowance." He waited until they had left the room before he turned back to Ry. "Do you remember seeing anyone around the place, maybe earlier that morning or the day before?"

Ry wondered what he would say if she mentioned seeing her Granny Jeter. She decided it was probably something she should keep to herself. "No. I didn't see or hear anyone."

"I didn't want to mention this in front of your mom, but we found the tree where the shooter waited."

"What do you mean waited?" she asked as her stomach began to churn. Immediately, the machine started beeping.

He looked at it with concern. "Are you okay?"

"Yes, it's just that blasted monitor. It's worse than a lie detector. Just ignore it. What did you mean he waited?"

"There were marks on the tree bark where he ground out at least three cigarettes. The grass was worn down like he stood there for quite a while."

"Was there anything to tell you who he was?" she asked as she tried to keep herself calm enough not to upset the machine.

"Not really. We managed to get one decent cast of a shoe print and we made a casting of tire prints we found about a half-mile down the road." Victor cleared his throat. "We found a cigarette butt over by where the car had been parked. It was the same brand as the one we found beneath the window at your shop." He hesitated.

She could see he wasn't finished. "What else?"

"Ry, you were shot with a thirty-thirty. We found the casing in the grass by the tree."

She closed her eyes and fought to control her anxiety. "The second shooter at the house last week used a thirty-thirty."

"Yes, he did."

She tried to convince herself it wasn't the same guy. Nobody was following her, trying to kill her. She had been shot by accident by a poacher. "That doesn't prove it was him," she said. "It's not as though a thirty-thirty is a rare weapon. Plenty of people own one. A Winchester is a common hunting weapon." She stopped and moved the conversation back to something less scary. "Did you find out anything on the identity of the two dead men?"

"No. We haven't gotten any of the results from the tests we requested."

"It's been a week."

He shrugged. "It's not like on television. We won't know anything for a few more days."

She didn't want to believe it was the same man, but something deep inside her told her it was. She took a deep breath. "Victor, what the hell is going on? Why is he after me?"

"Are you sure there's not something you forgot to mention that you bought out there, or maybe you saw something that didn't seem like much at the time?"

"No." She stopped. "Well, this doesn't amount to anything, but when Kate and I went out there last Sunday, we had two boxes of books and magazines. The one I'd accidently taken with my purchases. Then, a second one that contained some old magazines from the shop and some books I didn't think I could sell. I intended to drop the second box off at the nursing home. When we arrived at the house, I took the metal file box that had the pistol in it. Kate came in later with the box of books and magazines that was destroyed during the shooting."

He was nodding slowly, patiently waiting for her to get to the point.

"Anyway, it turned out that she took in the wrong box. The other box is now at my parents' house."

He straightened sharply. "What's in it?"

"Nothing worth shooting anyone over. Just some old magazines and a few hardback books. It's not as if they're really valuable or anything."

"I'd like to take a look at the stuff," he said.

"The box is in my room at Mom and Dad's house."

He frowned. "It doesn't make sense." He stopped and stared down at her for a moment. "I'm only telling you this because you don't strike me as being the faint-of-heart type, but I think this guy is stalking you. He knew where you were and he waited for you. And, it's only you. He hasn't made any move toward Kate." He shook his head. "Ry, when you get out of the hospital I think it might be a good idea for you to take a vacation somewhere away from here. You know, get out of town for a while."

"I appreciate that, Victor, but if he's truly stalking me, he wouldn't have any trouble following me. I think I'd rather stick around where there are people like you that I know I can depend on."

His face turned red. "It's nice of you to say so," he mumbled, "but I'm worried about you."

"Thank you, but I can't start running. But I promise you that from now until you catch this guy, I'll be a lot more careful."

He nodded. "I'll let you rest then. If you think of anything let me know," he said and gave a small wave. He stopped at the door. "If you don't mind, I think I'll ask your folks for that box of things and go through them. Maybe I'll see something you missed."

"I don't mind. But it's a waste of time. There's nothing there."

"I'll get it back to you as soon as I finish going through it."

"It's not mine," she said.

He waved again with his hat. "You rest now. We'll settle all that later."

Ry closed her eyes. She felt as though she could sleep for a week. She had hardly begun to doze before the door opened. It was James and Michelle, the first wave of her three siblings.

When each of her brothers and their respective wives entered, Ry smiled and greeted them as cheerfully as she could. She was happy to see them, but she was so tired she could barely focus on what they were saying. She repeated answers to the same health questions with each of them and listened to stories about and messages from each of her nieces and nephews. Rest didn't come until after visiting hours had ended.

CHAPTER THIRTEEN

A nurse woke Ry at five the following morning. It was the beginning of another long day. Instead of an endless stream of visitors, today consisted of an endless array of tests. It was almost six before she was finished and back in her room. The only good thing to come of the long day was that they removed the catheter and she was finally free of the irritating cardiac monitor.

She was sitting up in bed that evening when her parents came in. They stood at either side of her bed. She was happy to see they looked more rested. They both looked freshly showered and dressed in jeans and crisp shirts.

"How are you feeling?" her father asked as he patted her arm.

"Like I'm ready to go home," Ry grumbled. She kicked the sheet off her feet. She was tired of lying around all day.

"That will be a wonderful day," her mom said. She leaned down and kissed Ry's cheek. "We saw Dr. Price in the hallway about an hour ago. He said your test results were extremely positive. He's amazed at your recovery. He said he'd never seen anything like it in all his years of practice."

"So I can go home soon?"

"He still won't commit to a release date," her mom said.

Ry tried to shake off the blanket of grumpiness that had begun to envelop her. She was sick to death of this place. Her parents were probably much more tired of being there than she was. The past few days must have been a nightmare for them. She clasped their hands. "I can't thank you both enough. I don't know how I would have gotten through this without you." She saw the emotional wave she had created wash over them.

"We just want you home," her mom replied. She dabbed a tissue to her eyes.

Her father cleared his throat loudly before he spoke, "We're fixing up Granny's old room. The doctor said you'd still have to take it easy for a few weeks after you're released. He didn't want you going up and down the stairs."

"Thanks, I really appreciate that." She was again reminded of the dream in which she had seen Granny Jeter so clearly.

"What's wrong dear?" her mom asked. "You look worried."

"No. I'm not worried." If she told them about her dream, would they think the bullet had knocked one of her mental gears off-kilter? She glanced at them and decided not to worry them. "Has the insurance guy ever gotten out there to check the shop?" she asked. She hoped the sudden change in topic would derail her mother's scrutiny.

"Rylene, you can't be lying here worrying about that store," her mother scolded. "Your father and Kate are taking care of all that."

"Kate?"

"Her name is also on the deed," her father reminded her.

"Yes, I know. I'm just surprised that she would bother."

Her mom fussed with the sheet and tucked it back down over Ry's feet. "I don't want to hear anything else about that store."

Ry fought the urge to kick the sheet off again. She knew she was being difficult, and her parents had already been through enough. They didn't need her tantrums.

Her father patted her arm. She glanced up to find him smiling at her.

He winked at her. "Doreen," he said. "I'm a little tired. Why don't you and I go on back to the hotel and let Ry rest?" He leaned over and kissed her cheek. He stared at her for a moment. "This probably isn't the best time for this, but the doctor says you're much stronger and some things can't keep being put off. Kate's outside waiting," he said. "She's been here every day since you were hurt. Now, I don't know what's happened between you two. Frankly, I don't want to know, but she sure seems to be carrying a heavy load of guilt. You know I love you Ry, but you're no saint, so I'm betting some of that guilt lies at your doorstep. You two need to make peace, one way or the other. It's not good for either one of you to stretch these things out."

"You're right, Dad. Would you ask her to come in?"

He smiled and nodded. "Remember the good times and let the rest go," he said and stepped away from the bed.

"We'll see you tomorrow," her mom promised after she kissed Ry's cheek.

Ry watched her parents leave and couldn't stop the twinge of festering fear that never seemed to be very far away. Now everything and everyone around her seemed extremely vulnerable. She had grown up in the country where the cycle of life could be observed almost anywhere you looked. Until all this had happened, tragedy and death on a more personal level had only touched her briefly when Granny Jeter died. Even that had been softened by the fact that her life had been a long and happy one. While it was true that Granny Jeter's life had been touched by several moments of tragedy there had been many people who loved her and were loved by her. Ry couldn't imagine how she could possibly bear losing either of her parents.

Kate walked into the room and brought a halt to Ry's morose thoughts.

"Thanks for seeing me," Kate said as she approached the bed.

"Why wouldn't I see you? I saw you the other night." She stopped and shrugged. "At least I think I did." She was surprised to see Kate dressed in sweats. She wore them around the house occasionally, but she never wore them when she went out.

Kate gave a strained smile. "How are you feeling?"

"You probably know more about that than I do. I can only imagine how badly my mom is pestering the doctors and nurses."

As Kate stepped closer, Ry could see the dark shadows beneath her eyes. She looked exhausted.

Kate sat in the large chair beside the bed. "Doreen has actually been very brave about the entire thing. You should be proud of both your parents. In fact, since you've been here the entire Shelton clan has pretty much taken over the waiting room."

"You never were much of a fan of the Shelton clan, were you?"

Kate looked surprised. "I love your family. They're just so… so…alive!" She shook her head. "Ry, you have to remember I grew up an only child. Sometimes, when I think back to when I was younger, I wonder if I was ever a child. You've met my parents. They're both so stiff-necked and concerned about public opinion that nothing else matters. Your parents are everything mine aren't." She stopped.

An uncomfortable silence fell over the room. Ry finally broke it. "You look tired."

Kate dropped her head and began to fiddle with the hem of her shirt.

Ry saw a tear glisten in the light as it fell. "Kate, please don't cry."

The plea simply made Kate cry harder. "Ry, I'm so sorry. I swear I never meant to do anything that would hurt you." She wiped the tears from her cheeks. "When I first saw you in the emergency room, I thought you were dead and there were so many things…" Her voice broke. "I'm sorry."

Ry wanted to hold Kate, but she was out of reach. "Don't cry. It's all right. I know things hadn't been right between us for a long time. Most of it was my fault. I got too wrapped up in work."

"I should have been there to help you and support you," Kate said. "I know sales had dropped a little."

Ry suppressed a snort. "Actually, sales had all but stopped. If things had continued as they were, I would have been forced to close the store in two months. I might not have even made it that long."

Kate gasped loudly. "You never told me things were that serious. Why didn't you say something?"

"I don't know. Just too stubborn, I guess. I didn't want you to think I had failed again."

"What do you mean again? What did you ever fail at?"

"Come on, Kate. Don't patronize me. My God, I've blown five relationships. I can't hold a job. I've failed as a business owner. I could never shoot a deer but I killed a man without hesitation. How much more should I list?" She was glad the cardiac monitor was no longer attached, because she could feel her heart racing.

"At least you had the gumption to do something. Don't you realize that had it been left up to me, we would both be dead? I just hunkered there under that couch like a scared rabbit." She took a deep breath and looked up at Ry. "I was so angry with myself about that and I took it out on you. I'm sorry."

"The night before I was shot I had a dream," Ry began. "I dreamed that Granny Jeter was back at her cabin. It was so real, Kate. I sat on the side of my bed and talked to her. She told me there was a storm coming. She told me I had to be strong and fight."

Kate leaned forward in the chair. Ry looked at the woman with whom she had thought she would spend the rest of her life. "She also told me to be kind and forgive. At first, I thought she was talking about you, but I realized she wasn't, because there's nothing to forgive. We're both equally responsible." She swallowed the lump building in her throat. "This time I mean it when I say I hope you have a good life. And, I hope you and I can always be friends."

Kate stood. "Can I still give you a hug?"

"I certainly hope so."

They held each other and cried for a moment before Ry pulled away. "So, who is this nameless woman who stole your heart?"

Kate laughed through her tears and returned to the chair. "Are you sure you want to know?"

"No. Not really, but if I don't know her real name, I'm guessing you'll soon grow tired of the names I choose for her." She smiled to take some of the sting from the words. She prayed she'd be able to maintain some manner of civility when she finally met the woman.

"Her name is Destiny."

Ry looked at her in disbelief. "Kate, tell me she's old enough to buy beer."

Kate made a face at her. "She's only three years younger than me."

They talked for several more minutes, until the door opened. At first all Ry saw was a large bouquet of flowers. She couldn't stop from smiling when saw who was delivering them.

"I thought these might brighten your room." Nicole stopped when she saw Kate. "Sorry, I didn't realize you had company. I seem to have an awful sense of timing. Anyway, I just wanted to drop these off and check to see how you were doing." Nicole sat the flowers on a table beside the bed.

"They're beautiful. Thank you," Ry said.

Kate hopped up. "Don't go. I was about to leave. I need to drive back to Jackson City tonight and should get started."

Ry didn't like the idea of Kate being on the road alone. The crazy guy hadn't shown any interest in harming her so far, but who knew, he might change his mind and think she knew something. "Are you sure you want to drive back tonight?"

Kate nodded. "It's okay." She hesitated a moment. "I won't be alone, so don't worry." She gave Ry a quick hug. "Besides, it's you he seems to be interested in, so I'll be fine."

Her flippant remark worried Ry. "Kate, I'm serious. This guy is crazy."

Kate seemed surprised by Ry's sudden concern. "I'm sorry if I seemed glib. Trust me, I've been watching. I promise I'll lock my doors as soon as I get into the car. You know what a chicken I am. I never stop for strangers." She turned her attention to Nicole. "You're the game warden who brought Ry in, aren't you?"

"Yes. Nicole Matthews. You were in the emergency room, weren't you?" Nicole placed her hat on the foot of Ry's bed.

Ry watched as Kate introduced herself and the two women chatted. It seemed slightly surreal to watch them. Her ex-lover and the woman she hoped to… She stopped herself sharply. What in the heck was she thinking? She had just ended a relationship. The last thing she needed was to start another one. She found her eyes traveling the long line of Nicole's back. As she did she was struck by a wave of desire so strong she felt sweat pop out on her brow. She glanced away and flushed when she found Kate watching her with a slightly amused looked on her face.

"Nicole, it was nice to actually meet you. I wanted to thank you for everything you did for Ry," Kate said as she started toward the door. "Ry, I'll give you a call tomorrow to check on you." She turned back. "Oh, Ry, you should be careful about doing anything too stimulating that would raise your blood pressure." She pointed to her own forehead and smiled. "It might give you a headache."

Ry felt her face turn several shades of red as Kate giggled and left.

Nicole continued to look at the door for a moment after it closed. "How long were you two together?"

Ry scooted back against the bed trying to find a more comfortable spot. "We were lovers for six years. We've been friends for about six and half years."

Nicole nodded slowly.

"She's involved with someone else. I'm honestly not sure what we are now." She stopped. "I guess I should be angry she cheated on me, but I don't seem to feel anything."

Nicole looked at the flowers and rubbed her hand over her cheek. "I'm sorry if I came on so strong the other day. It was just—" She picked up her hat and began to spin it. "When I first saw you at the fundraiser, I couldn't take my eyes off you. I couldn't quit thinking of you. Then when I found you at the cabin," she swallowed. "I thought you were dead and all I could think of was I never got to know you. I had blown my chance and it was too late." She glanced at Ry and smiled. "I don't want to make that mistake again."

Maybe it was the two recent brushes with death, but for whatever reason Ry felt compelled not to waste a single moment.

"Well, it's not too late," Ry said. "I have to admit I'm sort of looking forward to seeing how far this would go."

Nicole stepped closer to the bed. "How far do you want it to go?"

Ry smiled. "How far are you willing to go?" Her heart was racing. She couldn't remember the last time she had wanted anyone so badly.

Nicole continued slowly to make her way toward Ry. "I'm willing to take you all the way there and back." As she came alongside the bed, she trailed her hand along Ry's leg.

A sharp pain shot through Ry's head. She grabbed her head and winced.

Nicole suddenly paled. "Oh, I'm sorry. Are you okay? Should I call for a nurse?"

The pain slowly subsided enough that Ry could grin. "I always hated it when Kate was right," she said.

"Maybe I should go so you can rest," Nicole offered.

"If you don't mind, I'd like for you to stay and just talk to me."

Nicole nodded. "I can do that." She looked at Ry and winked, "but I have to warn you that all the time I'm talking to you, I'm probably going to be thinking about all the other things I *could* be doing with you."

Ry smiled back. "You should be careful telling me things like that. I'm liable to be thinking the same thing."

Nicole clutched her chest. "You're a cruel woman, Rylene Shelton."

She had called her *Rylene*. "Dear God, you've been talking to my mother." Ry closed her eyes and covered her face with her hands. "I'm terrified to even think of what she's probably told you."

"Hey, your mom and I are tight. I've been officially invited to dinner on the first Sunday after you're released. She's going to bake me a carrot cake."

Ry dropped her hands and stared at Nicole. "She won't even bake me a carrot cake. How do you rate so highly?"

Nicole studied her nails before slowly polishing them on the front of her shirt. "All I had to do was save her little girl.

She's already taught me to crochet a basic stitch. And, your dad is going to show me how to use my new router as soon as you get home."

"Well, I'm certainly glad I could be of such service to you."

Nicole sat in the chair beside the bed. "That's just the beginning." She tapped her finger on her chin. "Let me see if I can even remember it all. Michelle is going to make *enchiladas verdes*."

"No, she's not. She only makes those for special occasions."

Nicole ignored her and continued. "Annie has already sent me a batch of her fudge pecan brownies."

"Oh my gosh, they are so good," Ry said and practically drooled.

"Elise is going to make fried chicken."

"Stop. Please. Stop. I've had nothing but an IV drip and hospital food for days." She looked at Nicole and rolled her eyes. "And trust me the IV drip was the better of the two."

Nicole started laughing as she stood and stepped closer to the bed. She leaned over and kissed Ry softly. "I promise to take you to all of your favorite places as soon as you're able."

Ry kissed her and slowly traced a finger along Nicole's cheek. "You should be careful. I have an extremely healthy appetite."

"I'm counting on it," Nicole whispered as she kissed Ry deeply.

CHAPTER FOURTEEN

Two days later Ry finally received word that she was being released. She was told she would have to wait until the doctor signed the release papers. By six in the morning, she had showered, dressed and packed her meager belongings into the small bag her mother had brought earlier in the week. She was more than ready to leave.

By the time her parents arrived at nine she was so anxious she could hardly sit still. When the doctor hadn't arrived by noon, Ry was ready to leave without his signature. She had to force herself to remain calm. When he finally did arrive at three, Ry was sleeping in the chair. Her father woke her.

"Dr. Price is here," he said quietly.

Ry sat up. "I didn't realize you were actually coming in," she said. "I thought you were just going to sign the paperwork."

He nodded. "I just wanted to chat with you a minute before you leave." He glanced at her parents. "I'd like to speak to her privately, if you don't mind."

Her parents left, but not without a worried backward glance.

"What's wrong?" Ry asked before the door was even closed.

"Nothing's wrong. I just wanted to tell you something." He sat on the side of the bed across from her chair. "I wanted to let you know I found my dog." His salon-perfect tan looked out of place in the nearly colorless room.

"That's great." She noticed that he kept gazing around the room rather than looking at her.

He nodded again. "How did you know where he was?"

Ry wondered how much she should tell him. The last thing she wanted was to spend another week here.

He seemed to sense her hesitation and finally looked at her. "I've already signed your release papers and you must know that I can't repeat anything you tell me."

Ry tapped her finger on the chair arm. "I believe you're limited to what you can tell someone about my health records. I'm not so sure about anything else," she countered.

"Would it make any difference if I give you my word that anything you tell me will never go beyond these walls?"

Ry shrugged. At the moment, she really didn't care who he told as long as it didn't delay her release from the hospital. "All I can tell you is when I shook your hand that day, I saw something. I suppose the best way to describe it would be an image. I saw a German shepherd sitting next to a tree with that swing beside him."

"That's all?" he asked.

She tried to recall exactly what she had seen. "I saw the dog tied to a tree."

He clicked the pen he was holding several times. "Has this happened before? I mean, have you had other visions, either before or after you were shot?"

"Nope. It was just that one time," she lied. She didn't see any point to telling him about the other times.

He looked at her as if he doubted her, but finally stood. "If it happens again, let me know. It might be an indication there's something deeper that we missed."

"The CAT scan didn't show anything else, did it?" she asked slightly worried.

"No. It looked normal. But, if you continue to have these hallucinations we need to be concerned."

She promised to call him if anything else happened.

He suddenly held out his hand. There was something about the deliberate way in which he offered his hand that made Ry wonder if he was testing her.

She took his hand and smiled. "See, no hallucinations."

Before she could dwell any deeper on why she had lied, he started talking. "I wouldn't worry about it. People respond differently to medications. You were on a fairly strong sedative." He nodded, as if he were satisfied with his conclusion.

"It's time to get you home," he said cheerfully. "I believe they've already set you up with an appointment to be in my office in two weeks to have the stitches removed."

"Yes," Ry said.

"Good. You probably won't have much of an appetite for a while, so it's important that you eat good, healthy food. Drink plenty of water. For the next six weeks, I don't want you to do anything more strenuous than walking. You can walk, eat, sleep or sit quietly. You shouldn't try to read too much or watch much television. It could cause you to experience headaches." He glanced at her chart. "Did they go over the prescriptions I ordered?"

"Yes."

"Good. Take them as directed." He motioned to the bruising on her face. "That will disappear in a few days."

An orderly came in with a wheelchair. "Are you ready?" he asked.

"Call my office if you have any problems or you have questions," Dr. Price said as stood and left the room.

Ry had to force herself to get sedately into the wheelchair rather than run past it. She was so happy to be leaving she felt as if she could have easily floated down the three flights of stairs and right on out into the parking lot.

As she allowed herself to be wheeled out, she ran a hand over her face. She had lied to Dr. Price. When she shook his hand, she had seen the dog again, still tied to the tree. Why had he lied about finding the dog? She was too tired to give the matter any serious thought, but felt certain he had been testing her.

* * *

As soon as her mom's car turned off the main highway onto the road that led back to her parents' house, Ry felt a sense of peace settle over her. "I'm so glad to be out of that place," she said more to herself than her parents.

"Amen to that," her father said as he leaned forward in the driver's seat and stretched his arms over the steering wheel. "You'd think a place as big and expensive as that hospital could offer a decent cup of coffee."

Her mom swatted his arm. "Seth, enough with the coffee already. I'll make you a pot when we get home. I swear. I've heard nothing but complaining about how bad the coffee was for a solid week." She dug through her purse. "I swear I can't find anything in this purse," she grumbled.

"What are you looking for?" Seth asked.

"I can't find my keys. I don't know what I've done with them."

Seth glanced at her and shook his head. "See what happens when you can't get a decent cup of coffee," he said and grinned.

"Horse hockey. What does coffee have to do with me finding my keys?"

"Doreen, sweetie, your keys are here in the ignition. We're in your car."

She looked at the ignition as if she had never seen it before and shook her head. "I swear I'm getting senile."

Seth swung the car into the driveway and stopped in front of the house. "Nope, you just need a good cup of coffee and some rest." He opened his door. "Let's get you two inside. I think we could all use a long lazy day."

"Ry, if you'd like to take a nap, we have Granny's room made up for you," her mom said as they entered the house.

"I think I'll sit in the living room for a while," Ry said. "I'm sick of being in bed."

"That sounds like a great idea for both of you," her dad said. "I'm going to go put the car in the garage and then I need to tend to a couple of things. You two should sit down and rest."

Ry sat on the couch. From there she had a great view of the front field.

"All I've done is sit," Doreen protested, but she looked relieved when she settled into the recliner and kicked the footrest up.

Ry's father returned with a pillow and a couple of light blankets. "I thought you might need these if you decide to take a nap." He handed one of the blankets to his wife before he placed the remaining items beside Ry. "I'll be back in a few minutes." He went outside.

"He looks happy to be home," Ry said.

"You know how he is," her mother said. "Never still for more than a few minutes. I swear if I hadn't made him sit down, he'd have started doing repairs to the drywall in the waiting room."

Ry smiled. "I'm sorry you two had to go through this, and I want you to know I appreciate everything you have done for me."

Her mom closed her eyes and gave a slight wave of her hand. "Rylene, we're your parents. That doesn't stop simply because you're grown."

Ry studied her mother for a long moment. She hadn't mentioned the dream about Granny Jeter to her mother. "Mom, do you or did you ever have a pair of sapphire earrings? There was something about a little gold heart."

Her mom blinked in surprise. "My goodness, what made you ask about those earrings?"

"You don't have earrings like that, do you? I don't remember ever seeing you wear anything even similar."

Her mom sat staring at her. "I had a pair years ago. My grandmother gave them to me. They had belonged to my mother." She frowned slightly.

"What happened to the earrings?" Ry persisted.

"I don't know. I lost one of them just after you were born." A shadow of sadness darted across her face. "Why are you asking me about those earrings? You never saw them. How did you even know about them?"

Ry licked her lips. "This is going to sound a little weird, but when I was at the cabin, I had a dream. Granny Jeter was in the dream. She told me to tell you that the earring you lost fell behind the baseboard at the back of your dresser. She described it as a little gold heart with a sapphire in the center."

"Was this before or after you were hurt?" her mom asked with a worried look.

"It was the night before." Ry hesitated. "Mom, I know this sounds a little crazy, but I think Granny Jeter tried to warn me about what was going to happen."

"In what way?"

Ry told her mom everything she could remember about the dream.

Her mom nodded after Ry finished telling her story. "Granny believed in the old ways. On rare occasions, she would start talking about how things were when she was a child. She always told us her mother had what she called 'the second sight.'"

"What was that?"

"According to Granny, her mother could see things before they happened. I guess we would consider her a psychic now."

"Do you believe that's possible?" Ry asked.

Her mom tilted her head. "I believe the vast majority of those places where they claim to read your palm or see your future in tarot cards are a fraud." She stopped and slowly nodded. "But, I have to admit that I've seen and heard, from people I trust, of things happening that are beyond explanation." She took the blanket off the chair arm and spread it over her legs. "I'm going to tell you something I've never told anyone. Not even your father." She looked at Ry. "I was afraid if I told, everyone would think I was being silly, or worse." Her eyebrows shot up to emphasize her concern.

Ry pounded the pillow into a comfortable wad beneath her head and stretched out on the couch.

"When I was about eleven or twelve, Ray Grayson, the man who usually delivered eggs and milk to Granny, disappeared. He left one morning with a load of eggs and milk and seemingly dropped off the face of the earth. The police organized search parties of the local men and they searched for days but never found anything. Then one night long after we had gone to bed, I heard a knock at the door." Her eyes took on a faraway look as her memory went back to that night. "I slept in that same little cubby you did in the cabin. There was a knothole in one of the boards separating the cubby and the living room."

Ry smiled and said, "I know what you're talking about. It's still there. The board would be hidden when clothes were hanging on that rod."

"That's the one," her mother said and nodded. "So, on that night when I heard someone knocking, I peeked through the hole and saw it was Mrs. Grayson. She and Granny were talking low, but I could hear them. Mrs. Grayson had come to ask for Granny's help. They sat down on the couch. I could tell Granny was sad, and then, she tells Mrs. Grayson that her husband was dead. He had been shot and robbed by a man in a green truck with a tent."

"A tent?"

Her mother nodded. "That's what Granny said. And of course, it didn't make any sense to Mrs. Grayson or me at the time, but a week later, a circus arrived in town and there was the green truck with a tent. The tent was a sign on the truck door advertising the circus. I never knew how or why, but the police investigated and they found the man. He still had Mr. Grayson's pocket watch."

"Do you think it was just a coincidence that Granny was right?" Ry asked.

Her mom seemed to consider the question a minute before answering. "Honestly, I've never known what to make of it. I just sort of put it out of my mind."

"Did you ever ask Granny how she knew?"

Her mom shook her head vigorously. "No. I would never have wanted her to know I'd been spying on her."

They sat in silence for a while, each seemingly lost in her own thoughts.

"Do you think she was right about the earring?" Ry asked cautiously.

"There's only one way to find out," her mom said as she lowered the footrest on the recliner. "You stay here and rest."

"No way. If you're going to look, I'm going with you."

"I'll grab some tools," her mom said as she scurried off.

As soon as they stepped into the kitchen, they ran into Ry's father.

He stared at the tools in his wife's hands. "Doreen, what in the dickens are you doing with those?" He glanced at Ry. Aren't you supposed to be resting?" he asked.

"I was walking. The doctor told me to walk."

Before he could say more Doreen thrust the tools into his hands. "Since you're so handy, follow me and I'll show you where you're going to use them." She turned and left without waiting for him to say anything further.

He looked at Ry. "What in the devil is that woman up to?"

Ry gave a half-hearted shrug. "I think we should do as she says."

"Honey, I always do as she says," he said as he took off after his wife.

In the bedroom, her mom was already removing items from the dresser top. "You'll need to drag this away from the wall," she told him.

He pulled the dresser out from the wall. "Okay, what am I doing now?"

Doreen turned to Ry. "Did she say where exactly?"

"Did who say?" Seth cut in.

They both ignored him. "No. She just said behind the baseboard at the back of the dresser."

"Who?" Seth asked again.

"Granny Jeter," both women answered at once.

Seth closed his eyes and took a deep breath. Then he picked up the tools and turned to his wife. "So you want me to remove the baseboard now, I suppose?"

Doreen smiled sweetly at him.

He shook his head as he knelt down and pulled the board free. "Now what?" he asked.

Before they could answer, he leaned down closer to the opening. "What's that?" He reached behind the baseboard. When he turned to face them, he had a tiny gold heart in his hand. Sunlight caught the small sapphire as he turned the earring.

Doreen took it from him. "Oh my goodness, I lost this earring a few months after you were born, Rylene." She held the earring before her. Tears glistened in her eyes. "I was sick over losing it. This pair of earrings is the only thing I have that belonged to my mother." She continued to stare at them. "My parents didn't have life insurance. So, when Granny took us in she had to sell off practically everything my parents owned to help pay off their debts. She refused to sell three pieces. She gave me Mama's earrings. She gave Daddy's watch to Donny and his gold cufflinks to Hank."

Seth hammered the baseboard back in place. After it was secure, he stood staring down at it.

Ry knew he wanted to go get his caulk gun. The man was obsessed with caulking.

Instead, he sighed and moved the dresser back against the wall. Only then did he turn to his wife and daughter.

"Will someone please tell me what's going on?"

Doreen hugged him suddenly. "Rylene, take your father back to the living room and tell him the dream you had about Granny Jeter." She took the tools from him. "I'll put these back, *exactly* where you had them," she added.

As they made their way back to the living room, Ry told him about the dream. How Granny had told her about the earring and about the coming storm. "Do you think she was trying to warn me?" she asked him as he helped her back onto the couch.

He sat in the recliner and popped up the footrest. "I can't answer that, but your Granny was different."

She frowned. "Different? What do you mean?"

He rubbed the back of his hand and glanced toward the hallway that led to the kitchen. "I've never told anyone this, not even your mother."

She knew better than to push him, so she sat quietly waiting.

He kept his eyes directed toward the hallway as he spoke. "Did your mom ever tell you anything about the day you were born?"

"No."

He nodded. "Granny Jeter was already living over by the pond, but she moved in here for a few weeks to help your mom. You weren't due until the end of March." He smiled. "But you always had a mind of your own. I'll never forget. It was just before midnight when your mom woke me and told me it was time to go. Granny stayed here with the boys. When your mom and I reached the hospital I saw right away that something was wrong." He looked at her. "You know how doctors sometimes tell you a lot by not telling you anything?"

She nodded.

"Time just kept dragging by. I'd ask about your mom and they'd put me off with some lame explanation. They kept it up for thirty-six hours. I was almost crazy." He smiled sheepishly. "I called Granny and started blubbering about how the doctors wouldn't tell me anything and they weren't letting me back to see your mom. Next thing I know here comes this short, paper-thin, seventy-seven-year-old powerhouse. She'd called your Uncle Hank and Aunt Minnie, left Minnie with the kids and made Hank drive her to the hospital." He rubbed the back of his hand again. "She marched in. The word 'no' wasn't in her vocabulary that day. It took her about fifteen minutes to pin that doctor's ears back. We both went back to see your mom. I'll never forget how small she looked lying there." He shook his head as if trying to erase the image. "Granny started pressing around on your mom's abdomen. That young doctor stepped in to try to stop her and she just went totally wildcat on him. She had him by the ear and asked him which catalog he'd ordered his medical degree from, and before he could even think of a response she started asking him why he hadn't done this or that for Doreen. Then she turned to a nurse and tells her to go get a stack of towels and a pan of warm water and that nurse did exactly as she had been told." He laughed aloud. "She soaked those towels and placed them on your mom's abdomen. When they'd start to cool, she'd wet them again. You were born an hour later at two forty-five in the afternoon." He grew serious again. "When you were born, Granny looked down at you and I saw tears in her eyes. It was the only time I ever saw her cry and it scared me. I just stood there and prayed that your mom didn't see. She'd already been through so much. I couldn't bear the thought of her having to hear there was something wrong with you."

Ry wondered why she had never heard this story.

"Later when Granny and I were alone, I finally got the courage to ask her what was wrong with you. She looked me square in the eye and told me there wasn't a thing wrong with you. But I knew better and told her so. I told her I saw her crying." He looked at Ry for a long moment before he continued. "She sat me down and told me you would be our special child. You would be the child who kept me awake nights and who would turn my hair gray. You would create your own world."

"Dad," Ry protested. "I never caused you sleepless nights, did I?"

He tilted his head. "I did worry more about you than the boys, I suppose, but it was just because the world can be so much more dangerous for women."

Before she could say anything, he held up a hand.

"She also said you'd be the child who brought the most joy not only to us, but to multitudes."

Ry's eyes popped. "Multitudes? Jeez, what did she think I was going to do, become a comedian?"

Her father didn't join her levity. "She said if you weren't careful, the joy would come at a high price for you. I sense a difference in you, Ry, and honestly, it frightens me."

She started to protest, but again he stopped her.

"I'm not saying I'm frightened of you. I'm frightened for you." He glanced toward the hallway again. "This past week has been crazy and I'm scared it's only the beginning. I don't want you to go through this alone. If there's something going on with you, your family needs to know."

They both heard the footsteps at the same time.

"Think about it," he added softly as her mom entered the room.

CHAPTER FIFTEEN

Ry gave a sigh of relief when she finally stretched out between the cool, crisp sheets. She tried not to think about the bed she truly missed sleeping in, the bed she had shared with Kate. Tonight she wouldn't have to worry about the endless stream of nurses coming in to check on her, or to wake her to give her a sleeping pill, or to ask her silly questions about what day it was or how many fingers they were holding up. Tonight she was home. She turned out the lamp.

There was a full moon. She watched its warm yellow glow cast shadows of the gently swaying pecan tree limbs across her window shade. As she watched the gracefully moving shadows, she imagined them conducting a mighty symphony. She could almost hear the beautiful strains of music as she drifted off to sleep.

She hadn't slept long before the voices started. At first, they were merely hushed whispers, but they steadily grew louder. It took a while to realize that she had heard some of the voices before. She struggled to remember where and finally it came to her. They had been there when she was talking to Granny Jeter.

She tried to call her Granny, but couldn't make her voice rise above those clamoring for her attention. There were so many speaking at once that she couldn't distinguish what they were saying. She tried to ignore them. She sang as loudly as she could to overpower them. She put her hands over her ears to block them. The harder she fought to drive them away the louder and more insistent they became. Ry began to run. She ran as fast as she could. Soon her lungs were burning and her heart pounded against her chest. Sweat burned her eyes. When she could no longer run, she fell to the ground. The voices pounded at her like angry fists. They poured over her until she could no longer move. Soon she was unable breathe.

Ry's eyes flew open and she sat bolt upright. She fought to control the waves of terror washing over her. The last thing her parents needed now was to be awakened by her hysterical screaming. They had been through enough already.

It took her a moment to determine that what had bound her arms and legs together in almost mummy-like style were sheets drenched with sweat, the top sheet holding her completely entangled. When she finally freed herself, she got up and sat in the rocker beside the bed. She knew she'd had a bad dream, but couldn't remember the details. What had happened in the dream? Slowly she realized that nothing had actually happened, other than she ran from the voices. The voices had been what frightened her so badly.

Ry began to shiver. Her sweat-drenched pajamas were making her cold. She got up as quietly as possible and found another pair in the dresser.

She opened the shade on the window, wrapped herself in the blanket from the bed and sat back down in the rocker. Time slipped by unnoticed as she stared out the window and tried to make sense of the voices. Maybe there was brain damage after all. The doctor had warned her that problems might continue to appear several months after the initial injury.

She tried to recall the voices, to remember what had they been saying. Should she have her parents take her back to the hospital? She'd heard of people who heard voices, voices that told them to do evil things. Was she a danger to people? Her parents! Her heart nearly stopped with the thought. Could she be endangering her parents? She stood up. If the doctors decided she was dangerous, they would commit her. That would kill her parents. She couldn't put them through that. She needed to leave. Sweat was pouring down her face. She shook the blanket off and started toward the window to open it. Suddenly, a movement at the edge of the moonlight caught her attention. She stood frozen as a doe with a fawn stepped into the light and made their way over to drink from the small garden pond. As she watched, the doe lifted her head and seemed to stare directly at her. A sense of peace settled over Ry.

She collapsed into the rocker and pulled the blanket back up around her shoulders. Her pajamas were damp again and she was cold. She continued to stare out the window long after the doe and fawn had left. The clock in the entryway chimed one... two...three and still she sat. It was only after she caught the soothing aroma of freshly brewed coffee that she climbed back into bed and slept.

When Ry woke, the room was flooded with light. She fumbled for the clock beside the bed and squinted to read the time. It was after three. Shocked, she got up and went to shower.

She found her mom in the front yard working in her flowerbed.

"There you are," her mom said, and beamed. "I'm so glad you were able to sleep and finally get some rest."

"I can't believe I slept so late," Ry said. Torn over whether she should tell her parents about the voices or not, she brushed her hand across the top of an Esperanza bush. Maybe the voices would go away as her brain healed.

"Sit down on the bench and keep me company. I'm almost finished here."

Ry sat down. The sun felt good on her shoulders.

"Your brothers will be over for dinner on Sunday," her mom said. "They would be here sooner, but you know how busy they are at this time of year."

"I'm sure they're behind with all the time they spent at the hospital. Even before that they spent a day or two working on the fence at the store," Ry said.

"Don't worry about them. They're young and strong; working a few extra hours won't hurt them." She started gathering her garden tools.

Ry stood to help her.

"No. No. You sit down. You don't need to be bending over or doing anything strenuous for six weeks."

"I feel fine. I can't go six weeks without doing anything." She stopped and sat back down. "Sorry. I'll try not to be a grumpy patient."

"I would greatly appreciate that," her mom said and smiled. "Since you seem to be feeling so rambunctious, what would you think about inviting a few other people?"

"Who did you have in mind?"

"Your uncles, of course. The people who dropped by the hospital—Victor Orozco and his wife, Wilma Brown and Nicole Matthews." She stopped working. "Rylene, I don't know any other way to do something than straight out, so what's going on between you and Kate? She practically lived at the hospital while you were there. I tried to talk to her, but she seemed so evasive and I didn't want her to think I was trying to grill her."

"You mean like you're grilling me?" Ry said with a smile.

"Oh, sweetie, I'm your mom. That gives me license to make your life miserable. So what's going on with you two?"

Ry felt a strange sense of betrayal at even considering telling her mom about Kate's affair. It was something private between them. Or was she simply ashamed that she had been so indifferent to their relationship that Kate had felt compelled to cheat on her? She took the easy way out. "We've decided it would be best for both of us if we went our separate ways."

But, her mom wasn't so easily put off. "Is there someone else involved?"

"Yes." She couldn't lie if asked directly.

Her mom was quiet for a moment. "Is Kate still speaking to you?"

"Mom, it's not me having the affair," Ry sputtered, stunned that her mother would think it was her. As soon as the words left her mouth, Ry realized her mom had outsmarted her. How many times had she and her brothers ratted themselves out in response to their mom's simple questions? "You played me."

"Nonsense. I was just trying to find out if I should invite Kate on Sunday or not."

"We're still friends. So if you want to invite her, that's fine."

"You don't think she'll bring her new girlfriend, do you? That might be a bit awkward."

Ry laughed. "Mom, the Shelton clan scared Kate half to death when we were together. I'm not sure she'll even show now that she doesn't feel obligated."

Her mom seemed on the verge of saying something else. Instead, she stood up quickly. "Are you hungry?" she asked. "I had a club salad for lunch. I made enough for both of us. I'll go get it."

Ry went to the other end of the garden and sat on the glider. Even though she had only walked a short distance, it felt good to sit down. She wondered how long it would be before she felt like her old self. How could she still be so tired after sleeping all day? The voices hadn't completely disappeared after she had gone back to bed that morning. She vaguely remembered they had kept trying to wiggle their way back into her dream, but something held them just out of reach from her.

Her breath caught as a hummingbird zoomed up and hovered less than a foot from her. It wavered from side to side a moment before speeding off to investigate a trellis filled with Turk's Cap. A wave of fear gripped her as she began to search the area around her. The man who had shot at her was still out there somewhere. Could he be watching her now? She glanced about. There were numerous outbuildings and trees where he could hide in complete safety. Her heart began to pound harder until she could barely breathe. The horizon seemed to tilt at an odd angle and she grew dizzy.

Relax. I'm here. You're safe. He'll never hurt you again.

"Granny Jeter?" Ry forced herself to slow her breathing. Soon the world around her returned normal. The brilliant green wings of a hummingbird reflected from the flowers on the trellis. As she continued to watch, she began to spot the flying jewels throughout the garden. Not only were there hummingbirds everywhere, but butterflies as well. By the time her mom reappeared with a plate and a tray, she had regained control of herself.

"I saw a doe and fawn out back last night," Ry said, hoping no residue of her moment of panic was visible.

"Really?" her mom said.

"I woke up and had trouble going back to sleep." Ry rushed on with her story. "There was a full moon. I raised the shade to look out. They came up and drank from the pond for a bit and then left."

"We used to see a large buck occasionally," her mom said. "But we've not seen him in a few weeks." She set about scrubbing the birdbath. "Your father thinks a poacher might have shot him."

"Nicole said that Nat Zucker was right about a poacher being over there around his place."

"She seems very nice," her mom said casually.

Ry tried to see if her mom was working up to something. "She seems to be," Ry agreed.

"I'm glad you agreed to invite her for dinner on Sunday. You know she spent several hours at the hospital with us. She has a horribly busy work schedule, with only two game wardens for this entire county. Can you imagine being responsible for protecting all that territory?" She used the water hose to refill the birdbath. "Did you know game wardens are certified police officers? If she catches someone speeding she can give them a ticket."

"Yes. I think I heard that somewhere." She wondered where her mother intended to go with this conversation.

"She can be on the job for days at a time." She turned off the hose and started in on the feeders. "I can only imagine how hard that must be on a relationship."

Ah, there it was. "If she's that busy, I doubt she even has time to think about a relationship," Ry said as nonchalantly as she could.

"Oh, there's always time to start things," her mom said. "It's finishing them that most people don't have time for."

Ry felt a bit of a bite in her mom's words. "Do you not like Nicole?"

Her mom stopped working and looked at her. "That's not it at all. I'm eternally grateful to her for saving your life." She held Ry's gaze. "I was only saying that anyone in a relationship with her would have to be extremely understanding about her job, the long hours and the constant danger."

Ry sat quietly while her mom continued to work. Flirting with Nicole had been fun and she wouldn't be opposed to taking it further, but she certainly hadn't been contemplating a relationship. Had she?

Her mother finished filling the last of the feeders. "I'm going in and get cleaned up. Then I'll start dinner."

"I think I'm going to sit and watch the birds for a while," Ry said.

Later that night when Ry went to bed, the previous night's scenario repeated. It happened again on the third night. As before, after the voices woke her, she would sit staring out the window until she heard her parents get up. Only then could she go back to bed and sleep until late afternoon. It wasn't until the fourth night when the voices started that she finally found some relief.

As the voices pulled at every shred of her sanity something within her suddenly snapped and a raw power unlike anything she had ever felt before surged through her. As the power intensified, the voices grew calmer. They didn't go away or lessen in number. They simply seemed to become less aggressive. Somewhere deep in her core she heard herself requesting only one voice at a time and it happened.

The single voice was eerily familiar. It took her a moment to realize she had heard it the night she had spoken to Granny Jeter. It was the voice of the young woman who had wanted her mother to find her diary. As soon as Ry recognized the voice, a visual image appeared. It didn't appear in a human form but rather in shades of dull colors. Sad colors.

"Please help me," the image pleaded.

"Who are you? Who is your mother and how do I find her?"

"I'm Lilly. My mother's name is Jankowski. You have to tell her about the diary, please."

"Where does your mother live?"

"She's at home. You have to tell her about the diary. It's hidden behind the fake panel in my closet."

"I need to know where your mother lives. What's her first name?"

The image faded.

When it disappeared, so did the other voices. Ry stretched her body until her leg muscles threatened to cramp. She felt at peace. She fell asleep with a smile on her face and slept soundly through the night.

CHAPTER SIXTEEN

Ry woke to the sound of birds chattering around the backyard feeders. When she got up to shower she sensed a new power within her. She felt her shoulders straighten and she stood a little taller. The biggest change was she knew who she truly was and her purpose in life. She had been searching for something all her life. It was so painfully clear; she marveled that it had taken her so long to figure it out. She was a searcher, a seeker and had been her entire life.

Dressed in jeans, a long-sleeved shirt and boots, she stood in front of the mirror and combed her hair, being careful of the surgical wound on her forehead. The bruises on her face had faded completely. She would continue to be respectful of her recent injuries, but she knew without a doubt that she had nothing to fear from them. She stared at herself in the mirror. In essence, today was the first day of her true life. Today she would begin searching. She would find Lilly's mom somehow and she would pass on Lilly's message. Seeking people and things would be her life's work. She placed the comb on the dresser. It was time to start.

When Ry walked into the kitchen, her parents were at the table having coffee. "Good morning," she called cheerfully.

They looked up, clearly surprised by her sudden appearance. Both of them frowned as they watched her pour her coffee.

"You look...rested," her mom said.

"I slept straight through the night."

Her father glanced at her boots and then back at her. "Dr. Price said it would take a while before you started to feel better." He looked more closely at her. "Did you use something to cover those bruises?"

"No. They're just finally starting to fade." Ry sat at the table with them. "So, what time is this shindig kicking off?"

Her mom was still watching her. "Your brothers will be here around ten. The girls are going to help me cook."

After breakfast Ry used the computer in her father's office to search for Lilly Jankowski. She finally found an obituary. Lilly had committed suicide in 2001. Her mother Irene Jankowski had discovered the body. According to the obituary, Lilly and her mom lived in Los Angeles. Ry checked the white pages and found a listing for Irene Jankowski.

She reached for a notepad that rested beneath a small box with a glass top. Inside the box was an arrowhead she and her father had found when she was about six. She opened the box and lifted out the arrowhead. The world spun as images of a battle filled her head. She dropped the arrowhead back into the box and closed the lid. It took her a moment to catch her breath. She pushed the pad and box away and extracted a smaller notepad from beneath a stack of envelopes. Her hand shook as she jotted the number and address on the notepad. She forced herself to focus on Irene Jankowski. How should she go about contacting this woman? She shut down the computer, but continued to stare at the blank screen.

The contact had to remain anonymous. She had seen too many bad movies where the individual who had started out intending to help someone, ended up being the one who needed help. Whatever method she chose had to be completely safe. She had to ensure that the information she sent could never be traced back to her.

Ry drummed her fingers on the desk. There had to be a way. Then she saw the box of envelopes and smiled. It was time to go old school. She could send Irene Jankowski a letter through the postal system. The only drawback was that she would never know if Irene found the diary or not. She could mail the letter from San Antonio. There would be no way to trace it back to her.

Ry started back to the kitchen to see if she could help her mom with dinner. The front door burst open and James and Michelle's three kids came running to her. Before she could get away, the rest of her siblings and families poured in, each of them toting something intended for dinner.

Things were going great until Elise gave Ry a hug. As soon as they hugged, Ry's world melted into the burst of colors. She saw folded money tucked beneath what appeared to be fabric. She looked closer. "It's caught under the lining in your purse," she whispered.

Elise leaned back and stared at her. "What?"

Ry kept her voice low. "The money you lost. There's a hole in the lining of your purse. The money is in there."

Elise was about to say more but stopped when Lewis joined them.

"How are you feeling, Ry?" he asked. "You look amazing."

"I feel good," she said as she hugged him.

He stepped back and stared at her a moment before nodding. "You really look good."

Annie leaned in to hug Ry and again the burst of colors blinded her. She couldn't stop the cry of happiness when the image appeared before her. She managed to cover her excitement by announcing she was so happy to be home. Annie's eyebrows rose slightly at Ry's sudden outburst, but she seemed to accept it and move on. Ry had to bite her lip to keep from screaming out that Lewis and Annie would soon have a son.

The steady stream of people kept coming in. Victor Orozco along with his wife and son among them. He told her that the county cops still had her phone. She would have no problem getting it back since it wasn't considered evidence.

It was after two before Nicole arrived. She was dressed in her uniform. "I'm sorry to be so late," she said to Doreen. "I'm working today. I made an excuse to run by and check Nat Zucker's place again." She smiled. "Of course, I told them I intended to stop for lunch first."

"You go sit down by Ry and I'll find you a plate," Doreen said.

Ry saw the same look of surprise on Nicole's face as she had with everyone else. She simply smiled. She knew there was no way she could feel so special without looking different.

"Wow, you look amazing," Nicole said as she gave Ry a quick hug. "Getting out of that hospital has really done wonders for you."

"It should. All I do is sleep and eat," Ry said.

Doreen set a full plate in front of Nicole. "I got you a little of everything," she said as she handed Nicole a set of silverware and a second plate with a piece of carrot cake. She rushed off as someone called her name.

Nicole smiled and dug into the food. "Gosh, this is so good. I can't remember the last time I had a home cooked meal."

"I take it you don't cook?" Ry asked.

"I'm never home to cook. We're so shorthanded. Sometimes it seems like all I do is work."

Ry's uncles, Allen and Zack Shelton, joined them. They immediately began to question Nicole about this or that hunting law. Nicole was extremely gracious in answering their questions. As soon as Nicole had finished her meal, Ry pried her away from her uncles and led her outside.

"You should leave your hat off more often," Ry said as she ran her hand over Nicole's short, glossy hair.

Nicole smiled. "You don't like my Smokey Bear hat?" Before Ry could respond, she rushed on. "Your uncles certainly love hunting."

"I'm sorry about that. Once they get started it's hard to change the subject," Ry said as they strolled across the backyard.

"Don't worry about it. Stuff like that happens all the time." She glanced at Ry. The sunlight seemed to enhance the mischievous twinkle in her eyes. "So tell me what's going on with you. I can't believe how good you look. And you seem to be as good as new."

"I feel great," Ry admitted. "I'm chalking it up to good, clean country air and an extremely vigilant guardian angel."

Nicole shook her head. "You scared me half to death when I found you on that porch. I've been a game warden for eight years and I've seen my share of some horrible stuff. I've even seen a gunshot victim, but whew," she blew loudly. "I really thought you were dead."

They had reached the edge of the yard and had started along the road that ran alongside the barn. Ry slipped her hand around Nicole's arm. "They say I would have died without your quick thinking." She grinned and added, "I don't know how I can ever repay you."

Nicole's eyes twinkled. "Is this a working barn or just here for decoration?"

"There's no livestock in it, if that's what you mean."

"Really. Maybe I should check it out. You never know what might be hiding in there."

Ry turned to face Nicole. "I need to tell you something."

"That sounds rather ominous."

Ry shook her head. "I don't think so. I just want to be upfront. I'm right out of a relationship and I'm not looking for anything permanent right now."

Nicole nodded. "So, you're telling me you just want an occasional booty call."

Ry winced. "It sounds so much worse when you put it that way."

"Ry, I love my work. There are more days than I would care to tell you when I literally live in my car. I have more clothes in my car and my locker at the office than I do at home. I have no pets and I rent a room above my sister's garage. And as appealing as a booty call with you sounds, I honestly couldn't commit to it." She rubbed Ry's shoulder. "All I have to offer is what's right here. In all honesty, my phone could ring at any time."

Ry gave a quick glance back to make sure none of her nieces and nephews had decided to trail along. "Then I guess you should get in there and start checking the barn." She took Nicole's hand. "It could be dangerous. Maybe I should go with you."

"Are you sure you're okay?" Nicole asked in a serious tone. "I mean you were just released from the hospital."

"I'm actually sort of miserable right now," Ry admitted, "but I'm betting you'll be able to cure me again real soon."

They walked into the cool interior of the barn.

"There is a great hayloft up there," Ry said as she started for the ladder.

"Oh, no. I'm not about to be responsible for you climbing up a ladder. The last thing you need is to fall from that thing."

Ry turned to stare at her. "I swear to you I am fine."

Nicole didn't budge.

"Okay, come on, let's see what's back here." She led the way to the old feed storage room where miscellaneous items of unused furniture were now stored.

As soon as they were inside, Ry reached for her. "It's hard to believe someone hasn't snared you." She saw a sudden shift in Nicole's gaze and stepped back. "You're not involved with someone, are you?"

"There's no one here," Nicole countered.

Ry sighed and stepped farther away from her. "But, there is someone somewhere."

"Yes, but she understands that I'm not there for more than a couple of weeks a year, and her job keeps her from moving here." She reached out her hand.

Ry fought the temptation to take it. If the other woman didn't care, why should she? "I can't."

"I swear we have an understanding."

Ry shrugged. "I'm sure you do, but I just can't."

Nicole rubbed the back of her neck and finally nodded. "I understand."

They stood in silence for a moment.

"I guess I should go," Nicole said. "My lunch hour is over. I need to drive over and have another look around Nat Zucker's place." She looked at Ry. "No hard feelings, I hope."

"How can I be angry? You saved my life." She gave Nicole a quick hug before they started back toward the house.

CHAPTER SEVENTEEN

Ry had just entered the living room when she spied Daniel coming down the hallway from the kitchen tugging at his tucked in button-down shirt. Daniel normally wore T-shirts and jeans. He owned more T-shirts than anyone she knew. She suspected Elise had made him wear a dress shirt and slacks for today's get together. At five-foot-ten inches, Daniel was the shortest of her brothers. The majority of his height was in his torso, and because of this she had once teased him that he looked like Yogi Bear. As he got older and a little paunchier, the resemblance increased. She suppressed a smile as she envisioned him with a little hat and wide tie.

"Stop fussing with your clothes," she said as he walked into the room.

"Where have you been?" he asked as he studied her closely. He didn't wait for her to answer. "What's going on with you? You look different." He looked her up and down. "You look taller."

"I'm not slouching." She was normally five-foot-eight and today she was practically eye-to-eye with him.

He shook his head. "No. It's more than that. You look different. I don't know what it is exactly." He stared at her a moment. "You look like you should be in charge or something."

She laughed. "What would I be in charge of?"

Again, he shook his head. "I don't know. You're sort of intimidating, like if you weren't my sister, I think I'd be afraid of you."

"As well you should be afraid anyway, brother." She laughed as she grabbed his cheeks and pinched them sharply.

"Quit that. You know how much I hate that," he complained. He rubbed his cheeks. "You're as bad as Aunt Sophie. I came in here to hide from her."

Ry looked around quickly. "I didn't know she was here. Where is she?"

He continued to rub his cheeks. "In the kitchen the last time I saw her. She and Uncle Carl came in about twenty minutes ago."

Ry put an arm across his shoulders and lowered her voice. "Daniel, it's the weirdest thing. I feel better now than I've ever felt in my life." She arched her shoulders. "I swear I feel like I could take on you, Lewis and James and give you all a good thumping. I feel like there's nothing I can't do or see."

He snorted. "You couldn't thump a single one of us, even if it was our worst day and your best."

"You do realize that you sound as though you're about six years old," she teased.

"Hey, I'm just being realistic. And, what do you mean you're seeing things?"

She glanced around them to be sure they were still alone. "Swear to me you won't tell a soul what I'm going to tell you, not even Elise."

He frowned and hesitated. "I don't know, Ry. You know I tell Elise everything."

She shrugged. "You're right, you do." She stepped away. "So what construction projects are you guys working on now?"

He looked at her incredulously. "What? You mean you aren't going to tell me?"

She shook her head. "Sorry, bro. I can't chance it. I haven't figured out how I'm going to handle this yet." She saw his look of surprise. "I need to think about the repercussions," she continued. She needed to tell someone what was happening to her, but at the same time, she was scared to tell. Once she told, it was out there and couldn't be taken back. "You never know how people will react to things."

"Dang it all, Ry. You know that sort of crap drives me crazy."

"Do you swear not to tell anyone, including Elise?"

He practically gritted his teeth. "Yes, I swear."

She glanced around once more to be sure they were alone. "Annie is going to have a boy," she whispered.

His face lit up. "That's wonderful. When did they find out? I thought they didn't want to know."

She shushed him. "Keep your voice down. They don't know yet. So, you can't say anything to anyone. Remember you swore."

He frowned. "What do you mean they don't know yet? If they don't know, how did you find out?"

"I saw it."

"You saw what?"

"I saw the baby," she said. She watched the different emotions run across his face. Maybe this had been a mistake.

He glanced at her nervously, "Ry, you're scaring me now. This isn't funny. I know you think my practical jokes are childish, but joking about the baby is low. I wouldn't even sink that low."

"I'm not lying to you." She tried to think of a better way to explain, but nothing was coming to her. "Daniel, I don't know how, but I can see things now."

He started to walk away. "This isn't funny."

"Wait a minute. I can prove it."

He stopped and turned back to face her. "I'm waiting."

"Have you lost anything that means something to you recently?" she asked. "I mean something you'd like to find?"

He looked confused and shook his head. "No."

"Oh, come on. You're always losing things. There must be something."

He thought for a moment. "Well, my favorite Nirvana T-shirt is missing."

She made a face when she realized which shirt was missing. "You mean that god-awful, twenty-year-old gray thing that you ripped the sleeves out of?" she asked.

"Yeah, that's the one and I happen to love that shirt."

"Whatever." She waved away his protests. "I want you to think about the T-shirt while you shake my hand."

He stepped back. "See, I knew you were messing with me. What have you got in your hand?"

She held out her hand, palm up. "There's nothing in my hand. I promise it's not a trick. Come on, shake my hand."

He looked her hand over carefully before he grudgingly took it.

The burst of color instantly filled Ry's vision. As usual, it took her a moment to interpret the scene. When she recognized what she was seeing, she sighed. The colors faded. "Gosh, Daniel, now I feel bad."

"Why?" He let go of her hand.

"I think your T-shirt is in the dump. I saw it in what looked like a ripped up trash bag and trust me, bro, you don't want it back."

He started to say something, but was interrupted by a high-pitched squeal.

Ry's first instinct was to cover her cheeks. Aunt Sophie had found her. Daniel ran, leaving her to face the cheek pincher alone.

Twenty minutes later, Ry made her way out to the side patio where Victor stood talking on his phone. He waved her over.

"I just received a call from Deputy Sheriff Ward over at county," he said.

Ry recalled the quiet deputy sheriff who had stayed with her while the Emergency Medical Technician removed the splinters from her face. "Did they catch the guy who shot me?"

Victor shook his head. "No. But thanks to that revolver, his days are numbered."

Ry felt a jolt of adrenaline flash through her veins. "What about the revolver?"

"I guess you noticed those silver grips?" Victor asked.

"Who could have missed them? They were beautiful and probably cost a small fortune."

Victor nodded. "A couple of the deputies were looking it over at the station a few days ago when another deputy sees it and gets all excited. She remembered hearing her grandfather, a retired cop, talk about two guys who robbed four banks in 1932. One of them used a revolver just like this one with the silver grips. She couldn't remember too many details and her grandfather was dead, so the county guys started going through the archives here in Jacks County. Then they called Bexar County and got them to digging and between the two counties, they found the whole story."

Ry waited patiently.

Victor sipped his coffee before he began. "Back in 1932, these two guys robbed all four branches of the South Texas Farmers' Banks. They hit two of the branches on July thirty-first and the other two the following morning. They robbed the main branch of the bank last. It was there that the shorter one took a pocket watch from the bank manager. Then he pistol-whipped the manager half to death. Apparently, they weren't satisfied with just robbing these banks because on the night of August first, all four of the banks were burned to the ground. There weren't many clues for the police to follow but they did manage to pull a single fingerprint from a gas can they found at one of the banks."

Ry frowned, not certain how this related to her.

He rushed on. "The robbers wore masks so the only description the police had to go on was the bigger guy carried a shotgun, the shorter one a revolver with fancy silver grips." He sipped his coffee. "Now six months later, there's another robbery, but this time it's a liquor store in San Antonio. Again, two guys wearing masks, one with a shotgun and one with a silver-grip revolver. Things don't go quite as planned. The two left the store just as an off-duty police officer happened to drive in. The big guy panicked and opened up with the shotgun. The police officer was hit and eventually died. But he did manage to put two slugs into the big guy that resulted in him being apprehended along with the cash, but the shorter one got away." He stopped long enough to sip his coffee.

"Soon as they began interrogating the guy he starts telling them everything he knows. His name's Harvey Jenkins and his partner's Raymond Dodd. He tells them they buried the money from the bank robberies in an old abandoned cemetery west of Floresville. They hadn't spent any of the money because a lot of it was new bills, and they were scared it could be traced."

"Could it?" Ry asked.

He shrugged. "Probably not, but they didn't know that. Anyway, when the cops ask him where they can find his accomplice, he tells them Dodd is in school. Turns out the guy with the silver-grip revolver is a twelve-year-old kid. So the police go out to arrest Raymond Dodd, but he's gone. Then the police go out to the cemetery where Jenkins claimed the money had been hidden and all they find is a recently dug hole where it might have been buried, but no money. Dodd wasn't heard of again until December 1941."

Victor grinned slightly. "Yeah. After the bombing of Pearl Harbor, Raymond Dodd, like many other young men, walks into a recruiting station in San Antonio and tries to enlist in the navy using the name Zachary Lawson. As part of the enlistment process, they run his fingerprints. They get a hit from the print found on the gas can in the bank arson. Dodd's arrested. They charge him with armed robbery and felony murder in connection with the death of the police officer. He's sentenced to life in prison in Huntsville. He died there at the age of ninety-four." He looked at Ry. "Five weeks ago."

Ry's head was spinning. "So how does all of that relate to me being shot?"

"The two dead guys out at the house were identified as Roger and Larry Lawson. They were cousins. We now believe the guy who shot you is Dennis Lawson. He's Roger's older brother." Victor stared at her with a look of satisfaction. He took his time as he sipped his coffee and methodically dabbed at his immense mustache.

Ry held her breath.

His eyes narrowed slightly. "They are the grandsons of Raymond Dodd."

Somewhat dejected, Ry released her breath and sat down. That still didn't answer her question. "I still don't understand why he's after me."

"That's a question we can ask him when we bring him in," he assured her.

"Do you really think you'll be able to catch him?"

Victor looked at his watch. "We know who he is and what he looks like. The county guys issued a BOLO, so every cop in South Texas is on the watch for him. It's simply a matter of time. If he's moving around, we'll find him." He gave her a short nod. "I feel confident in predicting that Dennis Lawson will be in police custody within the next twenty-four hours."

CHAPTER EIGHTEEN

Tired from the day's activities, Ry crawled into bed. It felt good to be alone. A lot had happened since she had gotten up that morning. Her body tingled when she thought about Nicole. She liked Nicole a lot, but getting involved with her was out of the question. In fact, she didn't think she was ready to get involved with anyone at this point in her life. She had always tended to jump from relationship to relationship. It was time to see what she could do on her own.

She knew she still loved Kate, but they always seemed to be at odds with each other. One of their biggest issues had been Kate's reaction to Ry's family. Even today, Kate had called to say there had been an unexpected change in the work schedule and she had to work. She wondered if Kate really had to work or if she had bailed because she didn't want to come. She told herself it didn't matter anymore. Kate was no longer an integral part of her life.

Ry gave herself a mental kick in the rear for telling Daniel about the baby and the T-shirt. He had tried to talk to her a couple of times afterward, but they had never gotten the opportunity to speak privately. When they were leaving, she promised him she would call him later in the week and talk to him. She knew she would have to follow through. He would hold her to that promise.

If she wasn't careful, this new ability might turn out to be more of a curse than a blessing. She would have to get better at hiding it or else she was liable to find herself being committed.

Ry yawned and turned on her side to watch the faint shadow of tree limbs on her window shade. Would Victor be correct in his prediction about Dennis Lawson's capture? She could feel herself drifting off to sleep. How had she gotten herself involved in a bank robbery that happened more than eighty years ago? Why had they burned the banks?

As soon as she began to doze, the voices started. She listened for a while and made mental notes of some of the requests. She eased herself away from the voices when a series of disjointed and incomplete images began to flash through her thoughts. She concentrated on them and tried to slow them down enough to make sense of what was there. The flashes slowed and gradually settled into a complete image. She found herself in a dark, frigid room that reeked of despair. A profound sense of hopelessness dropped over her, heavy, cold and suffocating. She struggled to shake it off. The harder she struggled, the heavier the burden grew. Desperate to escape, she latched on to a dim glimmer of light across the room. She strained against the invisible bonds weighing her down until she drew close enough to identify what was before her. The light was concentrated around a middle-age man with stooped shoulders who sat a table. Across from him was a young boy dressed in ragged overalls and no shirt. They appeared to be eating. She made her way closer. The glow around them grew stronger and warmer. She realized it emanated from the deep love between the two. The glow wavered slightly as a sense of outrage surged through her when she saw the battered metal plates before them. Each plate held only a meager serving of boiled potatoes. Such poverty was foreign to her. She had never been hungry or cold.

As she attempted to determine where she was and how she could help these two, she heard a knock at the door. Instantly she found herself standing outside on the front porch of a dilapidated house. Boards were missing from the porch. The railing on the front steps had pulled loose and hung at a dangerous angle. One of the front windows was covered with something that looked like burlap. The shredded wire on the screen door seemed to mimic the sad lives of the home's inhabitants.

Something white on the porch post caught her attention. She moved closer. The print faded in and out, but she finally managed to read the words "foreclosure" and "South Texas Farmers' Bank." As she tried to read the rest of the notice, the sound of car motors filled her ears. She turned to see three police cruisers. Not cars like Victor's, but antique cars, like those she and Kate had seen at the car show. As she stared at the vehicles, the sound of breaking glass came from behind her. She turned in time to see a rifle barrel slide through the broken window. There was a short volley of shots before a deathly silence fell over the area. She started back into the house, but stopped when she saw the crimson stream running from beneath the screen door. Sickened by the sight, she stepped back. The front wall of the house seemed to dissolve allowing her a clear view inside. The man lay on the floor by the window, a rifle at his side. The boy leaned over him crying. She could hear footsteps crunching the dry grass behind her and knew it would be the police. The boy suddenly turned his father over and removed something from his hip pocket. As the boy stuck the object into his own pocket, Ry caught a flash of silver. She watched the boy disappear out the back door seconds before the police officers tore through the front. She followed the boy as he sped into a nearby grove of trees. He sprinted in a seemingly haphazard style until he ran directly up to what looked like a solid rock wall.

Ry watched as he walked up to the wall and disappeared. She followed and found that a natural outcropping of the rock hid a small opening. A twinge of claustrophobia threatened as she wriggled her way through the narrow gap into total darkness.

A match sputtered and the boy lit a lantern.

Ry looked around. The cavern wasn't much bigger than the interior of a car. There were three cardboard boxes stacked to her left. The faded lettering on the side indicated they were quart-size canning jars. Next to the boxes was a large metal object. A closer examination revealed the rusted remains of an old moonshine still.

The light wavered as the boy set the lamp down and sank to his knees. She watched over his shoulder as he rolled aside two basketball size stones to reveal another opening. When he reached in and removed a shoebox-size wooden box, she peeked inside the hole and was surprised to see it was quite large beyond the opening. He opened the box and removed an old rag that smelled of oil. He unrolled the rag and removed the rusted skeleton of a much older pistol. He wrapped the rag around the silver grip revolver.

Ry glanced into the wooden box and saw a cigar box that seemed oddly familiar. She tried to get a better view, but the boy placed the bundle with the weapons back inside the wooden box.

He put the box back inside the hole and replaced the stones, picked up the lantern and a limb that had been lying nearby. He used the limb to wipe out his footprints as he backed out of the cave. At the opening, he tossed the stick back to where it had been, blew out the lantern and left it by the opening.

Curious as to his next move, Ry followed him. Her curiosity turned to confusion when he ran back to the edge of the woods and waited until the officers were close enough to see him. As soon as one looked his way, he sprinted across the open field. They caught him with little effort. She tried to follow as they led him toward the cars, but something dark blocked her way. Uneasy with the darkness, she retreated and gave in to the swirling colors that never seemed far away.

Ry sat up in bed, shaking with cold. She didn't need to look at the clock to know the approximate time. The faint aroma of coffee wafting from the kitchen let her know it was after four in the morning. She took a quilt from the bed and wrapped it tightly around her shoulders, the dream still fresh in her memory. She raised the window shade, sat in Granny Jeter's rocker and stared out into the early morning darkness.

She had clearly seen the words South Texas Farmers' Bank on the foreclosure notice. The young boy must have been Raymond Dodd. Had his father's death been the reason he had robbed and burned the banks? Although it by no means justified his actions, it at least helped to explain them.

The phone rang in the kitchen. Ry knew it was Victor even before she heard the soft knock at her door.

Ry followed her mom back to the kitchen and picked up the phone.

"I apologize for calling you so early," Victor began, "but I knew your folks would be up and about, and I promised you I'd give you a call as soon as I knew something."

"You caught him?" she asked.

"Yes. A state patrol officer spotted him at a café near Hondo. When he tried to make the arrest, Lawson pulled a gun and started firing."

"Is the officer all right?" She really wanted to ask if Lawson was still alive, but human decency demanded that she inquire about the officer first.

"He was hit in the shoulder, but he's going to be fine."

"What about Lawson?"

"Shot twice. He lived long enough to confess he'd shot his cousin Larry. His story was that after Raymond Dodd went to prison, his wife divorced him and took his sons Sam and Truman to live with her folks in Corpus. Years later, Dennis Lawson overheard his father and uncle speculating on where Dodd had hidden the money. When Dennis got old enough, he started visiting his grandfather in prison, but Dodd denied knowing anything about the stolen money."

"Do you think Dodd knew where the money was?" she asked.

"It had to be him who moved it after Harvey Jenkins was arrested or else the police would have found it then."

"Maybe Jenkins lied about where they hid it," Ry said.

"I doubt it. He sounded like a real wimp. I don't think he'd have had the stones to lie to the cops back then."

Ry couldn't help but think of the grieving young boy leaning over his father's body. She shook off the reverie when she realized Victor wasn't finished with his story.

"When Dennis couldn't get anywhere with the old man, he convinced his cousin Larry to try. Apparently, Dodd took a liking to this grandson. Larry went to see him consistently for the last year of the old man's life. Then he died and Larry swore he never told him anything about the money, but a couple of weeks after Dodd died, another relative tells Dennis that he saw the gun at Larry's house.

"Dennis and his brother, Roger, became convinced that Larry had found the stolen money and planned on keeping it all for himself." Victor cleared his throat. "Dennis claimed he and Roger got to Larry's house just before you were leaving with a truckload of stuff. They didn't know who you were. They decided Larry might be trying to hide some of the money, so he followed you home. Roger stayed with Larry to make sure he didn't take off.

"Dennis watched you and Kate through the shop window and saw you with the pistol. He realized you two didn't have the money, so he goes back out to Larry's and confronts him with what he saw. Larry denies knowing anything about the cash and claims to have found the pistol while going through some of his father's stuff. There's an argument and Dennis kills Larry. He and his brother had just left the house when you and Kate show up on Sunday morning. When they see you again they get nervous and decide they'd better kill you as well just in case Larry did tell you something about them."

"So he was there at the house the entire time his brother was shooting at us," Ry said, trying to absorb it all.

"No, he claims he was only there at the beginning. They'd parked their car down the road in a field. He told Roger to take care of you and Kate while he went to get the car. When he came back, he saw Roger's body lying in the yard. He said he could see you standing in the window. He started to go after you, but he saw a police car flying down the road. He panicked and took off. He said he wrecked your place in retaliation for you killing his brother." He sipped his coffee loudly.

"And that's why he shot me," she said faintly.

"Yes. You killed his baby brother."

She traced the grout line of the counter tile with her fingertip. "All this happened because I picked up the wrong box."

"Sounds like it."

She took a deep breath. "So what happens now?"

"Any investigations that were pending against you will be dropped. When you feel up to it, you'll need to stop by the Bexar County Sheriff's Office and sign a couple of forms. By the way, your cell phone is here in my office. If you or your folks are in town stop by, or I'll drop it by when I get the chance."

She thanked him and hung up.

Ry turned and found her parent anxiously watching her. She filled them in on everything Victor had told her.

Her father slowly shook his head. "What a waste," he said, "all those deaths and ruined lives."

"Why didn't Dodd just tell his grandsons he'd already spent the money?" Ry asked. "Ten years passed before the police caught him. He was married with at least two kids. What made them think anything was left?"

"Greed," her mom said. "Rational thought disappears as soon as greed enters the picture."

"How did they plan on spending it?" her father asked. "Those bills would have been over eighty years old. Can you just walk into a store and use them?"

Ry shrugged. "They're probably collector's items by now. There are a lot of coin and paper money collectors out there."

"Even if Dodd had hidden it somewhere, it would probably be ruined by now," he added.

Ry had studied many books on a variety of antiques and vintage items, one of them had been on coins and paper money. "The robbery happened in 1932," she said. "Gold coins were still in use. It's likely that at least part of the money would have been in twenty-dollar gold pieces. That's certainly not something they could have casually sold off in volume. The sudden appearance of a large number of new sales in gold coins should have raised some questions."

"Couldn't they have melted the coins down into bars?" her mom asked. "I saw on television where these companies buy up gold all the time. They melt it into gold bricks. How do they sell those?"

Both Ry and her father shrugged. "The only bricks I know anything about are the ones I promised to pick up and deliver to James. And you know James. He won't be a happy camper if I keep his crew waiting."

Ry sat at the table as her parents left the kitchen. She smiled when she thought of their morning ritual. Every morning rain or shine when he left for work her mom would walk out to his truck with him and wave until he reached the road.

Her mom returned just as Ry closed the dishwasher. "Mom, how would you like to go to San Antonio and Jackson City today?"

Her mom made a face. "What do you need from town?"

"I need to pick up my phone from Victor and sign some paperwork in San Antonio." Ry grabbed an apple from the bowl on the counter and went to her father's office. She intended to use the trip as an opportunity to mail a few letters, including one to Irene Jankowski. She struggled with what she wanted to say. She finally settled for: *Dear Mrs. Jankowski, You probably don't remember me, but I was a friend of Lilly's many years ago. I only recently learned of her passing and wished to offer my condolences. I'm sure you find great solace in reading her diary. We used to have such fun hiding our childish treasures behind that fake panel at the back of her closet. I sometimes wonder if she continued to keep her diary there. Sincerely, Carolyn Smith*

Ry re-read the letter. She tried to convey enough information to lead Irene Jankowski to her daughter's diary without making her intent obvious. With luck, Mrs. Jankowski would no longer remember the names of all her daughter's friends and the fake name wouldn't cause her any concern. She folded the letter and prepared it to mail. She hoped both Irene and Lilly would soon find some sense of peace.

She answered two other requests she had received the previous night. One came from a man who wanted his wife to know where he had hidden some money. The second was from a woman who wanted her daughter to know where the mother had hidden her life insurance policy. She didn't bother trying to explain how she had come about the knowledge, she simply told them where to look and left the letters unsigned. These two requests had come complete with names and addresses. As soon as she had finished with the letters, she rushed back to her room to get ready.

CHAPTER NINETEEN

When they arrived at the Bexar County Sheriff's Office in San Antonio, Ry was relieved that her mom elected to stay in the car. She could drop the letters into the mailbox outside without having to make up answers for her mom's curiosity. She was grateful to find that the paperwork had already been completed and was there waiting for her signature.

As Ry made her way toward the exit, she glanced over a copy of the papers she had just signed. A sudden burst of familiar laughter made her look up. Nicole and another woman had just entered the building. Ry cringed slightly when she saw the sudden disappearance of Nicole's smile. They stood staring at each other for a long, awkward moment.

Ry spoke first, "Hello."

Nicole nodded and quickly recovered. "Hi. What are you doing here?" She stopped short and added. "I meant I'm shocked to see you're able to get out and about so soon."

"I had to come here and sign some papers."

Nicole nodded. "I heard they had caught the guy who shot

you." She turned to the woman beside her. "Ann, this is Ry Shelton, the woman I was telling you about."

The woman extended her hand and murmured a weak, "Hi. How are you?"

Ry shook her hand or rather her fingers and forced herself not to grimace at the woman's limp handshake. Why would Nicole be attracted to such a mousey woman? "I'm fine, but I certainly wouldn't have made it without Officer Matthews' help," she said.

The woman looked up at Nicole adoringly. "Isn't she something? I worry so much about her being out in the woods all alone."

Okay, so Ann adored Nicole. Maybe that was the attraction. Still, Ry had to exert control to keep from rolling her eyes. Struggling for conversation, she asked the obvious, "You're not from here, are you?"

Ann grinned. "Atlanta. I'm here to visit Nicki. I surprised her. She wasn't expecting me until next month." Again, she looked up at Nicole with big cow eyes.

Nicole shifted nervously from foot to foot.

Ry gritted her teeth and held out her hand again. "It was nice to meet you, Ann. I hope you enjoy your stay." She nodded at Nicole. "Officer Matthews, it was good to see you again." She gave a quick wave and rushed out.

* * *

Rain began while they were driving back to Jackson City. It was a little after two when they parked in front of the sheriff's office. The rain had slackened to a heavy sprinkle. Ry shivered when she stepped out of the car into the cold, damp air.

"I'm going in to talk to Alma while you get your phone," her mom said. "I heard her mother is doing poorly again. I want to see if there's anything we can do to help her."

Ry nodded. Alma Diaz had been the dispatcher for the Jackson City Police Department for over twenty-five years. "Victor's squad car is in the parking lot, so I'll go see if he has my phone and meet you back at Alma's desk," Ry said.

As soon as they stepped inside it was obvious something was going on. Alma was at her desk, but too busy dispatching messages to and from deputies in the field to notice them. Ry heard her reading off a description. It sounded as though an elderly man was missing.

"Rylene, something's wrong," her mom said. "Maybe we should come back later."

They were leaving when Ry heard her name being called. It was Victor. He was standing in his office waving something at them. Ry assumed it was her cell phone. As she approached him, his phone rang and he grabbed it.

When she grew nearer she noticed Jamison Bradley, the director of the nursing home. She had known him since they were kids. Ry nodded to him as she stepped into the office. Victor was talking on the phone and leaning over a map on his desk.

"What's going on?" she asked.

Jamison wiped a handkerchief over his face. "Clarence Reed has gone missing."

Ry remembered the frail elderly man who suffered from Alzheimer's disease. Whenever she had gone to the nursing home, she had always tried to include him on her round of visits because he seldom had visitors. His only living relative was a brother who resided somewhere up north. The only visitors Clarence had were a couple of old friends who managed to find a way out to the nursing home occasionally.

"He was there when they took his lunch in at eleven, but when they went back to get the tray he was gone." He wiped his face again. "We've turned the facility upside down looking for him. I'm afraid he somehow got out."

Victor hung up. "Jamison, they need you back at the nursing home. They need your key to the back gate. Find Deputy Ross. He'll tell you what he needs."

Jamison jumped up and rushed out.

"Is there anything I can do to help, Victor?" Ry asked.

He hooked his thumbs over his belt. "We're trying to organize a search party, but you've got no business being out there."

Ry was about to protest, but was stopped when her mom came into the room.

"I can help," her mom said.

They looked back to see her in the doorway.

"I'm perfectly capable," her mom said.

He nodded. "All right. If you don't mind waiting a couple minutes, you can ride over with me." He looked at his watch. "Nat Zucker is bringing his hounds. We're hoping to track him."

"Won't the rain be a problem?" her mom asked.

He looked worried. "Depends on how long it keeps up and how hard it rains. According to Jamison, Clarence hasn't been doing too well."

Ry noticed a faded shirt in a clear plastic bag on Victor's desk. What would happen if she touched it? Before when she sensed something it had been when touching an individual. She remembered the incident with the arrowhead. "Is that one of Clarence's shirts?" She tried to keep her voice casual.

Victor nodded. "We'll need it for Nat's dogs." He glanced at his watch again. "I wish he would hurry up and get here."

Ry bit her lip and glanced nervously at her mom. She knew she should keep her mouth shut, but she couldn't stop thinking about poor Clarence. She took a deep breath and prayed she wasn't about to make a huge fool of herself. "Would you mind if I looked at the shirt?"

"There's nothing there to tell us anything," he said absently.

"Victor, please let me see the shirt."

Something in her voice made him look up. "What good would that do?"

"Just please give it to me."

He shook his head. "No. The dogs might get confused if too many people handle it."

"Is that the only shirt he had?" Ry's tone was sharper than she intended.

"Rylene," her mom began.

Ry held out her hand. "Please, Victor. I wouldn't ask if I didn't think it was important."

He frowned at her and hesitantly handed it to her. "I guess it's okay since it's in a bag."

She tore the bag open and reached inside before they could stop her.

Ry was thrown into a swirling vortex that seemed hell-bent on ripping her apart. When she finally freed herself of its spinning fury, she found herself in a field covered in brush and cactus. She felt as if every bone in her body might explode with each movement she made. Despite the cold rain that drenched her, her skin burned. Her lungs hurt when she breathed. She raised a hand to wipe away the rain on her face, but stopped and stared in horror. The hand she saw wasn't her own. The hand before her was old and withered. The knuckles were swollen and bruised. It took her a moment to realize she was seeing the world through Clarence Reed's eyes. She forced herself to ignore the pain as she turned in a complete circle and searched for anything that would identify her location. Each step was tentative and painful. All she saw was endless waves of brush and cactus. She tried to walk, but exhaustion weighed her down. She sat down on a rain-soaked tree stump. The pungent odor of pine tickled her nostrils. As she struggled to breathe, she heard the soft jingle of bells and the distant sound of a donkey braying. The next thing she was aware of was coming to on the floor of Victor's office with him and her mom hovering over her. She was exhausted and her body ached. She struggled to sit up.

Victor helped her to a chair. "Rylene," her mother gasped. "Are you all right?"

Ry stared at her hands, relieved to find they were her own.

"He's in a field covered with brush," she said without preamble. "We have to find him. He's really sick." She shivered. "I heard bells. They sounded like sleigh bells and there was a donkey braying." She realized they were both staring at her as if she had lost her mind.

Victor looked at Doreen, confused and concerned. "I'm sorry. I don't understand what's going on here."

"Rylene, what are you doing, honey?" Her mom put a hand on Ry's arm. "My goodness, you're burning up. You have a fever." She grabbed Ry's arm. "Come on. We have to get you to the hospital. It must be an infection. Dr. Price warned us it could happen."

Ry grabbed her hands. "Mom, I'm not sick. If we don't get to Clarence soon, he's going to die. I could feel it." She stared into her mother's eyes. "Do you understand me? I could feel him suffering."

"Should I call an ambulance?" Victor asked, staring at Ry as if she were possessed.

Ry pressed on. "It was raining. I smelled pine trees. He's really sick," she repeated.

"You smelled pine trees?" Victor asked incredulously.

"Yes. I didn't see them, but I could smell them."

"Ry, there are no pine trees around here."

She remembered the strong odor. It was unmistakable. "I'm telling you there was a pine tree. I could smell it. It smelled just like Christmas." She heard Victor's breath catch.

Her mom must have heard it too. "What's wrong?"

He stared at Ry. "There's that Christmas tree farm out on Old Pecos Road."

Ry remembered the place but he couldn't possibly be there. "That's at least twenty miles from the nursing home," she said, beginning to doubt herself.

They were all shaking their heads. Only her mother expressed what each of them was thinking. "Clarence couldn't have walked that far."

A hard chill shook Ry's body and for a brief moment she again felt his pain. "I don't know how he got there, but if those are the only pine trees around here then that's where he is. Come on, Mom. We're going out there."

"Rylene, I think I should take you to the doctor," her mom said.

"I don't need a doctor. I need to find Clarence."

Her mom again started to protest and then stopped. "Okay. Let's go." She began digging in her purse for her keys.

Victor gave a low growl before he snatched his hat off a table. "Come on. I'm not letting you go out there alone." He glared at Ry. "The last thing your mother needs is for you to get out there and have some kind of relapse."

"I'm fine," Ry said, although she wasn't feeling fine. She couldn't remember ever being so cold.

"We'll go look, Victor," her mom said. "You stay here and continue on with what you were doing."

He shook his head as he opened a closet door, grabbed a blanket and wrapped it around Ry's shoulder. "Seth would kill me if I let you two go off alone with her sick." They followed him out. "Alma," he yelled. "I'll be in my car if you need me."

The rain was coming down harder. Low visibility and slick roadways slowed their progress. When they reached the Christmas tree farm, Victor turned to Ry. "Does anything seem familiar?"

She tried to look around but was having trouble focusing. She rolled the window down long enough to sniff the air.

"That's the smell, but it's too strong. He's not this close to the trees. There was a donkey. I heard bells."

"We used to keep bells on the goats," Doreen said from the backseat. "It made them easier to find when they strayed off. Someone with goats or sheep might have a donkey to keep the coyotes away."

Victor tapped his finger against the steering wheel and then grabbed the mike to the police radio. "This is Sheriff Orozco," he shouted into it. "Does anyone know who owns goats or sheep and a donkey in the vicinity of the Christmas tree farm out on Old Pecos Road?" He lowered the mike and waited. A second later, there was a crackle and then a voice.

"Sheriff, this is Ross. Ms. Rollins has goats and a donkey. I had to go out there last week. The donkey had gotten out and was over at Dink's place."

Victor glanced back at Ry. "Are you sure about this?" He rubbed a finger over his mustache. "If you're wrong it could mean Clarence's life."

Another chill hit Ry. "I'm sure," she replied. "Please hurry."

"Ross," he said into the mike, "how many people have shown up to help search?"

"I guess there's about a hundred."

"Split them into four groups," Victor instructed. "You take one group and get over to Ms. Rollins' place and start looking around. Find out where that donkey is. I need to know."

There was a brief silence, "What am I going out there to look for?" he asked.

"Clarence Reed."

"Um. Sheriff, that's nearly twenty miles from where—"

"Just get out there," Victor yelled. "Gomez," he continued. "You take a group and go over to Ralph Dink's place. Brock and Pierce you two grab teams and come in from the east and west sides of that area. I want everyone to converge on that big ridge that runs across the back of Dink's property. There's a lot of brush out there so go slow. I want every inch of that area covered. Make sure you have flashlights and a flare gun. It's going to be dark soon. If you find him, shoot off a flare. Alma, are you there?"

"I'm here, Sheriff."

"Send a couple of ambulances out here. I want to be ready for whatever happens."

He set the mike down and put the car back into gear. After a few miles, he parked the car at the edge of road by a field. The rain grew heavier. It seemed determined to fight them every inch of the way.

Victor tried to convince Ry and Doreen to stay in the car. When they refused he found a couple of slickers in the trunk and gave them to the women. "Sure you're up to this?" he asked Ry again.

She nodded. "Let's go."

"You tell me if you see anything remotely familiar," he said as he took a flashlight and a flare gun from the car. "We'll spread out about six feet apart and make our way straight toward that ridge over there."

They began to walk. As the rain continued to beat down on them, Ry began to worry. What if she had made a mistake? After all, she had never been able to prove her visions were accurate. Dr. Price claimed he had found his dog, but she had still had the second vision. Her body began to ache. Each step became more difficult. Because of her, Victor had moved the entire search twenty miles away from where they had originally estimated Clarence might be. Common sense told her the elderly man couldn't have possibly walked this far. Because of her, Clarence might be dying within a mile of the nursing home with no one there to find him.

Ry looked at the sky. It must be after four. It would be dark in a couple of hours, less if the cloud cover continued. As soon as darkness fell, their chances of finding Clarence decreased greatly. He was too frail to survive the night.

They trudged through rain and muck shouting for Clarence and straining to see or hear any sign of him. Ry's heartbeat accelerated each time Victor's radio crackled. After about an hour, she began to see small flickers of light. She stumbled but managed to stop her fall by grabbing onto the branch of a scrub oak. The lights she had seen were those of the other searchers. They were all converging on the ridge. Any hope of finding Clarence was quickly evaporating. Darkness began to settle over them. Ry wished she had a flashlight. Soon she would have to depend completely upon her hearing. The pain in her stomach grew until she could hardly walk. Why had she butted in? Victor was a great sheriff. He had protected the county for more years than she could remember. What had made her assume she could help?

A pain so intense she fell to her knees struck Ry. She tried to stand, but her arms and legs could no longer lift her. She fell facedown into the mud. It took all her strength to turn her head enough to breathe. Again, she felt the burning pain and weakness of old joints and muscles. Only vaguely aware of her mom and Victor trying to help her, she managed to grab Victor's hand. "He's nearby," she said, her voice no more than a whisper. "Hurry."

Victor looked around frantically. "Clarence," he shouted at the top of his lungs.

"Help him, Mom," Ry pleaded.

"I'm not leaving you, Rylene. Honey, I've got to get you to the hospital."

"Mom, he's dying. Please, help Victor find him. He's nearby."

Ry saw the struggle in her mother's tear-filled eyes. She tried to reach for her, but she could no longer lift her arms. She closed her eyes against the raindrops that felt like stones being hurled against her aching body. A brilliant red glow seemed to burn through her eyelids. She scrunched her eyes tighter against the light and tried to fight the black void threatening to engulf her. The cold ground stole the last bit of warmth from her body. She felt herself slipping. She could no longer fight. All she could do was watch as the dark void crept steadily closer.

"Rylene, they found him." Her mom was patting Ry's face. "He's alive, honey."

Ry gave in and let the darkness take her.

CHAPTER TWENTY

When Ry opened her eyes, she was no longer freezing.

"We really have to stop meeting this way."

She blinked until the face above her finally came into focus. It was June, the Emergency Medical Technician, who had removed the splinters from her cheek after the shooting.

"How's Clarence?" Ry asked.

June's face sobered. "He's in bad shape, but thanks to that anonymous caller, he has a chance."

Ry started to ask about the caller, but stopped when the back door to the ambulance opened.

"How is she?"

Ry recognized Kate's voice. "I'm fine," she replied. She started to sit up, but June stopped her. "Where's Mom?"

"With your dad," Kate said as she moved to stand behind June. "They're waiting outside in his truck. In fact, your entire family is waiting out there."

Ry tried to sit up again and found she had wires attached to her. "Can you get this off me?" she asked June.

"No." June pushed her back again. "Lie down and stay there for a while longer." She moved toward the door. "Kate, you keep her company while I go let her folks know she's fine."

"Tell Dad to go on home," Ry said. "I'll catch a ride with one of my brothers."

"Tell them they can all leave," Kate said. "They were out there searching, and they're wet and cold. I'll take her home."

June nodded briefly and hopped out of the ambulance.

She noticed that Kate still looked tired. Dark circles smudged her eyes and there was an unusual listlessness in her movements. She considered asking what was going on, but hesitated. "You're wet too," Ry pointed out instead.

"I'm fine," Kate said as she sat down on June's stool. "I can't imagine what possessed your mother and Victor to let you go out there. You should be home in bed."

"I wanted to help."

"Why are you so dang stubborn?" Kate asked, clearly upset. "You're going to kill yourself."

Ry didn't know how to respond. An awkward silence fell between them. She heard Kate take a deep breath.

"I received a call from Wilma Brown this afternoon," she said. "She said the claims adjuster's finished and you can start cleaning up anytime you want. She's supposed to call me back tomorrow with the settlement figures."

Ry sensed that Kate was struggling to control her anger. "Good. I was wondering how much longer it was going to take." Ry fought the urge to pull the wires off and sit up. She fidgeted as silence once more filled the ambulance.

"I ran into your friend, Nicole, again the other day," Kate said. "She seems nice."

Ry stared at the ceiling of the ambulance and wondered if Kate had met Ann also. "She is nice."

"Your mom sure seems to like her."

"Yes, she does. She invited her to dinner last Sunday."

"I'm sorry I wasn't able to attend," Kate said. "There was a last-minute shift change, and I had to work."

"That's fine. Mom understood." Ry tried to think of something to say. "Are you still living with your parents?" The question sounded disapproving. She gave herself a mental kick. So what if Kate was still living with her parents? Wasn't that exactly what she was doing herself? It wasn't as if Kate could go back to their place. Before she could say more, Kate surprised her.

"No. I found an apartment in that new development over by the hospital."

"Dad's company worked on some of those buildings," Ry said. "He mentioned they were nice places."

"I didn't realize your family had worked on them."

Ry sensed something in Kate's voice. "So, I guess you'll move now."

Kate looked at her sharply. "Why would you say that?"

"It's no secret you never approved of my family."

Kate's mouth flew open. "*I* never approved of *them*? Don't you have that reversed? Your family never approved of my father or me."

Ry frowned. "Why would my family disapprove of your father?"

"God, Ry, are you really that dense? When your family got together, all they could talk about was the greedy Republican Party doing this or that. How a working man couldn't catch a break because of them. It was a fairly easy conclusion to draw that your family didn't care for mine."

Ry started to deny the accusations but stopped. Part of what she had said was true. Her family was blue to the bones Democrat. She had once joked that it had been easier to tell her parents she was a lesbian than it would have been if she'd had to tell them she'd turned Republican.

Yet another awkward silence fell between them and lasted until June returned several minutes later. She looked at the two women and shook her head. "How are her vitals?" she asked.

Kate checked the machine monitoring Ry's vital signs. "She's still stable."

"In that case, I guess it's safe to let you go home."

Ry sat up. "Good. Get me loose from these wires."

June took her time removing the leads to the machine.

"Maybe I can still catch one of my brothers."

"No," June said. "I'm sorry. They left before I came back inside. I told them you were stable, and Kate was taking you home."

Ry stared at her, wondering if June had deliberately waited until they left. She shook off the ridiculous thought. Why would June care who drove her home? She glanced at Kate, who was busy rolling up the wires. Was she regretting making the offer to drive her home?

Ry retrieved her boots and sat on the cot to put them on.

Kate squeezed past June. "Ry, I'll wait for you outside."

When Ry stepped out of the back of the ambulance a couple of minutes later it was Victor, not Kate, she found waiting on her.

"I told Kate to go on home. I needed to talk to you," he said. "Come on." He turned and left, leaving her no choice but to follow.

When Ry got into the car with him, he was on the radio.

"That was Alma," he said. "She'd just gotten off the phone with the hospital. Clarence has pneumonia, but the doctors seem to think he's got a decent chance to pull through, barring complications."

"That's good to know," Ry said.

Victor eased the car onto the road before he spoke again. "Do you want to tell me what happened this afternoon?"

Ry stared out the side window. "I don't exactly understand it myself." She took a deep breath and slowly exhaled. "Since I was shot, I sometimes see or sense things."

"So this wasn't the first time something like this had happened?"

"Victor, you're not going to try and have me committed or anything, are you?" She turned to face him.

He glanced at her quickly before returning his attention to the road. "Are you hearing voices?"

"Sometimes I do," she admitted.

He hesitated a moment. "What do they tell you?"

"They always seem to be people who have died and…"

"Holy crap." He shot her another quick glance. "Are you joking?"

Ry rubbed her thumb across the back of her hand. "No, I'm not. It seems to be people who have died and left something unfinished." She told him about the letters she had mailed that morning.

It was his turn to take a deep breath. "Have you told your folks about this?" he asked.

"No." She thought about the conversation she'd had with her father. He knew there was something different about her. "I've been trying to find a way to tell them."

He gave a short laugh and shook his head. "Well, I think you did this afternoon. Your mom is pretty upset."

"I didn't mean to upset her. I couldn't help it."

He smoothed his mustache. "The reason I wanted to talk to you was to tell you people started asking how I knew where to look for Clarence. I said it was an anonymous call from a trucker who'd picked Clarence up. That's probably what really happened. It had to be a stranger who picked him up. He certainly didn't walk out there, and everyone around here knows him. Anyway, I said this mystery trucker got worried and called me after Clarence insisted on being let out in the middle of nowhere." He glanced at her. "I didn't know what else to do. You know if the truth gets around, people will start looking at you differently. There's no telling how far it could go."

"I know. I've sort of thought about that. I appreciate you covering for me and I'm sorry I put you into a position where you had to lie."

"Ry, I'm not worried about a little white lie. You saved Clarence's life. If it hadn't been for you, it might have been months before we found that poor old man's body. He wouldn't have made it through the night."

She rubbed her hands again. "My parents have been through so much already with this shooting. I'm just not sure they're going to want to hear more."

He stared at the road ahead for a moment before he spoke. "Your folks are levelheaded. Your mom was there today. She saw the same thing I did. You just need to open up and tell them what's going on. Let them help you, when they can. There's no need for you to try to handle all this on your own."

"You're right." The dashboard lights cast a dim red glow across them.

"Do you mind talking about what happened?" he asked. "I mean what do you see and hear?"

She listened to the hiss of the tires on the rain-soaked road. How could she describe what happened to her without sounding like a nutcase? She couldn't stop the involuntary flinch when the radio suddenly squawked. He lowered the volume slightly as she explained what she had experienced.

He shook his head. "You know, this isn't the first time I've heard of things like this. There's a woman over in Harris County who can sometimes see things before they happen. She's actually helped the police a couple of times. They never release her name, but my brother-in-law's on the police force there and he mentioned her. There was another woman in California who does the same thing." He frowned. "I wonder if there are any men who are able to predict the future."

Ry tried to move the conversation away from her. "My brothers always seemed to know exactly when Mom was going to show up to get someone to take out the garbage. They were never around for that."

"Now, you sound like my wife," he said and grinned.

They rode in silence until he turned onto the road leading back to her parents' house.

Ry could see the lights through the living room windows. As they drew nearer, she saw several vehicles parked in the driveway.

"Looks like your brothers are all here," Victor said as he stopped the car.

"Would you like to come in for some coffee?" Ry asked.

"I have to get back and start doing the paperwork." He sighed. "The never-ending stream of paperwork, worst part of the job." He turned to her. "Besides, I think this is going to be a long night for you and your family. Best if you get in there and get started."

"Thanks for the lift."

He gave her a quick wave and drove away.

As Ry walked across the yard, she tried to anticipate how her family would react if she told them about her new ability.

Her parents had already experienced the incident with the earring and knew something was going on. Her mom would have certainly told her dad everything that had happened with Clarence Reed, but she wouldn't have mentioned it to the boys. Or at least Ry didn't think she would have. Daniel had already had a preview, but would still be suspicious of her trying to pull a prank on him. Lewis would be his usual stoic self and not say anything unless asked directly. James was the unknown factor. How would he react to something so esoteric? He was the responsible, dependable one. His world was composed of black and white. The one thing she was sure of with all of them was that they loved her unconditionally.

When Ry reached the door, she took a deep breath. She didn't need any sort of psychic powers to know what she would find when she stepped inside. They would all be sitting around the kitchen table quietly talking. But she opened the door to a sound she had never heard. They were shouting, not the easy-going, loud boisterous noise that her brothers occasionally resorted to over a basketball or football game but ugly, angry shouts. She ran into the kitchen and arrived just in time to see Lewis grab James's collar.

"Lewis!" Her scream froze the room. "What are you doing?" All eyes turned toward her. She received a worse shock when Lewis suddenly released James and rushed toward her.

"What the fuck are you trying to pull?" he shouted.

Her father's voice boomed through the room. He was warning Lewis about using that sort of language in his mother's house, but Ry was too terrified to feel any shock over Lewis's language. All she could see was an insanely enraged man looming over her. She was only vaguely aware of Daniel and James grabbing Lewis and dragging him away from her.

"What's going on?" she asked in a voice that she could barely hear herself.

Lewis glared at her. "What is it with you?" he spat. "Why do you always have to be different? Being the spoiled little princess wasn't enough for you. You had to spit in all our faces and become a lesbian. Then you get yourself shot and become a fucking psychic."

"Lewis, I'm not going to warn you again," her father said as he stepped forward.

Lewis's words struck her as if he had used his fist. A cold anger settled over her. When she spoke, her voice low and menacing sounded strange to her own ears. "Let him go," she commanded.

Lewis shook loose and took a step toward her. She stepped forward to meet him.

"First of all, I didn't *choose* to be a lesbian."

"Of course, none of this is your fault, is it?" he sneered.

She stared him in the eye. "Well, sure it is, Lewis. I woke up the other morning and decided, oh poor me, I'm just not getting enough attention. What do I need to do to get some attention? Then it hit me. I could go out and piss off a homicidal maniac who'd give me a free lobotomy?" She stepped closer until she was mere inches from his face. She lowered her voice until it was little more than a whisper. "So why don't you just tell me, what the fuck is wrong with you!"

"That's enough from both of you," her father shouted.

Ry and Lewis stared at each other. She watched the conflicting emotions rush across his face. When his shoulders finally relaxed, she released the breath she hadn't realized she'd been holding.

"That's enough from everyone," her mom said. "I want all of you to sit down, so we can discuss this rationally."

Lewis turned to Annie. "Come on. We're leaving."

"Lewis," Annie pleaded. "Please do as your mother said. You can't leave it like this."

He looked at his wife. "Why stay? Everyone here will defend what she did. How I feel doesn't matter."

"Lewis, that isn't true," her mom said.

"At least tell me why you're so pissed off," Ry demanded.

He spun back toward her and for one terrifying second she thought he might actually strike her. "I'm pissed off because you pulled my unborn child into your mumbo-jumbo crap."

Ry had never wanted to slap Daniel alongside the head as badly as she did at that moment, but she knew she only had herself to blame. Everyone knew Daniel was completely incapable of keeping a secret.

"You're right," she said. "I shouldn't have said anything." She looked at Annie. "I'm sorry. I was just so excited that I needed to tell someone."

Annie wiped tears from her eyes and nodded slightly before looking away.

"It's my fault," Daniel replied. "I should have kept my mouth shut."

Ry had never seen him look so lost and sad. She looked around the room. She had caused this. Why hadn't she kept her mouth shut? Her family had always acted as a cohesive unit. They didn't always agree with each other, but they always respected the other person's opinion. Not only was this ripping her family apart, it could also destroy their business relationship. Her father and brothers had to work together. She had to do something to stop this.

"I'm really sorry," she said. "I thought I could handle this, but obviously it's going to be a much larger issue than I imagined." She swallowed the lump in her throat. "Lewis, you can be as mad as you want at me, but you can't let it come between you and them." She motioned to Daniel and James. "They were only doing what you'd have done before tonight. You're brothers and you need to remember that. Direct your anger where it belongs, at me." She looked around the room. "I'm sorry, but I'm tired. I'm going to bed."

She locked her bedroom door, opened the window shade and sat in Granny Jeter's rocker. Thankfully, there was no more yelling from the kitchen. There were a couple of light knocks at her door, but she ignored them. Later she heard the sound of car engines cranking. When the house grew quiet, she turned on the lamp and packed her meager assortment of clothes into two large shopping bags. She couldn't continue to live here. She knew Lewis well enough to know he wouldn't come back as long as she was here. That would break her mother's heart. Her family needed time to think, and either accept or reject the changes in her life. To do that, they needed distance from her. In the morning she would return to the store and start cleaning it up.

She didn't want to think too far beyond that, but the horrible knowledge of what she had to do weighed heavily upon her shoulders.

It was a little after two when she took her keys from the table by the door. She placed a note to her mother beside the coffeepot and slipped out the back door. Her truck had been parked in the barn to keep it out of the weather. When she climbed into the truck she tossed her phone on the seat and then noticed that the broken side window glass had been replaced. The tears she had been fighting all night blinded her. She brushed them away, but they were quickly replaced. Rather than drive back up to the house to the driveway and risk waking her parents, Ry took the bumpy farm lane that looped around and connected with the main road farther up. She couldn't shake the feeling that her life would never be the same. Why had she been so careless as to take that blasted box to begin with? That's what started all this. If only she'd driven past that estate sale sign.

Jackson City was dark and quiet when she drove down Main Street. When she turned onto the side street, which led to the back of the shop, she saw the new fence and gate her father and brothers had built. The remote control to the automatic door opener was clipped to the visor above her head. She pushed the button and watched as the gate slowly swung inward. Kate would have loved that, she thought with a smile. Thinking of Kate only made her feel worse. As she parked behind the shop, she noticed a new security light lit the area. She sent a silent "*thank you*" to her dad and brothers as she backed her truck up to the door of the shop. She hadn't entered the shop since that dreadful night. The thought of doing so now caused a knot of pain to twist in her stomach.

She found her gloves beneath the seat and then went to retrieve the wheelbarrow from the shed. After she had gathered her tools, it took her a moment to muster the courage to unlock the door, step inside and flip on a light. Even though she knew what to expect, the complete destruction of everything in sight still caused her knees to weaken. She grabbed the wall for support and took several deep breaths. Slowly her determination started to build. With one final deep breath, she squared her shoulders.

It was time. She pulled on her gloves, rolled the wheelbarrow inside and picked up the first handful of debris. Each handful got a little easier. As she worked her way down the hallway toward the stairs, she occasionally found some small trinket that hadn't been destroyed. By the time she heard someone pounding on the front door, she was drenched in sweat and covered with dust.

She looked toward the front windows and instantly recognized the silhouette of her parents. She cupped her hands around her mouth and shouted for them to come around back. A moment later, the shadows started toward the side street. Ry went to her truck and used the remote to open the gate. For one small moment she considered sneaking out the front door because she knew she was about to catch hell from her parents.

"What in the devil are you doing?" her father demanded as soon as he saw her. "Why didn't you answer your mother's calls? How could you be so thoughtless with everything that's been going on?"

"I'm cleaning," she said. From the set of his mouth she could tell he was really upset, something he rarely was. Ashamed that she had needlessly worried him, she rushed on. "I'm sorry. I guess my phone is in the truck. I left you a note."

"Yes. I found your note." She patted her husband's arm. "Rylene, why did you sneak out?" her mother demanded. "What time did you leave anyway?"

Ry knew there were no right answers to those questions and tried countering with one of her own. "Mom, what would you have said had I waited until you got up?"

"I would have told you it was too soon for you to be doing this. Dr. Price said you had to take it easy."

Ry took a deep breath. "I know you're worried, and I appreciate your concern, but honestly, I feel fine."

"You could have waited until the weekend and your brothers and I would've helped you," her father admonished.

"No." She quickly held up a hand to stop what she knew was coming. "I'm not angry with Lewis. He had every right to be upset. I'm not angry at anyone," she added. "This is something I need to do by myself." She looked at her father. "I need to make this right, Dad."

The three stood staring at each other for a long time.

Her father finally broke the silence when he scrubbed his hand roughly over his face. "Lord, Doreen, I don't know why you had to have such stubborn children."

"They're no more stubborn than their father," she replied as she took his arm. "Come on, let's go and let her work."

He stood for a moment longer staring at Ry. "Promise me you won't overdo it. And, you'll get home at a decent hour so your mom won't worry."

Ry prepared herself for the second round. "Actually, I'm moving back in here." She felt sorry for them as they struggled to find that thin line that allowed her to be her own person and them to be protective parents. "The holidays are almost here and I need to have the store ready."

"Seth, she's right," her mom said so brightly that both Ry and her father turned to stare at her.

Her father seemed on the verge of saying something but time had taught him to follow his wife's lead. He simply nodded and waved to Ry. "Come on," he said as he took his wife's hand. "Let's go see if we can find a decent cup of coffee."

Ry went to the truck to get her phone. In truth, so much had been going on that she had barely looked at it since she picked it up from Victor. She was shocked to see her voice mail was full. She sat on the tailgate of her truck and started checking the calls. A few had been from other antique dealers, but the vast majority was from old school friends and people she knew calling to check on her. There were two missed calls from Nicole, one from Kate and seven from her mother. She considered calling Kate, but what would she say. Slowly, she slipped the phone into her pocket.

CHAPTER TWENTY-ONE

Ry worked through the day until exhaustion forced her to stop. She made the third and final run to the dump so that the truck would be empty for the following day. She considered calling Daniel to see if she could borrow the trailer again, but held off.

She tried to ignore the fact that the only call she had received that day had been a text from Kate. The text had been to let her know the insurance settlement checks had arrived at her apartment and she had deposited them into the business account and the personal account they had once used for the household. She told her to use however much she needed to have the shop repaired. There hadn't been a single call from her family. She'd started to call her mom a few times, couldn't make her mind up as to whether they were giving her space or she had hurt their feelings so badly they weren't speaking to her. Scared that it might be the latter, she refrained from calling.

She called a local motel and found a room she could rent for a week, promising herself that before the week was over she would have cleared enough debris out that she could make herself a small living space.

Despite the early hour, she showered, went to bed and slept straight through the night. At some point a voice had tried to intrude, but she kept it at bay.

The next morning, Ry's leg and shoulder muscles were so sore she could barely get herself out of bed. She stopped at a local diner and ordered breakfast. She was enjoying the last of her coffee when Kate came in alone. Kate looked uncertain for a moment, but finally went over to where Ry sat.

"What are you doing here?" Kate asked.

"I started cleaning out the shop yesterday," she said. She was glad to see Kate looked more like her old self in a carefully tailored suit that accentuated her figure and the dark circles were gone from around her eyes.

"By yourself?" Kate asked, clearly surprised. "You shouldn't be doing anything that strenuous. Didn't your doctor tell you not to do anything for the next few weeks?"

Ry nodded, embarrassed by the tears that stung her eyes.

Kate stepped closer. "What's going on?"

Ry glanced around the diner. There were too many people close by. She didn't want the entire town to know her business. She wasn't sure she even wanted to tell Kate what had happened between her brothers.

Kate took her coat off. "I hope you don't mind if I join you. I woke up craving pancakes and was too lazy to make them."

Ry motioned to the chair across from her.

They were interrupted as the waitress appeared and took Kate's order.

"Are you planning on reopening the store?" Kate asked after the waitress left.

"I don't know. I'm hoping I'll make my mind up by the time I finish cleaning." She stopped. "I'm sorry. I'm just bumbling along here assuming you wouldn't want the building. I was thinking that we'd either sell it and split the money, or I could buy your half. Did you want the building?"

Kate seemed to hesitate before she shook her head. "I don't have any use for it. Let's wait until you decide what you want to do and then we can worry about the best way to settle everything."

Ry sipped her coffee. "I promise I'll make a decision in the next couple of weeks. Of course, I'll keep making the payments until we settle."

Kate traced the pattern on the tablecloth with her fingertip. "Please use the insurance money. I know things must be tight for you now."

The waitress arrived with Kate's order of pancakes.

Ry stared at them. "It's hard to believe that it was just two and a half weeks ago that I promised to take you out for pancakes."

Kate nodded. "A lot's happened since then."

"You don't know the half of it," Ry said sadly. She scooted her cup back. "I should get going. If I sit here much longer, I'll be too stiff to work."

Kate looked concerned. "Is your head bothering you?"

Ry stood and suppressed a groan. "My head is fine. It's my butt that's dragging."

Kate chuckled. "If your mom isn't planning anything special for you, why don't you come by for dinner and see my new apartment on Friday night. Friday and Saturday are my days off with this new schedule."

Ry nodded again. She didn't bother to tell Kate she was staying at the motel. "What time?"

"Around seven would be good. I'll make spaghetti."

She left enough cash on the table to cover Kate's breakfast. "It's a little late, but I did promise you a pancake breakfast."

When she arrived at the shop, she backed her truck up to the door and started working. After she had cleared a path from the back door all the way to the stairs, she started up the stairs intending to start cleaning a living area. Once she was up there, she realized that she would have to find a way to get the debris down. The easiest way would be simply to toss the debris out the window into the truck, but the truck bed was so small most of the stuff would probably end up on the ground and have to be picked up again. That was double work. She would have to think of another way.

Again, she thought about Daniel's nice wide trailer with the high wire sides. She took out her phone and stared at his number for a long moment. All she would have to do was ask. She put the phone back into her pocket. It had been her choice to give them time away from her. She needed to stand by her decision.

In the meantime, there was still plenty of work left to do downstairs to keep her busy for days.

She moved from the downstairs hallway to her workroom and started clearing things out. The desk she had bought from the estate sale caught her attention. The top was now split in half. As she carried the destroyed desk out to the truck and tossed it in the bed of the truck, she tried not to dwell on the stupidity of the destruction.

Back inside she began tossing broken strips of wood from what had once been a bookcase into the wheelbarrow. When she came across the cigar box that had held the folk art animal carvings, she picked it up. The animal carvings had been dumped out onto the floor and smashed. Only the partially carved rabbit was still intact. She picked it up. Instantly the burst of colors filled her vision and pulled her inward. When she was finally able to see again, she found herself in a familiar location. She was back in the cavern where the young boy had hidden the pistol. The person in the room now was no longer a young boy, but rather a man. Ry moved closer and gasped when she saw the pile of money on the ground before him. He was busy stuffing large rolls of bills into quart canning jars. She recalled seeing the boxes of jars there by the moonshine still. After he filled a jar, he screwed a lid onto it and placed the jar deep into the hole where he had stored the box holding the pistol. She watched him fill jar after jar. Some of the jars contained bills while others held gold coins. He rolled two basketball size stones back in front of the hole. Then he picked up the stick and erased his tracks, tossed the stick back inside, blew out the lantern and left it just inside the entrance, as he had before.

She followed him outside and instantly found herself back in her workroom kneeling on the floor. The carving had fallen from her hands. Tentatively, she reached out and picked it up, but nothing happened. She pulled herself up and went outside.

She was still sitting on the tailgate ten minutes later when Victor parked his squad car beside her truck.

"You look like you've been working hard," he said as he motioned to her dusty clothes.

"It's beginning to feel like a lost cause," she admitted.

He sat on the tailgate beside her. "Did you talk to your family the other night?"

"I guess the better description would be they were waiting to talk to me," she admitted. A streak of loneliness hit her.

"That doesn't sound too good."

"It was horrible, but it's my own fault. I should have handled things differently."

He shrugged. "Don't be so hard on yourself. It's not as if you could've gone out and bought a how-to book." He shook his head.

"I can't blame them. I screwed up and did something stupid. Lewis had every right to be angry with me."

"Oh, it was Lewis. I can see where he'd have problems accepting something like this. He always was a down-to-earth, no-bull kind of guy."

They sat quietly for a minute before Victor spoke again. "I came over here hoping I could ask for your help."

"Please tell me Clarence isn't missing again," she said as a knot started in her stomach.

"No. It's not a person exactly." He seemed to struggle for words.

"Just tell me Victor."

"You know Jack and Tina Dempsey?"

"Yes. I went to school with them. They have a little boy who's sick, right?"

"He's autistic. The kid has a cat that for whatever reason helps keep him calm. Whenever the cat gets out of his sight he starts getting anxious."

"My gosh that must be horrible." She thought about her own nieces and nephews and how fortunate they were to be healthy.

He cleared his throat. "The cat disappeared sometime last night and the family is frantic to find him. I've looked everywhere I can think of."

Ry realized why he was there.

"I don't mean to offend you or anything, I mean, with it being a cat and all."

"Victor, please. If it will help that poor kid, I don't care if you ask me to find cat poop. Did you bring something that belongs to the cat?"

He took a plastic bag from his pocket and handed it to her.

Inside she found a small stuffed mouse with a bell on its tail. She reached in and touched the mouse; instantly she saw the cat. She carefully studied the area around the cat by turning in a complete circle. As soon as she saw the enormous pot of begonias hanging from a tree, she snapped herself back. She handed him the bag back. "The cat is on the back patio of the Silver Spur restaurant."

He hopped off the tailgate. "How can I ever thank you, Ry?"

"Just keep my secret," she said.

He nodded gravely. "Don't worry about Lewis. He'll come around." He gave a quick wave and rushed to his car.

Ry put her gloves back on and went inside. Suddenly, the work seemed a lot lighter and she felt a glimmer of happiness. When she heard a car drive into the back lot an hour later, she was actually humming.

She rushed to the door, hoping it would be someone from her family. It was Victor. Her regret faded when she saw his smile. "From that smile on your face, I guess everything went well with your cat hunt," she said.

"You should have seen the difference in that poor little boy. One minute he's screaming his lungs out and as soon as he sees the cat, it's as if he sees something magical. He starts laughing and the next thing you know he's sitting there next to the cat, coloring away in his coloring book."

Victor reached into his pocket. "I also came by to give you this." He took money from his pocket. "His parents had already posted flyers offering a fifty-dollar reward. I told them I couldn't take it, but they kept insisting. I thought that since you're the one who actually found the cat, it should go to you."

Ry stepped back quickly. "I can't take that."

He looked confused. "You have to. I can't keep it."

Ry looked at the money and tried to think what he could do with it. Finally, the solution came to her. "Why don't you start a special fund at the police station? Whenever you see someone who needs a little help, give it to them."

He slowly nodded. "Okay, if that's what you want. I'll get Alma to take care of it."

"Hey, since you're here I have a question for you," Ry said.

"Okay. What's up?" He smoothed his mustache.

"You know the money that Harvey Jenkins and Raymond Dodd stole from those four banks? If the money was ever found, who would it legally belong to?"

His eyebrows rose. "Did you find it?"

"I don't have it," she answered honestly.

He didn't seem to notice the vague answer. "That's a good question. The banks never reopened. I seem to remember reading that Aaron Lassiter died a few years after the robbery." He looked at her and held up a finger. "Maybe the government owns it because of their having to pay out the insurance."

Ry shook her head. "The Federal Deposit Insurance Corporation wasn't operational yet. It didn't start until 1933."

Victor went back to smoothing his mustache. "Okay. Then I think the money would be given back to the account holders or their heirs."

"They burned the banks. I doubt they had any type of backup files then, so the information they had on the account holders would have been destroyed."

"I see you've given this some thought," he said and then sat quietly.

Ry could see he was really getting into figuring out the ownership.

He held up a hand again to emphasize his words. "I suppose if there was someone still living who had an account there and they still had the necessary paperwork to prove they lost their money during the robbery, then they might have a claim on whatever was due to them. Maybe they'd get the principal plus whatever interest over the years." He shrugged and dropped his hand. He hooked his thumb over his belt. "Who knows how a judge would rule? One thing I know for sure is that the only winners in the mess would be the lawyers. You can bet they'd walk away with most of the money."

"That doesn't seem fair," she mused.

Victor looked at her closely. "I think if I was a regular citizen and not wearing this badge and I found that money, I'd keep my mouth shut and find a way to make it do some good."

Ry nodded. "Victor, I like the way you think."

CHAPTER TWENTY-TWO

Ry continued hauling debris from the downstairs area. She made four trips to the dump. During the cleanup, she found several pieces of jewelry and a few small items of merchandise that somehow remained undamaged during Dennis Lawson's rampage. Unfortunately, none of the furniture or glassware had survived intact. It broke her heart to see the splintered remnants of once beautiful pieces lying in scattered heaps. The downstairs level, at least, had begun to look manageable.

Her body ached from exhaustion. She lost track of the number of times she had picked up an intact object and had a mental image burst forth in her head. After a while, she had started to notice that if she concentrated on trying to avoid seeing the visions, they happened less often. It was when she forgot and grabbed something without thinking that it happened.

On Friday, Ry decided to cut her workday short. She didn't want to be exhausted when she went to Kate's for dinner. She left the shop at three and drove to the motel. After showering, she stretched across the bed hoping to catch a quick nap before dinner, but sleep evaded her.

She couldn't stop thinking about her family. No one had contacted her since her parents left her shop on Tuesday morning. She wondered if things had gotten worse between her brothers. It wasn't as if they hadn't had minor spats before, but she had never seen any of them as angry as James and Lewis had been on Monday night. Maybe they were waiting for her to make the first move. She covered her face with her hands and suppressed the urge to scream. The one constant in her life had been her family. It was a given that they would be there when and if she needed them, and now she didn't even know if she should call or not. She cursed Dennis Lawson for shooting her. Then she cursed Raymond Dodd for robbing those banks and starting this entire fiasco. Her anger was cut short when she realized that had she not been shot, Clarence Reed would more than likely be dead. She got dressed. It was still too early to go to Kate's, but she couldn't stand the thought of staying in the small, dim room another minute.

Ry drove to a liquor store and managed to find a bottle of wine that she knew Kate liked. As she drove toward the downtown area, she noticed kids in costumes. It was Halloween and she had completely forgotten. She had seen the decorations around town, but lost track of the days. There would be all sorts of things going on in the town square for kids of all ages. Victor would have the town square closed to traffic allowing the kids an added measure of safety as they ran from shop to shop. Merchants would pass out candy, and the town council would have booths and games set up on the square. Later in the evening, there would be a dance with a live band at the civic center parking lot. She knew her brothers and their families would be out there somewhere. She drove slowly along the adjoining streets hoping to catch a glimpse of her family. On her third circuit, she noticed flashing lights behind her. She pulled over to the curb and waited. She had not been speeding and was ready to defend herself. The lights on the police car went out, and a moment later Victor stepped out of the car.

Ry relaxed and got out of the truck. "You had me going there for a minute," she admitted.

He grinned and rubbed his mustache. "I saw you cruising around and thought I'd harass you for a while."

Ry dropped the tailgate on the truck and they sat down.

"How's the cleanup going?" he asked.

"Slow, but I can actually see the floor in spots now."

He nodded. "Are you going to reopen?"

"I don't know. I like living here, but the shop was almost too much."

"Have you considered a smaller place?" he asked. "You could buy a little house to live in or even rent a place."

Ry swung her legs from the tailgate. "The idea sort of crossed my mind, but honestly, I never gave it any serious consideration." She glanced at him. "Do you know of any smaller shops for sale?"

"I heard that Lacy Wayne is looking for a buyer."

Ry nodded. She vaguely remembered hearing that from someone. "I'm not sure her shop is big enough. I remember it being small."

He waved at a passing car. "Have you considered doing something besides antiques?" He glanced around them. "I mean, with things being the way they are for you I'd think that handling so many things that belong to other people could be hard on you."

"Strange you should mention that," she admitted. "I've been having some problems with that very thing."

He nodded. "Have you thought about what's going to happen at, say, an estate sale?"

She shivered. "No. I haven't."

He stood. "I'd better get back to work. My wife and I are leaving in the morning. We're going to be gone for a few days to visit her sister's family in Houston."

"That sounds like fun."

He grunted. "You haven't been to Houston in a while, have you?" He smoothed his mustache. "Anyway, if you need me, you have my cell number. Feel free to call me."

"That sounded more like a plea than an offer," Ry said and laughed.

"I love her family," he said, "but I sure wish they lived somewhere else." He gave her a quick wave.

She got into her truck and sat staring out the window. A smaller shop would make things easier. Rather than antiques in general, perhaps she could specialize. Furniture was definitely out. It had been a problem for her from the beginning—too heavy to move alone. She loved old books and maps, but doubted there would be a big enough market here. Vintage glassware had been easy enough to find, but difficult to handle. One small chip and the piece lost most of its value. Antique toys and clothes didn't interest her. Farm tools had been somewhat cool, but every antique store in the county sold those. If she were to be brutally honest with herself, the only thing she truly loved about the store was finding the pieces. Once she found them, they held little interest to her.

"I don't want to be an antique dealer," she mumbled to herself. "I'm an antique seeker." She started to crank the truck when she heard. *You're a treasure seeker.* She glanced around to see who had spoken, but she was alone. "A treasure seeker," she repeated. She liked the connotation the words brought to mind.

As she drove to Kate's apartment, she dreamed of dashing off to exotic destinations in search of treasure. She thought about Dodd's bank robbery money. Victor had more or less said that as long as she kept her mouth shut, who would ever know she'd found the money? How would she get rid of it? Sell it, was the obvious answer. It wasn't as if she could take it to the bank and deposit it into her account. She could probably sell the old bills and coins on the Internet. She was still plotting when she rang Kate's doorbell.

When Kate answered the door wearing a form-fitting sweater and jeans, Ry felt a little leap in her pulse. She pushed the feelings away and reminded herself that there might be a third person here tonight, even though she didn't think Kate would have been that insensitive. She handed over the bottle of wine. "I remembered you liked this particular merlot."

Kate took the wine and glanced at the label. "This is what they served at that little steak house near the hospital in San Antonio. You used to meet me there sometimes when I worked the evening shift." The smile left her face as she turned and started back inside. "Come on in."

Ry followed her into the apartment. It was small, obviously a place meant for one person and somehow that made Ry feel better. It was certainly much nicer than the motel where she herself was staying.

She followed Kate into a tiny kitchen. Two glasses sat on the counter next to a corkscrew. The relief she felt made her realize that she hadn't been entirely sure it would be just the two of them. She wondered if she should ask about Kate's new girlfriend and decided to wait and see how things went. There was no need to get things off to a bad start.

"The pasta's ready," Kate said as she got busy at the stove. "There's a bottle of wine in the fridge. Would you mind pouring us a glass?"

She opened the wine and poured Kate a glass, but got a glass of water for herself. She set Kate's wine next to the stove.

Kate apologized when she saw the water. "I forgot you're not supposed to be drinking alcohol. You seem so normal, I forget."

Kate turned back to the stove. "Did he give you a ticket?" she asked and chuckled. "I heard Victor pulled you over while you were driving around town."

Ry shook her head. "It never ceases to amaze me how quickly news travels in this town. Who told you?"

"Ben Harrington, told my neighbor, Mrs. Montoya. She came by a couple of minutes before you arrived to tell me my dinner guest would be late since Victor had pulled you over." She stirred the sauce. "Ben always gave me the willies. I don't mean I thought he was dangerous or anything, but he never seemed to miss anything. It's like he's always watching."

He never missed anything except seeing the store being demolished.

Ry hadn't realized how hungry she was until they began eating. They chatted about the weather and other mundane things as they ate. Afterward, Ry helped her clean the kitchen before they went to the living room and got comfortable.

"How have you been feeling?" Kate asked.

"Great. I'm just tired from working at the shop."

"I'm sure you all will get it finished this weekend."

Ry didn't say anything.

Kate looked at her over her wine as she took a sip. "I assumed your family would be there to help you over the weekend," she said.

Ry took a quick gulp of water to wash the lump from her throat. When it didn't work, she shook her head.

Kate set her glass down and leaned forward. "Ry, what's wrong? Why are you so upset? Is there something wrong with your family?"

Again, Ry shook her head. How could she tell Kate what had happened without telling what had started it all? She didn't realize she was crying until Kate moved to the couch beside her and took her hand.

"What's wrong?"

Suddenly, everything that had happened since the shooting came pouring out of Ry's mouth. She told Kate about the voices and visions. She even told her about having a vision of Raymond Dodd hiding the money. When she finally stopped, they sat staring at each other.

Kate finally stood, retrieved her wineglass and drained it. "I'll be right back," she promised. She returned with the wine bottle and refilled her glass. She took a long swig before she sat down in the chair across from Ry. She cleared her throat and took a deep breath. "All right, let's go through all of that once more, only this time let's try it a little slower."

Ry retold her story.

Kate sat for a long while, tapping her wineglass and then she began asking questions. "So, it was your vision that led Victor out to the Christmas tree farm?"

"Yes, but I asked him not to tell anyone. He lied to protect me."

Kate nodded. "Are you absolutely sure someone didn't mention the sex of Annie's baby?"

"I'm sure."

"What about at the hospital? You were pretty heavily drugged. Maybe someone mentioned it to you and you forgot."

Ry frowned. "I guess it's possible, but I really don't remember talking to anyone about Annie."

Kate nodded and licked her lips. "Ry, I shouldn't tell you this but one of the nurses accidently mentioned the baby to me. She thought we all knew."

Ry held her breath.

"You're right. Annie's having a boy," Kate said. She stared into her wineglass before turning her gaze back to Ry. "Have you talked to Dr. Price about any of this?"

"No, and I don't intend to. I'm not about to become someone's guinea pig."

"I don't want to frighten you, but it could mean that there was more damage than anticipated. A blood clot could have formed after the surgery. He could have missed a tiny fragment of the bullet or skull. Any of these things could be pushing against your brain causing you to hallucinate."

"Is it a hallucination if what I'm seeing is real? How could I have known that someone named Lilly Jankowski committed suicide a thousand miles from here or that her mother's name was Irene? How could I know where Raymond Dodd hid that money?"

"The location of the hidden money remains to be proven," Kate reminded her.

Ry shrugged. "I know he put it there. I watched him."

"It doesn't matter. That's not something you can ever prove."

"Why can't I prove it?" Ry demanded.

"You have no idea where this rock wall is. It might be in Kentucky for all you know."

Ry shook her head. "I know I could find if I set my mind to it."

"I don't see how." Kate leaned back and sipped her wine.

"Do you have your laptop handy?"

Kate frowned. "What are you up to?"

"I'm going to find out where Raymond Dodd lived in 1930," she said.

Within a matter of minutes, Ry had accessed a search engine for the 1930 federal census records. It only took her a few minutes to locate ten-year-old Raymond Dodd. He was living in McDowell, Lupton County, Texas with his father Amos. Two hours later, they had sifted through newspaper archives, death records, the family histories of other citizens in the area and a host of other sites and learned that the town of McDowell had tripled in size after the discovery of a large oil field near there in 1930. Amos Dodd had gone to work in the oil fields. He and twenty-seven other workers had been severely injured when a platform gave way and fell. Afterward, he was unable to work. There were no records on how he and his son survived, but there was an entry in one historical account that told how the oil company had gobbled up as much of the surrounding farmland as they could. They also found an old newspaper story that related how Amos Dodd had been killed in a shootout when the Lupton County Sheriff had tried to serve a foreclosure notice. The shootout had taken place south of McDowell near Old Highway Twelve. It went on to say that Dodd's young son had been placed in an orphan's home in a nearby county. Copies of old county land records showed the bank had taken Amos Dodd's farm and then sold it to the oil company.

"No wonder the kid was so pissed at the bank," Kate said as they shut down the computer. She stared at Ry. "It's exactly as you saw it. I don't know whether to be awed by this or scared for you," she admitted. "I'm still worried there might be something wrong."

"I don't feel like there's anything wrong with me," Ry said. "My head doesn't hurt. I'm able to work all day. The only time I feel the least bit strange is when the colors start swirling around me. I get dizzy." She stopped. "It was different when I saw Clarence."

"How was it different?"

Ry thought before she answered. "It was almost as if I became him. I felt his pain. When I looked at my hands, I saw his."

Kate tapped the stem of her glass. "I'm an emergency room nurse. If you had a gunshot wound or a broken bone, I could tell you a little bit about what was going on with that, but the brain…" She shook her head. "All I know is the little we learned in school. Honestly, I've even forgotten most of that."

Ry stared at her. "Do you think there's something wrong with me?"

Kate glanced at the computer and slowly shook her head. "Even if there was something causing you to hallucinate, it wouldn't explain how you know all the things you've told me." Her eyes widened. "Oh, my God, that's how you knew about my keys. When you woke the first time in the recovery room, you told me where my keys were. The tube was still in your throat and I could barely understand you, but when I checked later, the keys were right where you said they were. I had meant to talk to you, but so many other things happened and I forgot about it."

Ry vaguely remembered the incident with the keys. "So what should I do?"

"I wish I could tell you. Obviously, you've already seen what can happen when people don't want to hear something. I'm not sure you should even tell Dr. Price. From the scuttlebutt I've heard about him, his dog probably wasn't even lost. He most likely tied him to that tree." She sipped her wine before continuing. "Price is big on research. That's where the real money is to be found. If the rumor mill at work is true, he likes expensive things." She shivered. "What if the government came after you?"

Ry laughed. "What would the government want with me?"

"Don't laugh. Think of what someone with your ability could do. You could shake a foreign dignitary's hand and know what his intentions are toward us."

"Judging from what I've been seeing, it's more likely I'd be able to tell him where his lost socks were."

"Don't joke about this. It's a gift. You told me you've been able to make the voices calmer at night, and you're learning to control the spells you have when you touch things. It's like any other talent, Ry, the more you use it, the more you'll learn to control it. There's no telling how far you could take this. I've heard the government used to do all sorts of experiments with mind control and things like that."

Ry was no longer smiling. "Now you're scaring me. You keep talking that way and I'm going to start watching for dark sedans with tinted windows parked across the street."

Kate looked her in the eye. "If you aren't careful, that might be exactly what you'll end up doing."

Ry blinked and swallowed. The wine bottle on the table next to Kate was empty. She sure hoped Kate's wild talk was caused by the wine and not facts.

"What are you going to do about the money?" Kate asked.

"I'm going to go get it." Ry was almost as surprised by her answer as Kate. "I now know about where Dodd's house was and I sort of remember how the kid worked his way back to the rock wall."

"You can't go alone. It's too dangerous."

"So go with me. You can stop the bleeding if some wild-eyed rancher shoots me."

"That's not funny. You know it's located on private land."

Ry thought about it and, considering approximately ninety-four percent of the state was privately owned, it seemed likely that the area with the rock wall would be on private land. "I'm still going. It's only illegal if I get caught."

Kate rolled her eyes. "That's probably what Raymond Dodd thought when he robbed those banks. It didn't work out so well for him."

Ry smiled. "You know what I always said. If I go to prison, I get three meals a day, a big screen TV and wall-to-wall women."

Kate made a snorting noise. "Those women would scare you fartless."

"Yeah, probably, but it's something to consider."

"When are you going?"

"I'll have to go in after it gets dark. So I guess I'll go tomorrow morning and scout around to see if I can find where the house was and hopefully I'll be able to find the wall and get the money tomorrow night."

"What will you do with it if you find it?"

"I don't want it for myself. It needs to be used for something good. There's too much blood on it."

Kate gave her an odd sort of smile. "You were always a better person than I am."

"How can you say that? You help save people's lives all day."

Kate shrugged and looked sad. "Sometimes it feels like all I do is ask people for insurance cards." She took a deep breath. "If you go, I want to go with you."

"Are you sure? Our last outing didn't turn out so well."

Kate gazed at her. "I was an ass to you that day. I'll never forgive myself. You saved our lives. All I could do was hide under that couch, and then I ran home to Daddy like a sniveling coward." Tears rolled down her cheeks. "I've never been very nice to you and for what it's worth, I'm sorry."

Ry forced her hands into the front pockets of her jeans. She had never been able to stand seeing Kate cry. She had to be careful or she might do something they both would probably regret later. She swallowed the lump that had formed in her throat. "There's enough blame on both sides to go around, so why don't we store all that on a shelf and start over?" She hesitated before adding, "I miss talking to you."

Kate nodded. "I'd like that." She rubbed away her tears with the back of her hand. "So what time do we leave in the morning?"

"McDowell is about a four-hour drive from here. I'll pick you up around nine." She glanced at the clock and was shocked to see it was a little after midnight. When Kate walked her to the door, it took all of Ry's strength simply to hug her goodnight. All the way back to the motel, she kept reminding herself that Kate had someone else in her life now. If she wanted to keep her friendship, she couldn't do stupid things like try and kiss her.

CHAPTER TWENTY-THREE

Ry parked her truck in front of Kate's apartment building at nine sharp. Kate had obviously been watching for her because she came out immediately.

"Good morning," she beamed as she climbed into the truck with a large bag. She was dressed in jeans and a pink polo shirt that enhanced the creamy highlights of her skin.

"I can't believe you're so cheerful," Ry said. "You finished that bottle of wine last night."

"I never get a hangover, you know that." She fastened her seat belt and patted the bag in her lap. "I packed a thermos of coffee and some muffins. I figured you probably hadn't eaten anything since you're living in that awful motel."

"I'd love a cup of coffee. The motel's not that bad. It's old, but they keep it clean," Ry said. "Besides, it's only for a few more days."

"How long do you think it will take you to finish cleaning the shop out?" Kate began pouring the coffee into a travel mug.

"It's hard to say. I've been working since Tuesday and I've only cleared about half of the downstairs." She took the cup of coffee and sipped it. "Thanks. Part of the problem is that I'm still finding some undamaged items mixed in with the debris so I have to sort of sift through it as I go."

"Are the pieces worth that much? Surely, the insurance settlement must have covered them."

"I don't know. I guess I'm being silly, but it seems wrong simply to throw them away. They've survived all these years. I have a little metal cup that made it through two world wars."

Kate looked at her. "Did you see that in one of your visions?"

"No. The woman at the yard sale told me that when I bought it from her."

Kate's eyebrows rose. "And you believed her?"

Ry shrugged. "Who cares whether it's true or not? The cup is certainly old enough for it to be true, and besides, everything has its own tale." She sipped the coffee and set the cup into the holder. "I never pass the stories along to my customers unless I know for certain it's true."

Kate fiddled with her coffee cup. "I was thinking that maybe I could help you clean out the shop when I'm not working."

Ry spoke before she took time to think. "Doesn't the new girlfriend object to you spending time with me?" She instantly wished she could take the question back.

Kate stared out the window for a second before answering. "That's no longer an issue. It didn't work out between us."

Ry felt an overwhelming urge to shout with joy. Instead, she forced herself to keep her eyes on the road. "I'm sorry to hear that," she said and hoped she sounded sincere. In her peripheral vision, she saw Kate turn to look at her before she began digging in the bag again.

"What's the plan for today?" Kate asked as she tore the top off a muffin and passed it to Ry.

"Once we find Old Highway Twelve, we'll drive down it until, hopefully, I see something that looks familiar. Then we'll take it one step at a time. If the area is heavily populated we'll have to wait until it's dark before we start prowling around off-road. If no one's around, maybe we can snoop before it gets dark."

"If it's there, do you really intend to take it?"

Ry looked at her sharply before returning her attention back to the road. "You don't think I should?"

"Well, it is on someone else's property. It doesn't really belong to you."

"Yes, it's probably on private property, but it doesn't belong to them either."

"What do you intend to do with it?" Kate picked at her muffin.

"I don't know yet, but I promise you it's not for me."

"I believe you," Kate said. "You're kind and you have a good heart. I'm sure you'll do something good with it."

"If I find it guess I should put it in a safe deposit box. I don't want to keep it around the shop. Victor said it's tainted money. What if he's right?"

Kate waved her hand as if to dismiss the thought. "It's not as if you're doing this out of greed," Kate said. "I think it would be rather ironic that eighty-plus years after it was stolen, the money ends up back in a bank."

It was a little after one when they finally reached the small community of McDowell.

"What a sad little town," Kate said as they drove through what must have once been a booming economy.

The dilapidated buildings along the main street showed a town that had been deserted and forgotten. For the past several miles the landscape had been dotted with rusted-out tanks and other debris that Ry assumed had been left behind by the oil company.

"I guess the oil ran out," Ry said. "I just hope there's someone still around who we can talk to."

At the far end of the street, they finally found signs of life, a rundown gas station and a bar whose walls leaned so severely, Ry would have been leery of entering. She pulled the truck into the gas station parking lot and shut the engine off. "Maybe you should stay here," she told Kate as she looked the building over.

Kate threw the truck door open. "You're not leaving me out here alone." She scooted off the seat and scurried around the truck to stand by Ry.

"Okay. Let's go see if anyone here knows where Old Highway Twelve is." Ry led the way. She could feel tension building in her body as she approached the dark, crumbling building. There didn't seem to be anyone around. Tentatively, she turned the doorknob. A part of her hoped the door was locked. The door squealed in protest as she pushed it open. The filthy windows allowed very little light to enter and what did make it through was quickly lost in the wild jumble of display cases, shelves, tables and counters that were piled two and three feet high with a crazy assortment of items. On the table closest to her Ry saw baby clothes, camouflage hunting pants, an old bottle of Listerine that still had the cardboard-like tube around it and a garden shovel. She leaned forward to peek around the cabinet by the table and couldn't stop the small squeal that escaped her when a small fuzzy head popped up.

It didn't help any when Kate grabbed hold of the back of her shirt. When she finally managed to get her heart out of her throat, she gave a timid wave. "Hi."

The tiny white-haired woman who had frightened her half to death gave a huge toothless smile. "Scared you some, didn't I?"

Ry laughed nervously. "Yes, ma'am, you sure did."

"What'cha lookin' for? Ain't got no gas, if that's what'cha want. Ain't had none for twenty-odd years."

"No, ma'am. I actually want Old Highway Twelve."

"What'cha want with it?"

Ry blinked. "I meant. I'm trying to find where it used to be."

The old woman pointed to the road out front. "That right there is part of it."

Kate wiggled around from behind Ry. The narrow passageway hadn't left her much room to maneuver. "We're trying to find the old homestead of Amos Dodd."

Ry wanted to kick Kate. They didn't need to announce where they were headed.

"He's dead, you know. Nobody livin' out there no more. The dirt ain't no good for farmin' now."

Ry nodded. "Yes, I assumed he was dead." Now that Kate had spilled the beans, there was no reason to pretend. "Do you know where his homestead was located?"

"You're lookin' for that money, ain't you?"

"What money?" Kate asked innocently.

"People used to come out here all the time. Dug the whole place up out there. Some fool even tore the house apart. Tore boards plumb off the wall, ripped up the porch. People get plumb crazy when it comes to money."

"We're actually writing a story on the oil boom that hit here," Kate said. "During our research, we found an article on the accident that hurt several people. Mr. Dodd's name was at the top of the list and we thought we might expand our article to show how the boom didn't help everyone."

Ry kept quiet and let Kate continue.

"That oil didn't help nobody 'cept them there oilmen. Everybody else it hurt. They come in and sprayed stuff to kill everything. Then they dug all them there holes everywhere. Holes so big a young'un could fall in 'em. I was eight years old when they put that first big old nasty thing up right outside town." The old woman shook her head. "Caused all kinds of nastiness to come here. We had a pretty town." She shuffled sideways and pointed back over Ry's shoulder. "Used to have a big old fountain right back over there in a big, pretty green park and every year at Easter time us kids would have Easter egg hunts. There'd be pretty yellow daffodils growin' round the fountain. Then they sprayed that stuff and kilt all the flowers and grass. They tore it all up for another one of those nasty oil things. Nobody could stop 'em. One of them nasty things kilt my daddy and brother. Fell on 'em and crushed 'em." She wiped her eyes with a claw like hand. "Now everybody's gone. People are scared to try and farm. Too many holes everywhere. Oilmen dug 'em and left 'em. Just me and a few more old fools livin' here now. You tell that to your fancy paper readers."

Ry watched the poor woman and felt ashamed that she had dredged up bad memories for her. "We're sorry we bothered you, ma'am." She nudged Kate. As they turned, the old woman stopped them.

"Stay on this here road till you reach the crossroads, take a left there. Amos's place was about six miles out. Last time I was out that a way, part of the old chimney was still standin'. Been about thirty years since I was out there, though. Reckon some fool has probably done tore it down by now." She blinked and looked at them with clouded eyes. "Ray wasn't a bad boy. He just got even with 'em for what they did to his daddy. Nobody 'round here blamed him. He was just a young'un."

Ry nodded. "Yes, ma'am, I'm sure you're right."

They walked back to the truck and drove away. Ry had driven to the crossroads before either of them spoke.

"How many lives do you suppose were ruined here?"

"I'd rather not know," Ry admitted. "What do you suppose she was talking about them spraying? They don't need to clear the vegetation before they drill."

Kate shook her head. "Maybe they were trying to destroy the crops so people would sell them the land."

Ry was horrified by the thought. "Why would they do that?"

"Greed." Kate spat the word out so harshly Ry turned to look at her.

"Are you okay?"

"No. I'm sick to death of people caring more about a fricking dollar than they do about people."

"Kate, I'm sure it's been like that since the dawn of mankind."

"It still doesn't mean I can't be tired of it."

Ry turned the truck left. "She said it was about six miles from here." She rubbed her chin. "Do you realize that if she really was eight years old when they started drilling, then she's now over ninety?"

"I'm surprised the poor thing hasn't broken her neck trying to walk around in all the crap back there."

"Can you imagine having to live like that?" Ry asked. A glimmer of an idea planted itself in Ry's mind.

The old woman was right about one thing, the chimney was no longer standing. Ry drove past the place three or four times before Kate finally spotted part of the foundation sticking out of the weeds. There was a grove of trees behind the house, but they seemed much closer than what Ry remembered from her dream.

She parked the truck alongside the road and took two nearly empty backpacks from behind the seat. Each pack had bottles of water tucked into the side pouches, along with a flashlight. She handed one of the packs to Kate.

"I guess we don't have to worry about the area being overly populated," Ry said as they walked across the field toward the house.

When they reached the area where the house had once stood, they found a pile of crumbled bricks from the old chimney and part of a stone foundation.

"There's not much left, is there?" Kate said as she stared at the ruins. "Ry, I want my life to amount to more than this."

"What are you talking about? Kate, I've told you before that you've already made a difference. You make a difference every time you save someone's life."

Kate shook her head. "Everything is changing. The new hospital administrator doesn't care about people. All he cares about is the bottom line. He's already laid off so many nurses that we're working crazy hours. He's let trained people go and replaced them with people willing to work for a lot less money, but they're so inexperienced. It's only a matter of time before someone makes a mistake." She looked at Ry. "I couldn't stand it if it were me. We're so understaffed that there are days when I work an evening shift and then have to stay for a night shift as well. I'm bone tired by the time I finally get home. When you're that tired it's easy to make mistakes."

Ry put her hand on Kate's shoulder. "Is there anyone you can go to about him?"

"No. The head office doesn't care. He's cutting costs and that equals more profit. They're only interested in profits." She took a deep breath. "Ry, I've been thinking about quitting nursing all together."

Shocked, Ry stopped sharply. "You love nursing. How could you just walk away?"

Kate shrugged. "I don't know, but something has to change."

She looked so lost that Ry took her into her arms and hugged her. "I know you, and you wouldn't simply walk away from nursing without a good reason. You know that whatever you decide, I'll be there to support you."

"If I quit my job, you may have to support me," Kate joked as she pulled away and wiped tears from her eyes. She grinned at Ry before looking toward the trees. "Are those the woods he ran into?"

"I think so, but they seem to be a lot closer to the house than when I saw them."

"It's been eighty-plus years, so I guess things would be different. Lead the way and I'll follow."

It took Ry an hour to locate the rock wall. "There it is," she whispered and pointed. She could hear Kate breathing heavier. "Are you scared?"

"I think so," Kate admitted.

"I'm glad because I'm terrified." She swung the backpack off her shoulder and removed her flashlight.

Kate did the same.

"Come on, let's go get it," Ry said.

The hidden entrance was just as she had seen it. She turned on her flashlight and squeezed through. She glanced to her right and there sat the lantern. Since they had the flashlights, she decided not to try to light it. Who knew how the oil would react after all these years? She stepped out of the way so Kate could squeeze through.

The beam of Ry's flashlight caught the stack of cardboard boxes of canning jars to her left. She giggled with excitement when she saw the old rusted still next to the boxes. She carefully raised the flap on the top carton. The box was empty. "It's exactly as I saw it," she said as she turned the light down to the two basketball-sized stones. She handed her flashlight to Kate.

"Shine the light down here," Ry said as she knelt on the ground. The rocks were heavier than she had expected. The boy had seemingly rolled them away with ease.

Kate squatted down to help her.

As soon as the rocks were out of the way, Ry grabbed the light and looked at Kate. "Do you realize we're within inches of a small fortune?"

Kate nodded.

Ry moved the flashlight beam down and peered inside the empty hole. She stared at it, not believing what she saw.

"What's wrong?" Kate asked.

"It's not here," Ry said as she frantically ran the light around the perimeter of the hole.

Kate squeezed down and stared in.

They both sat down in front of the empty opening.

"This can't be right," Ry said. "I saw him put the money into the jars and then hide the jars in the hole. I saw him."

Kate didn't say anything.

Ry turned back to look in the hole again, then got up and went back to the boxes. She checked all three of them. The top two were empty, the bottom one still held eight empty jars.

"We should go," Kate urged. "The old woman at the store might tell someone we were there asking questions."

Ry nodded. She stopped and turned back to the hole.

"What are you doing?"

"I don't know. I just want to leave it as he left it." She rolled the stones back in place, restacked the boxes and finally found the stick she had seen him use. She carefully wiped out their footsteps. When she reached the opening, she tossed the stick back inside, just as the boy had done in her vision.

As they trudged silently back to the truck, she wondered if anyone would ever again find the hidden spot. Then she began to wonder where the money had gone.

When they finally reached the truck and were inside, Ry stared out across the land. "Perhaps it was best we didn't find it," she said. "Maybe it was never meant to be found."

"Do you think he came back for it and spent it?" Kate asked.

"I don't know. He was twelve when he hid it there and twenty-one when he was arrested. He had nine years to spend it."

"Yes. But, he was placed in an orphan's home. How old would he have been when he left there?"

Ry shrugged. "Eighteen, I suppose."

"That only left him three years."

"Within those three years he married and had two kids," Ry reminded her. "He may have told his wife where the money was after he was arrested."

"I thought Victor told you the grandsons knew he hadn't spent the money. Is that why Larry kept going to see him?"

Ry cranked the truck. "Who knows? I'm sorry I dragged you all the way out here on a wild goose chase."

Kate placed her hand over Ry's hand. "I had fun today. How often does anyone actually get to go on a real live treasure hunt?" She squeezed Ry's hand before she got busy fastening her seat belt. "I'm really impressed you were able to find the place."

"Let's go home. I'll buy you dinner at the café."

"Are you joking? I still have leftover spaghetti we have to finish. You know how I hate to throw away food."

CHAPTER TWENTY-FOUR

Ry arrived at the shop just after daybreak on Sunday morning. Sleep had been slow in coming the night before. At some point during the night, she realized she hadn't heard the voices since Tuesday night. She deliberately tried to hear them, but nothing happened. She had finally fallen into a restless sleep somewhere around three. Now she was in a foul mood and hoped work would put her back on track. As she worked she thought about the money and then about the voices. Why had they disappeared? She took off her gloves and looked around in the debris until she found an old metal cheese grater. She picked it up and waited, but nothing happened. After digging around a bit longer, she found a pair of furrier nippers and picked them up. Again, nothing happened. From the corner of her eye, she saw a gleam. She dug through the debris and found a gold wedding band. She had purchased it at an estate sale she had gone to over a year ago. She picked it up and gasped when she felt the wave of love wash over her. The image of a young couple in plain clothes wavered before her. She watched as he slipped the ring on her finger. A shout called her back. When she turned she found Kate at the back door watching her.

"Are you all right?" she asked as she came closer.

Ry nodded and smiled. "I am now."

Kate tilted her head slightly. "I don't have to be at work until tomorrow night. They changed my schedule again."

"They sure are changing your schedule a lot," Ry said.

"It's crazy," Kate said and sighed as she looked around her. "Where shall I start?"

Ry swept her hand across the mess. "All of this has to go. If you find anything intact, just put it over there in one of those boxes." She pointed to the row of boxes she had lined along the walls.

They worked steadily for over an hour. Kate heard the noise first.

"What's going on out there?" she asked as she turned to look toward the back door.

Ry frowned. "It sounds like car doors." She started walking toward the back, but before she reached the door, her brother, Daniel, stepped inside. Ry watched as one by one her family members walked into the room. She couldn't stop the tears when Lewis came to her.

"I'm sorry," he said as he hugged her tightly.

Her three sisters-in-law joined them and soon everyone was crying.

"Did we come down here to blubber or help your sister?" her dad bellowed as he came in. "Ry, give Daniel your keys so he can get your truck out of the way. We brought a couple of trailers." He took Ry's keys and turned to Daniel. "Move her truck and bring a trailer in. We'll fill it up and you and James can take it to the dump while we're filling the other one." He saw Kate. "Glad to see you two finally came to your senses."

"Dad, stop it," Ry said. "Kate came by to help."

"That's what I meant," he said. "What did you think I meant?" He gave her a slight smile and winked, before he started barking orders.

Ry hugged her mom. "I've missed you all so much."

"I'm glad you didn't call," her mom said softly. "I really missed you, but it showed some," she nodded toward Lewis, "what it would be like without you there for our weekly dinner."

"Where are the kids?" Ry asked.

"They're at the house. Your Aunt Sophie offered to stay with them."

Ry rubbed her cheeks. "I feel bad for the kids."

Her mom swatted her arm. "Stop it. The poor old thing means well, God bless her."

Daniel suddenly appeared before Ry and pinched her cheeks. "Aunt Sophie said to tell you hi." He ran before Ry could grab him.

"Daniel, stop horsing around," their father yelled. "I should have left you at home and brought the kids," he grumbled.

With her family's help, the debris seemed to melt away. In no time at all the ground floor was empty and they were heading upstairs. With the trailer parked beneath the back window, tossing the trash out was twice as easy. By nine thirty that evening the job was finished and everyone was starving. Her mom began to unpack a feast she had brought for them. Her family sat on buckets around an old door laid across a pair of sawhorses and ate their evening meal together. Everyone was exhausted, but Ry couldn't remember when she had been happier.

After they had finished eating, Lewis reached into his shirt pocket. "I almost forgot. I found this outside by the trailer. It's old so I assumed it was part of your inventory."

Ry reached for the item he was handing her. As soon as it touched her fingers, a wave of colors washed over her. As the image became clear, she began to smile. When her vision cleared, she found her family staring at her. She looked at the nickel in her hand. "It's a 1930 buffalo nickel," she explained. She glanced at Kate and smiled. "It has some condition issues, so it's only worth about forty cents. I like them because you rarely ever see one anymore."

"Let's get this mess cleaned up," her father said as he stood and pointed to the table. "It's getting late."

Together they cleared the stuff away quickly. In no time at all her family had left.

Kate stood at the back door with Ry. "It's late. I should get going."

Ry grinned. "Are you too tired to take a ride?"

Kate looked at her doubtfully. "Where are we going?"

"It's a secret."

Kate made a face. "I've never liked secrets very much."

"I promise you're going to like this one."

"I guess this secret can't wait until tomorrow?" she asked.

"No. If you don't want to go, it's okay. I can go alone."

Kate rolled her eyes. "You know that drives me nuts. This had better be good because bouncing around in that old truck of yours has already bruised every bone in my body."

"You're going to have to trust me on this, okay? It may be a little scary at first, but we'll be all right. I promise."

Kate looked doubtful but nodded.

Forty minutes later, they turned onto a small county road. When Kate realized where they were headed, she grabbed Ry's arm. "I don't want to go back out there."

"I promise you, we'll be safe."

"How can you promise that?"

Ry shrugged. "Just because I can. Trust me, okay?"

When she parked the truck in front of the house where they both had almost died, Ry had a moment of misgiving. The bullet-riddled walls and fluttering police tape did nothing to make the place look inviting. "If you'd rather not go in, you can wait here."

Kate smacked her arm. "I told you to stop that." She eased the truck door open and hopped to the ground.

Ry grabbed the backpacks that she had left behind the truck seat from their previous trip. They carefully picked their way through the rubble. She found the old upright radio in the back bedroom, exactly where it had been on the day she tried to buy it.

"Help me turn this around," she said as she sat her flashlight on the floor.

"What are you doing?" Kate hissed.

"Come on and help me."

Together they managed to turn the radio around. The back panel was loose and fell off as soon as they let go. Stuffed inside the case were two bags. Kate grabbed one and Ry took the other. Without saying a word, they quickly replaced the back panel and moved the radio into the same position it had been when they arrived. Ry grabbed the backpacks and flashlight and they ran from the building. Neither woman spoke until they were safely inside Ry's motel room. After closing the drapes, they slowly dumped the contents of the bags onto the bed. Even Ry was shocked by what came out. It wasn't the old money from the robbery, but rather a little over two hundred thousand in present-day currency.

"We have the wrong money?" Kate sputtered.

Ry shook her head. "Larry had already sold the old money. This is what he got for it."

"How did you know where to look?" Kate asked.

"Do you remember the nickel that Lewis found? It must have been from the stolen money. Maybe it was in the box with the woodcarvings and I never noticed it. I don't really know. But, when Lewis handed it to me, I saw an image of Larry Lawson stuffing the bags into the radio. I tried to buy the radio when I was out there, but he was adamant about not selling it."

"What are you going to do with the money?"

Ry stared at Kate. "I was sort of hoping that the two of us might find a way to make a difference with this money," she said.

"What do you mean?"

"Let's lease the store out," Ry said. "We can take some of this money, help those poor people in McDowell and use whatever's left to help others. I don't have it all figured out yet, but if I found this money, I'm sure I can find more. Who knows what all we can accomplish?" She took a deep breath. "Kate, I know we have a lot of issues to work through, personal ones I mean, but I want you in my life. I don't want you to quit your job here and run off to who knows where."

"So you're asking me to be your *business* partner?" Kate asked.

Ry nodded. "For now," she said and shrugged. "Maybe with time we could work things out and get back to where we used to be. Back to when it was good between us."

"What if that's not what I want?"

Ry swallowed her disappointment. "Then I still want you as my friend and a partner in whatever this leads to." She pointed to the money on the bed.

Kate looked at her for a long moment. "I'm willing to stay here for a while and see how it goes. But I need more than we had before. I want a partner to go through life with. Not one I see during her free time."

Ry nodded. It wasn't perfect, but it was at least a place to start. As long as Kate was still around there was a chance they could work out their problems.

The following morning, Ry woke before daybreak. She lay in the dark staring at the red blinking light of the fire alarm on the ceiling. It gave her an odd mixed feeling of security and annoyance. Surely, there was a better place in the room for it rather than directly over the bed.

Before Kate had left the previous night, they stuffed the bags of money beneath the bed and agreed that Ry would take them to the safe deposit box the following morning. They had made no definite decisions about how the money would be used, but they both agreed it should be used to help others.

Victor would be able to help with that, if they could find a way to pick his brain without telling him they had the money. Eventually he would figure it out, but she didn't think he would care if they weren't personally benefitting from the money.

Ry rubbed a hand over her face and wondered if she would ever be able to repair the damage she had caused in her relationship with Kate. The blinking light grew more irritating. Suddenly she sat up. She'd had enough of living in the cramped motel room. She got out bed and showered. The sun was just clearing the horizon when she dropped the key off and settled her bill. She had to wait for the bank to open. It only took her a few minutes to stow the money in her safe deposit box. By the time she parked her truck in front of her granny's old cabin the sun was shining brightly. She shut off the engine and sat staring at the front porch. She hadn't been back here since the shooting. Ignoring the fist that gripped her stomach, she got out of the truck and walked slowly to the porch. Other than a few new planks on the porch and the missing hummingbird feeder, it looked as it had when she stepped out the morning she had been shot. Either her father or one of her brothers had replaced the bloodstained boards and cleaned away the broken glass.

She sat in one of the rockers on the porch and looked across at the pond. The pair of mallards was still swimming about and a male cardinal flitted about among the cypress trees. A plan began to form as she relaxed in the rocker. The Antique Nook would not reopen. She would either sell or lease the building. She would move out here to the cabin. The solitude would allow her the opportunity to freely experience and learn to understand her new abilities. When she was ready, she would use these abilities as her grandmother had said—to help others. And, if she were truly lucky, a little treasure hunting would be involved occasionally.

Then, she began to reflect on her family. It was time she started thinking more about them. She had always thought of them as being there for her. It was time for her to start being there for them as well. Lewis had been right in some of his accusations. She was spoiled. It was time to grow up.

Kate—how could she regain Kate's love? She couldn't bear the thought of her leaving. How could she go through life without Kate?

Ry walked to the edge of the porch. As she gazed out at the serene landscape, a gust of wind hit and caused the cypress limbs to creak. She glanced up at the massive limbs and closed her eyes as a sense of peace settled over her. She was a treasure seeker. There was no way she was going to lose her greatest treasure of all. She opened her eyes and smiled as she dialed Kate's number.

Bella Books, Inc.

W   *r.*